John Doyle
and
the Pennsylvania Canal

David R. Stewart

PublishAmerica
Baltimore

ISBN: 1-60563-126-4
PUBLISHED BY PUBLISHAMERICA, LLLP
www.publishamerica.com
Baltimore

Printed in the United States of America

This book is dedicated to the thousands of Irish immigrants who left their homes and arrived on the shores of this continent with optimistic dreams of a better future.

Introduction

In the spring of 1982, Father Michael Barrett was doing research on obscure and forgotten Catholic cemeteries located within the Diocese of Harrisburg (Pennsylvania). One small cemetery was found on a hill overlooking the Susquehanna River and the town of Liverpool, 26 miles north of Harrisburg, the capital city of Pennsylvania. A single headstone, containing the name of John Doyle, was discovered buried there. It was the only headstone found in the cemetery and was consequently re-erected. From the inscription on his headstone, we do know that John Doyle was born May 1, 1795, at Ballylee[1], County Down, Ireland, and died November 17, 1828, at Liverpool, Pennsylvania.

Fr. Barrett, a member of the Irish Heritage Society of Central Pennsylvania, suggested to the membership that some sort of recognition be given to the site since Catholic Cemetery Records indicated that all the men[2] interred were born in Ireland. A fundraiser was held and a bronze plaque was dedicated on Saint Patrick's Day 1987 in front of John Doyle's headstone. Accompanied by a piper, the dulcet voice of Bill O'Connor singing "Danny Boy" echoed over the river valley following the blessing and dedication of the plaque by Fr. Barrett. The plaque lists the names of eight men interred and acknowledges five unknown men laid to rest within the cemetery.

The dedication of the plaque was not only to honor those Irish decedents buried at Liverpool, but for the thousands of Irish immigrants who left their homes and arrived on the shores of this continent with optimistic dreams of a better future. At that time, young men were the greatest export of Ireland. Many came to the new country to dig coal, work on the canal system, or build railroads, and took the jobs nobody else wanted. The work was done with pick and shovel.

It was a rough life. America was built with backbreaking work and the Irish contributed a lot of blood and sweat to build a new nation. Without them, this country wouldn't be what it is today.

"The Irish who came here and worked on the canals and railroads were powerful instruments in the building of this country," Fr. Barrett said at the dedication. "They had hard lives. They were close to their church and had tremendous faith."

There is no way to tell how the men interred at the Liverpool Catholic Cemetery lost their lives, but state and religious records indicate that at the time of their deaths, the Susquehanna Division of the Pennsylvania Canal System was under construction. Two canal locks were being built at Liverpool in the same year that these men were interred. (*Portions of the crumbling walls of the locks remain today a few feet from a modern four-lane highway.*) A few documents do indicate that in 1828 a cholera epidemic swept through the area and many local citizens died. Those local residents were interred in the Liverpool Cemetery, a non-sectarian site, located adjacent to the Catholic cemetery. Since none of the names within the Catholic cemetery match the names in the public cemetery, it has been assumed that the Irishmen buried there were not local citizens. And, since they all were interred within the same time frame, they are assumed to have been employees of the Pennsylvania Canal System. However, a *History of Perry County* written in 1922 by H.H. Hain, mentions that a John Doyle, a "hotel keeper," was interred in "the Irish Cemetery" during the same time period.

I was president of the Irish Heritage Society of Central Pennsylvania at the time the plaque was dedicated and Fr. Barrett asked me to write a remembrance for these Irish lads. Hence, I wrote the following poem, which was read at the dedication:

John Doyle

In seventeen hundred and ninety-five
To the Doyles a son was born.
They named him John, a family name,
He arrived on a rainy morn.
Born he was, in County Down;
In the town of Ballylee.
Within him grew a desperate need
To cross the northern sea.
To America, he set his sights,
The land of promised gold.
There he'd find his wealth and name,
His future he would mold.
His father shook his hand for luck,
His mother held him tight,
And off he sailed from Belfast town,
Beneath a star filled night.
Penn's Wood is where he put his roots,
On Susquehanna's Bank.
There he took up pick and spade
And joined the canal men's rank.
He labored long and labored hard,
And yet there was no wealth.
Cold and wet, but still he dug
And the canal soon took his health.
They laid him down in Liverpool,
In November of Twenty-eight.
There were no streets of gold for him.
Poor John had met his fate.

7

His granite headstone stands there still,
To tell us of his story;
And of the many Irish lads
That sought their fame and glory.

For many years, after the dedication, I thought about what it must have been like for these Irishmen to leave their homes, cross the northern sea, and arrive in a new country. Thus, I took pen in hand and created this book, which is pure fiction, as nothing is actually known about John Doyle other than what his headstone states, what Mr. Hain has written, and John's visits to me in my deepest sleep. However, in an attempt to offer the reader a sense of 'where and when,' I have tried to be historically accurate with dates and locations during John Doyle's travels. I have also included the names of the other seven men interred at Liverpool Catholic Cemetery in my book only to offer a perspective and to honor them. All else is guesswork.

David Stewart

Chapter 1

Late in the summer of 1838 a packet barge gently glided north on a remote canal paralleling the Susquehanna River in central Pennsylvania. The air was clear and fragrant with the warmth of the midday sun. Pure white clouds, like puffs of cotton, drifted randomly through the deep azure sky. The green leaves at the tops of nearby trees stir, moved by a gentle breeze. Birds, picked through balls of manure and twitter with annoyance at being disturbed as the barge team of chestnut horses trod along the dusty canal path. They flew away until the team passed, then quickly returned to their errand of selecting delectable seeds from the undesirable source as the horse-stirred dust settled back onto the ground. The steady clop, clop, clop of their hooves held a rhythm like the steady tick of a pendulum clock dwindling away the minutes of each hour. Their harness jingled softly, almost like music, as they made slow progress northward. They appeared to be sleepwalking in the warmth of the summer day as their team master led them slowly along the narrow towpath. Their tails swished placidly back and forth as they swept away the numerous biting flies from their flanks.

Inside the packet cabin several muffled voices could be heard having an indistinguishable conversation as the dozen or so passengers relaxed in the forward salon. A few gentlemen passengers lolling about on the forward deck chatted with the captain. The steersman, with tiller firmly in hand, watched carefully ahead for snags or logs that may be drifting in the casually swirling waters of the canal.

Beside the steersman stood a slender young woman seemingly in deep thought. Her plain dress indicated that she was from the working class. Her long blonde hair lightly fell from beneath her light gray summer bonnet. The young woman's blue eyes gazed forward over the passenger cabin, toward the north, without expression.

Steep walls of rock rose from the edge of the river forming tall mountains on both sides of the Susquehanna River Valley. She was told that this very narrow portion of the river is called Girty's Notch, named after Simon Girty Jr. who was born near Harrisburg. He was 15 when his parents died. Simon ran off to join the local Seneca tribe, which led attacks against the local settlers. He sided with the British during the Revolutionary War and later became a river pirate. For a few years the village of Girty's Notch attracted a wild gang of disagreeable characters. Almost cornered by the settlers, Simon fled to Canada and lived out the rest of his 77 years among Indian friends. Local lore reported that Simon Girty's gang hid its booty in a cave on the side of Mount Patrick; a treasure that has never been found.

Here and there on the steep slope the occasional tree grew from a precarious ledge exposing tree roots where the rocks had tumbled away and slid into the waters below. A thick green canopy of trees and shrubs covered the tops of the nearby mountains. The lush foliage gracefully flowed down the mountainside until it reached the bank of the canal and river. As the packet rounded a bend, the young woman could see thin, wispy columns of smoke emanating out from several chimneys of a town in the distance. The occasional glint of sunlight reflected from a window or two.

"Liverpool lies just beyond this lock, Miss," advised the steersman, a man easily twice her age. His deeply tanned, rugged face showed years and years of labor in the outdoors. His gravelly voice added, "It won't be long before we're there. It shouldn't take more than an hour to clear the lock. There are only a few barges ahead of us." He puffed on his old, worn pipe as he smiled at the young woman. His smoke chased away a pesky fly that persistently landed on the brim of his frayed straw hat. She nodded back at him and smiled demurely. A dragonfly buzzed gently at the shoulder of her navy blue dress, but in a second it was gone, off to seek other adventures.

The young woman's gaze swept out over the river, which lay just beyond the low levee separating the canal and the main body of water. Occasionally a barge, canoe, or large log-float slowly passed them as it drifted south following the meandering river current.

The young woman focused on a log-float as it lazily passed by heading south. She noted that chaining the outer logs together formed a floating corral with numerous logs enclosed within the center. Two men with pikes watched for loose logs that might slip under the outer ring. In her mind the two resembled shepherds back home in Ireland as they tended their herd, for these men on the log-float stayed alert for any wandering member of their flock that might drift away.

A tent was pitched on a rough-hewn raft in the center of the log float and she surmised that it was placed there to protect the men from the dampness of the night. She marveled at the way they deftly stepped, barefoot, from log to log without slipping, and she pondered for a moment as to where they are going with all that timber.

A gentle bump of her packet brought her attention back to her own boat as her passenger barge was steered to the side of the levee. She watched as two crewmen leapt ashore, ropes in hand, to secure the mooring lines. The team master boarded briefly to retrieve feed buckets for the large packet horses. As they stood, waiting patiently, they continued to sweep away the numerous flies with long swoops of their full tails.

The cook entered the passenger cabin and began cleaning up the lunch remains. He folded the tables out of the way giving the passengers more room in the cabin. Several passengers went up on deck as the crew placed a ramp leading to the towpath. Two nattily dressed gentlemen in top hats walked down the ramp and stood on the bank smoking cigars. They watched with avid interest as a cargo barge slowly entered the lock. The two discussed the merits of canal travel over that of the dusty stagecoach and rumors that steam railroads may soon reach this far north from Columbia, sixty miles to the south.

Two young girls emerged from the cabin and, covering their mouths coquettishly, giggled as a burly, shirtless young man strolled by on the towpath smiling at them. When he realized that his physique had attracted their attention, he cockily tipped his hat. That caused the girls to bashfully turn away and giggle all the more.

The waters of the canal lazily lapped at the sides of the packet making a gentle sound in the warmth of the day. Several ducks quietly swam around the barge hoping for a handout from the cook. Small fish could be seen as they jumped at darting mosquitoes, making tiny splashing sounds as they reentered the water. They created slight ripples that spread slowly outward.

After the dusty stagecoach trip from New York City to Philadelphia and the noisy, dirty train ride from Philadelphia to Columbia, the young woman had discovered that barge travel was very clean and casual with many interesting sights along the way.

At night, once the tables were placed out of the way, the berths folded down from the wall into fairly comfortable beds. A curtained doorway split the cabin in half at night, men at the aft end of the cabin and women and children at the fore end. In the morning, the berths were folded against the wall once again and the folding tables setup for the passenger's meals. When each repast was complete, and the tables were moved out of the way, the cabin became a roomy parlor. Of course, fish was a large part of their meals. Dry, smoked or fried.

The peacefulness of a serene afternoon was suddenly interrupted by a loud crash. A frightened horse could be heard snorting and loudly neighing. Just as the cargo barge was being towed into the lock, the inside horse stumbled and was now slowly sliding off the stone levee into the canal. The young woman gasped as she glanced toward the lock to see the animal hanging half in the water suspended by the harness tethering the team together. Ducks noisily scattered as its thrashing hind legs churned the canal into a frothy mixture. Its eyes filled with fright from the noise of its thrashing team member, the second horse began to lean far to its left to keep from being pulled off the levee by the connecting leather straps. His nostrils were wide open with a fearful snorting as he was slowly being dragged toward the edge of the canal levee.

Several men rush forward to render assistance as the team master jumped into the waist deep water of the lock to soothe the fallen horse. The captain of the cargo barge whipped out his knife as he rushed to the team. Risking his life, he jumped between the horses with his razor sharp knife in his hand. He quickly severed the leather straps that connected the fallen horse to the rigging. Once free the animal fell into the water on its side with a loud splash. The team master, already in the canal, grabbed the horse around its neck and hung on for dear life, as he tried to cover the horse's eyes with a rag. The panicky animal finally calmed to the soothing words of his team master.

With the weight of the fallen horse suddenly gone, the horse still on the levee path stumbled to the left. Its feet dangerously kicked out; one hoof barely missed the barge captain's head as the animal fell to its side. The rigging, caught beneath the captain who had fallen to his knees, flipped the man head over heels into the canal. He rose from beneath the waters with a boisterous laugh. Realizing that he was unharmed, everyone nearby broke into relieved laughter. The captain and team master led the calmed horse toward a dirt ramp located outside the lock.

On the packet barge, the steersman turned to the young woman and said, "Miss, it'll be a another hour or two before we get through the lock. The wall of the lock will have to be repaired where the stones were kicked loose. This barge won't arrive at Liverpool much before dark. If you'd like you could walk up the towpath to the town. It's about a half mile to Mrs. Gensler's Rooming House. She has a real nice place. I know you'll be comfortable there."

"My bags…" the young woman began.

"Oh, I'll see to it that they are unloaded and sent to Mrs. Gensler's place," the steersman responded. His friendly eyes smiled at her as she descended the several steps into the passenger cabin.

She stood in the cabin at the bow of the packet and took inventory of her possessions. The two small carpetbags, her employer had loaned her, sat near the door packed with her travel clothing. She had risen early in the morning when the packet had left the New Buffalo mooring and packed her bags. For the past several days she had called the packet cabin 'home.' Her berth was one of eight in the women's section and was now neatly folded against the wall. There she had slept pleasantly, falling asleep listening to the gentle splash of the water on the other side of the wall and drifting off to the singing of the canalmen as they sat around a fire next to the towpath. The folding table was now also fastened back into place and she momentarily wondered if the letter that she had written, while sitting there several days earlier, was now on a ship heading back to Ireland. She had promised to keep all her relatives back home advised on this trek she was taking. Looking around to be sure she hasn't forgotten anything, she picked up her light cream-colored shawl and went back up on deck.

Glancing toward the lock, she saw that the team master was taking careful inspection of his horse's legs after it was led up the slippery ramp. The cargo barge captain stood nearby with a concerned look as he chewed on a freshly lit cigar. Water was still dripping slowly from the brim of his hat. The two men casually discussed the expense of repairing the cut harness leather. The barge captain put his hands on his hips and shook his head with frustration over the incident.

The steersman, who had fussed over the young woman as if she were his own daughter since they departed Columbia, held out his hand to help her descend the steep ramp. At the bottom of the ramp she turned and said, "Sir you have made my trip to Liverpool a pleasant experience. I thank you kindly for watching over me. I just wish this trip could have been for a more pleasant cause. May God go with you, Mr. Thompson."

The steersman tipped his hat and replied, "And may God be with you on your quest, Miss Doyle."

Starting north on the towpath, the young woman followed a few of the other passengers who are now strung out along the path to town. Far ahead, almost at Liverpool, she could see the two men in top hats strolling casually along puffing on their cigars. They quickly disappeared into the first tavern at the edge of town.

As she approached the edge of Liverpool, the young woman noticed an older woman hanging her wash outside a small house. The house was neat as a pin with a split rail fence running along the road. A well-kept garden, on one side of the cabin, was filled with a lush green growth promising an abundance of fresh vegetables on the dinner table each day. Chickens searched frantically about the yard for a tasty morsel and a cat on the front door stoop grinned with wisdom as it dozed in the warm sun. The cabin reminded the young woman so much of her parent's home back in Ireland. She called to the woman, "Begging your pardon, Ma'am, but would you be kind enough to direct me to Mrs. Gensler's Boarding House?"

With a friendly smile, the woman walked to the rail fence and asked, "New in town, Dear? You can't miss the place. It's a fine white two-story house in the center of town. The house has green shutters and is surrounded by a white picket fence. Her inn faces the river with a lovely flower garden along the road. Mrs. Gensler's sign hangs over the gate. Are you there on holiday for a visit?"

The young woman felt comfortable in the presence of this older woman. Her smile was filled with kindness and concern. "Oh, no, Ma'am. I've come on the packet barge." She glanced back toward the lock and continued, "I'm not here on holiday, but on solemn business I'm afraid." Sadly she looked down at the dusty road.

"Liverpool? Solemn business? What strange business can bring such a young woman out here in the middle of nowhere?" The older woman wrinkled her brow at the mystery of it all.

"You see, Ma'am, I have a brother buried here in Liverpool. He died ten years ago while working for the Canal. I was born the year he left home in 1811. He was sixteen years of age at the time. I never knew him except by his letters home." The young woman felt comfortable in the presence of this friendly lady.

She added, "I came to America a year ago and now work as a domestic in New York City. I've come here while my employer's family is on holiday. My brother was my parent's eldest son, and I promised them that I would visit Liverpool someday and lay flowers on his grave for them." After a pause, she asked, "Could you tell me where to find the parish Priest?"

"Ah, he was just here last week. Father Barrett only comes here once a month or so on his rounds. We have no Catholic church here in Liverpool. The good Father comes up river from Harrisburg and holds Mass at some of the distant towns. Father won't be back this way for several weeks, now."

The young woman peered sadly down again at her dusty shoes. She had so hoped to visit the local priest for details about her brother.

"I'll tell you what, Dear," the older woman offered. "I'll walk with you and show you Mrs. Gensler's place and then we'll go up to the Catholic Cemetery. It's a short piece and I'm sure we can find your poor brother's grave. Just give me a minute to grab my shawl. By the way, my name is Myrtle Deckard. My husband, David Deckard, is the local constable. He may be able to help you find information on your brother's passing."

"Oh, thank you, Mrs. Deckard. It is so kind of you to trouble yourself." The young woman felt so relieved to find a friendly, helpful person so quickly upon arriving in Liverpool.

Mrs. Deckard removed her apron and went into her cottage and reappeared a few seconds later with her shawl wrapped around her shoulders. As they walked up the road the older woman inquired, "What was all that commotion down at the lock?"

"A horse slipped and fell into the canal," the young woman told her. "No one was injured, Thank God. Even the horse seemed unharmed."

"Such things happen along the canal. It's all in a day's work for canal men."

As they strolled into the town, they passed a group of young boys swinging on a rope out over the canal where they dropped into the cool waters with a refreshing splash. Their laughter demonstrated their pure joy in the fun of it. Mrs. Deckard asked the young woman, "What was your brother's name?"

"John Doyle. I'm Mary, the youngest of ten children. John was my parent's first born. He came to America to seek his fortune. Our Parish Priest back home notified the family of John's death a year after it happened. The Church in Harrisburg sent my family official notification of his death, however we have no idea of the cause of his passing. All we could find out was that he was buried in Liverpool. My parents and I would like to learn about the circumstance of my brother's death."

As they continued to stroll along the dusty, rutted street toward the center of town Mrs. Deckard pointed out a large whitewashed house just ahead, "That's the widow Gensler's Rooming House, there on the corner. Let's just stop for a minute and let her know you're in town and then we'll proceed up to the cemetery. It's on the hill only two blocks west of here."

Mrs. Gensler was pleased to see Mary Doyle and acknowledged that she had received Mary's letter the month before requesting a room. She told Mary, "I have a lovely room for you overlooking the Susquehanna River. I am sure you will find it to your liking. I'll have your bags placed in your room as soon as the men bring them from the packet. When you and Mrs. Deckard get back I'll have fresh baked cookies and a pot of tea ready for the both of you."

Mrs. Deckard and Mary continued on their way to the cemetery. "Mary, dear, would I be presumptuous to ask if you're from Ireland? I'm sure that's the accent I detect. We have several families from Ireland settled in this area."

"I am," Mary replied. "My family is from Ballylee, a wee town in County Down, in the north of Ireland. My father worked in

Belfast in the shipyards. He is now retired and wouldn't leave Ireland for all the gold in the world."

"How did you happen to seek work in New York City, Dear?"

"There simply isn't enough work for everyone back in Ireland. I was offered a lovely position as a maid for a barrister and his family through a mutual friend in Belfast. I decided to seek my fortune in America. Many young people seek employment outside of Ireland." Mary quickly included, "That's why my brothers came to America."

After a pause she sadly remarked, "Poor John lies here in Liverpool and my brother, Michael, disappeared on his way to California seeking gold. We haven't heard from Michael in years. My father thinks the worst."

But with a more cheerful sound to her voice, she said, "Perhaps, though, he's just fine and just hasn't had the opportunity to send a letter back home. The way men are, Michael may have not realized how much time has passed. Someday I just know he'll come home!"

Mrs. Deckard simply gave Mary an understanding smile.

At the entrance to the cemetery a simple wooden sign hung from a post, "Liverpool Catholic Cemetery." Mary paused and studied the sign for a few seconds.

"Oh," interrupted Mrs. Deckard, "we are in luck! There's the caretaker, Mr. Perkins. Yoo hoo, Mr. Perkins! Over here. Come and meet this young lady. She's come all the way from Ireland."

Mr. Perkins, with a slightly hunched back, hobbled over to the women steadying himself with a cane. His deeply etched face revealed many years of untold stories. "That you, Mrs. Deckard? What brings you here on such a fine summer day?"

"This is Mary Doyle, Mr. Perkins. Mary's brother, John, worked for the canal. He passed on ten years ago and is buried here in the Catholic Cemetery. Mary would like to visit his gravesite. Would you know where it is?"

"Well, Miss Doyle, I can tell you exactly where your brother lies." Mr. Perkins turned and casually began walking up the hill with Mary and Mrs. Deckard following close behind. He continued,

"You see, there are only eight headstones in this cemetery. All placed here by the Susquehanna Canal Company. There's several more lads laid to rest here as well, but they were only known by nicknames. No one knew their real names so they never got headstones.

"I cut the grass and keep the place in good order for the church and I know all the boys here by name. Knew most of them before they passed on. You see, I worked the canal with many of them. When the digging went north, I stayed here in Liverpool and worked in the company store. All that digging in the cold damp earth!" He shook his head in sadness he explained, "Took too many lives to dig that canal. It's a marvel today, to be sure, but the canal ended many a good man's days. It was a terrible job!"

"Oh, Mr. Perkins," moisture filled Mary's eyes, "Back home we never knew what caused my brother's death. Did you know him? What was the circumstance of his death? What was he like?"

"Now, now, young woman," Mr. Perkins firmly responded. "You go too fast. Your brother's headstone is just up here at the top of the cemetery." He continued slowly walking toward the far end of the cemetery. He looked at Mary and said, "We'll walk up there while I tell you what I know of John. But, please, only one question at a time."

Mr. Perkins slowly led Mary and Mrs. Deckard through the small cemetery. "John, as I recall, was a spry young man. He had the occasional nip, but he was a devout fellow who never missed the masses held by the circuit priest, Fr. Barrett. Father has come up this way for almost 20 years. Gets here about every five or six weeks. There is no Catholic Church in town so masses are held in someone's home.

"It was ten years ago that most of the lads here died," Mr. Perkins continued. "Some of the lads I barely knew, but I remember John well and can remember his passing as if it was yesterday. It was such a sad incident."

He stopped beside a small headstone at the uppermost portion of the cemetery and gestured toward John's gravesite. "Yes, he was a grand fellow. Enjoyed a good laugh with the lads, John did. He would play his guitar and could sing like an angel. Everyone liked John. Didn't have an enemy in the world." After a short pause to catch his breath, he added, "I don't recollect any one ever saying a bad word about your brother. John Doyle was everyone's friend."

Mr. Perkins removed his hat and lowered his head in sadness as he tells the ladies, "The fever took him."

Recalling the incident that occurred so many years earlier caused his eyes well up with dampness. With a sigh, Mr. Perkins continued describing the events that had occurred almost a decade earlier, "John was the supervisor of the crew. He was overseeing the lads as they were lining the floor of the upper lock with stone in preparation for the installation of the gates. They were working at the north end of Liverpool when an earthen dam collapsed between them and the river."

He reached into a rear pocket to retrieve a large red handkerchief and paused to dab at the increasing moisture in his eyes. With a quavering voice he went on, "The water and mud roared into the canal. As I said, the lads were laying stone at the bottom and sides of the lock when that wall of mud came at them. Most of the boys jumped out of the way, but there was a man who wasn't quick enough. The mud came in so fast it trapped the man's legs and he couldn't get out of the lock. The water was rising fast and was up to his chest. Your brother threw off his coat and jumped into the canal to save him. He dove under the freezing water, pulled the mud away from the man's feet and freed his legs." Mr. Perkins closed his eyes as he tried to remember all the details of the accident, "Oh, yes. Pat Hurley was the man's name, I recall now.

"Well, Pat survived thanks to John's heroic act. But the accident happened early in April. John and Pat were soaked to the bone in the cold damp air. The other lads built a roaring fire and got the wet clothing off both men as quickly as possible. Towns people brought blankets and wrapped both lads up, but they were shivering profusely."

As he wiped sweat from his brow, he continued with his story, "Young Patrick got over the experience quickly, but poor John came down with a fever. There were many diseases to be had along the river in those days and your brother's fever, as a result of the accident, had already weakened him.

"Pat owed his very life to John and spent every minute he could with him while he was in the company cabin. Even went to the Doyle home and helped tend him there. They gave him coffee with hot whiskey and sugar to ward off his fever. They kept feeding him chicken broth to give him strength. In these parts, chicken broth is the best medicine there is."

Mrs. Deckard nodded in agreement in support of that statement.

"John was terribly sick for about a month. For a week after the accident he was in an unconscious state most of the time. He did begin to slowly recuperate, but never got his strength back. And the accident affected his memory. He couldn't work on the canal any longer and needed another position."

He pointed to a gray, two-story building down in the town below and told Mary, "Well, that hotel on Front Street was available for rent. Had a nice pub in one room. The Doyles took over the place and made a pretty good go at it. John's music brought folks in from all around. He could sing and play his guitar like nobody else in these parts. They had a pretty good business going once the canal opened for business. Lots of boats stopped at Liverpool for the night and the hotel was in great demand.

"As well as the pub," he added with a grin.

Stopping to chase away a pesky bee, Mr. Perkins continued, "During the fall your brother's illness caught up with him. They had to give up the inn late in October. John had been such a young, healthy man, but was failing fast. Doctor Armstrong said there wasn't anything further he could do for him. Father Barrett was visiting here from Harrisburg and gave John the last rites. Your brother died about a week later. Died quietly in his sleep, praise the Lord.

"Pat Hurley was the worst of it for a while. He commenced drinking and bemoaning the fact that it should have been him that died and not your brother. John Doyle was a favorite with all the canalmen and townspeople. Pat, well, he finally moved west. No one has heard of him since the day he departed."

"Such a sad story," Mrs. Deckard lamented as the three sat looking at John Doyle's headstone. Mary gazed back down the hill toward the town of Liverpool. From this vantage point, high on the hill above the small town, she could see the sparkling blue waters of the Susquehanna River for miles in each direction. Boats and rafts drifted slowly downstream seemingly without a care in the world. Eagles and hawks lazily soared in the cloudless blue sky above them. For a long time she studied the mountain on the far side of the river. It soared steeply from the edge of the river to a crisp ridge and seemed to touch the sky. It was a serene panorama and Mary felt peace within her troubled heart knowing that her brother would enjoy such a place to spend eternity. This valley was so much like the family's home back in Ireland.

Mary reached over to touch her brother's headstone. Lovingly fingering the engraved lettering, she traced her brother's name. A tear slowly slid down her cheek. As she dabbed the tear away she told Mr. Perkins and Mrs. Deckard, "Tomorrow I would like to bring flowers for John. That is my parent's wish. I only have a few days here. Then the packet will return from Northumberland and I must return to New York City. I can't thank you enough, Mr. Perkins, for watching over my brother."

Gently touching Mary's shoulder, Mr. Perkins asked, "You never knew your brother, Mary? How did he ever come to be in Pennsylvania?"

"No, I was a babe when John sailed for America," Mary answered in almost a whisper. "I knew him from his lovely letters boasting about the beauty of this country. He had a special love for this country as well as his own. Why he came to America? Oh, that's a long story. My mother and father sat in front of our hearth many times telling us of John's dream."

"Before you leave Liverpool, Mary," Mr. Perkins interrupted, "you must visit John's wife and son."

"Wife and son?" Mary responded with a start. "No one in our family knew that John was married! There was no mention of it in his letters. He has a son?"

"John married Patricia Thompson a month before the accident." Mr. Perkins informed Mary. "I'm sorry. I thought you knew."

After a short pause he added, "Patricia was by his side constantly from the day of the accident until he took his last breath. She worked hard in their pub after his accident. They tried to keep it going, but John kept getting weaker. She was too frail a young thing to run a hotel and pub alone. Near the end of summer John began to once again grow ill. In the fall, just before John died, she had to close the hotel.

"Patricia is the daughter of Samuel Thompson, a local farmer just west of Liverpool," he advised Mary. "John and Patricia's son, Andrew, must be almost ten years of age now. He and his mother live with her parents on the Thompson family farm. You must go visit them."

"Oh, I shall, I shall!" The excitement of this fantastic discovery sent quivers through Mary as tears of joy poured down her cheeks. She and Mrs. Deckard hugged each other sharing the ecstasy of the moment.

As Mary dabbed away her tears of joy, she told them, "I can't wait to write mother and father with this wonderful news. Everyone at home will be so pleased."

"First thing in the morning, Mary," Mrs. Deckard said, as she holds the young woman's trembling hands, "I'll have Mr. Deckard hitch up the wagon and take us all to the Thompson farm. I know where it is, but I never dreamed that your brother had a wife and child living there!"

Later that night, Mary, with tears of delight in her eyes, sat down to write her parents: *Dear Mother and Father, I have the most wonderful news...*

Chapter 2

On a cool morning in 1811, twenty-seven years earlier:

A white washed, thatched roof cottage stood on a hillside overlooking the mist-shrouded town of Ballylee in the north of Ireland. Smoke gently swirled from the stone chimney and dissipated into the morning fog. The pungent smell of burning peat and frying rashers permeated the air. Muffled sounds of youthful chatter and laughter were heard within the confines of the small cottage as youngsters inside rose to greet the new day. In the early dawn, the hearth within cast a dim orange glow that flowed through the four small windows. Slowly the glow in the windows began to fade as the morning sun appeared from behind the distant mountain warming the front of the cottage and the sleepy village below. Several sheep in a field near the cottage began to stir as they sought out their early fare of grass painted with sweet morning dew.

As the sun touched the town, in the valley below, the sound of waking citizens disturbed the calm silence of another morning and roosters proudly announced that they had caused the sun to rise in the sky. Several barking dogs were demanding their morning repast, while a lowing cow urgently called to her owner reminding him that she had milk to be taken. Here and there, chickens began to appear from their coops scratching the ground in search of any grains dropped the previous day. Several children left the shelter of their warm cottages with wooden buckets to fetch water from the towns well in the central square.

In front of the cottage, on a stone fence, a young, blond haired man sat whittling aimlessly on an old chunk of briar. He stopped for a minute and wistfully peered off in the distance, out over the valley below. His mind was thousands of miles away, thus he didn't hear the red door of the cottage open behind him. A tow-headed boy, barely in his teens, emerged and paused as he looked at the young man sitting on the fence. He stepped out onto the stoop and quietly pulled the door shut behind him. The young lad halted a few feet from the fence and tilted his head to one side. His blue eyes studied the older boy's emotionless face. For a few minutes he gazed with admiration at his older brother. Without a word he stepped forward and placed his hand on the older boy's arm. Slowly becoming aware of his presence by the touch, the older boy affectionally put his hand on the younger boy's hand.

"John," the young boy spoke softly, shaking his brother's arm. "John, mother says breakfast is ready. You're to come now. She's made a special breakfast for us today."

John's blue eyes continued to stare off into the distance. His face remained expressionless. The young man was so enrapt by his own thoughts that he seemingly heard nothing.

With determination, his younger brother placed his hand on his older brother's shoulder and gently shook him again. "John, mother has our breakfast ready. What are you thinking about? America?"

At the word 'America', John at last became aware of his younger brother.

"Yes, America, Michael. America where the streets are paved with gold," John replied in almost a whisper as he continued to peer off at the distant horizon. He watched as the morning sun slowly melted away the swirling morning mist.

"Aw, John," scoffed Michael. "You don't really believe in those stories. Do you? Father says 'tis all blarney."

John dropped the piece of briar and slipped his knife back into its sheath on his belt. He looked at his younger brother seriously for a few moments, then with a grin he replied, "No, I know that the streets aren't really paved with gold." His expression changed to a mock look of gravity, as he quickly added, "No more than I believe that there's a pot of gold at the end of the rainbow."

The loud laughter broke the calmness of the morning just as Kevin, the Doyle's second born, came outside. "What are you two going on about?"

"Aw, me older brother thinks he can pick gold off the ground in America," Michael teased. "And he'll be coming back home a wealthy man."

"Sure, he will," Kevin joined in the teasing. "He's going to buy a fine manor with lots of land and ride a grand black stallion."

"Ride a horse?" John challenged. "Why I'll have a dozen fancy carriages in me stable with a driver for each. And a footman for each as well!"

The boys all laughed at the suggestion. Their high spirits were momentarily interrupted as a creaking jaunting cart approached on the road running past their cottage. All three boys paused to watch as a neighbor approached on his way to town. An old man, hunched over the reins, guided his shaggy pony as it pulled the small jaunting cart. With a toothless grin, he waved to the boys as he passed. The three boys returned his greeting and wished him a good day.

"What would you really do if you were a rich man?" Kevin asked John.

"For one thing, I'd buy a lovely cottage for mother and father. No longer would they have to pay some Englishman rent for a rundown place like this!" John firmly stated.

"Father keeps the place neat and in good order," Michael argued back. "I don't think our house is run down."

"Aye, Michael is right," Kevin said. "Father does a lot to our house with what little he has. I agree the chimney needs repair and father can only do so much with stone and mud." After a moments pause as he looked back at their home, he added, "And a few cracked windowpanes could stand to be replaced."

Michael interjected, "The landlord won't even fix little things!"

"If our parents owned their own place," John spoke up, "they wouldn't have to beg a landlord to fix such things. When I have my wealth, father wouldn't have to fix a thing. I'd hire a mason to fix their fireplace and their cottage would have high quality glass in all the windows."

Kevin shook his head, "It's all a dream, John. If there were such wealth in America, we would have heard about it from some of our cousins who have ventured there already."

"Ah, don't ruin his dream," Michael countered. "For all you know John could come back home a wealthy man some day."

"That will be some grand day, indeed," Kevin sarcastically snapped.

Jokingly John shoved Kevin's shoulder and returned to seriousness as he said, "But you know, Kevin, I've heard that there really is gold lying all around at the foot of some mountains in America. One just has to know where to look. I want to find that gold and make my fortune. Yes, my dream is to someday take our parents away from all this and give them a better life."

Michael laughed lightly, "Oh sure, an' me brother, John, knows just where to look for all this gold! That's as sure a fact as a leprechaun giving you his pot of gold if you nab him by the coat tails under the full moon!" Michael laughed even louder.

"Just you watch your funnin' of the leprechauns, Michael Doyle," John smiled as he jested with his younger brother. "One just never knows what goes on at the fairy rings in the wood."

John's somber gaze once again turned to the distant mountain and quietly, but with determination, he murmured, "I'm off to America this very day. I'll find some of that gold and bring you each a big chunk. That'll quiet the both of you."

As the boys all laughed, the upper half of the red door on the cottage sprang open. A burly man peered out into the thinning mists. He watched his sons' merriment for a few seconds then called to them, "Hey, boys. Get yourselves in here now, lads. Your mother has a lovely feast prepared to send John on his way. Come on now, don't be dallying about."

Almost in unison, the three boys responded to the summons, "Yes, father,"

John jumped off the wall and dusted off the back of his trousers. He affectionately put his arm around Michael's shoulder and together they slowly walk back to the cottage still chuckling at their recent exchange. Kevin followed closely behind his brothers as they began to enter the cottage.

At the door, John stopped, turned to Kevin and said, "You know, Kevin, once I am off on my journey you'll be the oldest son at home. It'll be up to you to take command and watch over mother and the others while father is away all week at the shipyards. You'll be expected to tend the sheep and the garden. You must be sure the little ones get off to their lessons each day. Its an awful big responsibility."

"Sure, John, sure," grinned Kevin. He jumped to attention, he gave John a mock salute and said, "and I'll do me best to fill your grand boots while you're off plucking all that gold from the trees in America."

They all laughed as they entered the warmth of the cottage. The smell from their mother's hearth immediately caught their attention. Only on special days do the boys feast on such delicate morsels as she had prepared this morning. Rashers and eggs sizzled in her large black skillet as blood pudding sausages churned in boiling water over the peat fire. The boys joined the rest of the family at the table where Mr. Doyle began slicing a loaf of freshly baked soda bread.

"Now where have you boys been?" Asked Mrs. Doyle, a woman of vast girth and jovial expression. "Your rashers and pudding are getting cold. I have a treat for you, John. EGGS! I traded some goat's milk with Mrs. McGinley for some fresh eggs. Told her I've got to build me boy up for his long voyage across the sea!" Her sparkling eyes gleamed from her flushed, round face, but the dampness below her lower eyelids revealed recently wiped tears, which gently reflected a soft radiance from the glow of the fire in the hearth. She reached up to John's much taller frame and gave him a loving hug about the shoulders then led him to the table. "Now sit you boys down and if yer father will give us all a grand blessing, we'll partake of the Lord's bounty."

Mr. Doyle reverently bowed his head. He was silent for a moment, as if in deep thought, then began in a soft, deep, slightly wavering voice, "Lord Jesus, we ask Thee to bless this meal we are about to share. We thank Thee for Thy bounty. But, today I will ask our Dear Lord and the Blessed Mary for more. Our son, John, leaves us for America this very day. Oh, it's so far away from us. We pray for Thee to watch over him. Be with him. Protect him. He's a good boy, Lord, but the Devil may try to lead him off to the wrong path. We beseech Thee, Lord; be with him and watch over him until he comes back to us once again. Amen." As he crossed himself, a single tear trickled down his cheek. He quickly wiped it away with his sleeve hoping that none would recognize his moment of fleeting male toughness.

But Mrs. Doyle no longer able to retain her composure began to silently weep. "Enough of that, Lass," Mr. Doyle understandingly demanded. "Your young bird has out grown the nest and flies away to chase butterflies! I just hope they don't taste too bitter!" The family all tittered at the suggestion and everyone began to talk at once.

This special farewell breakfast was shared for one last time by eleven of the Doyle family. Mary, the last-born Doyle, could be heard cooing happily in her crib waiting patiently for her mother to feed her.

"John," demanded Kevin, "Tell us again about the ship you'll be working on. I want to hear again about sailing across the ocean."

"Well," John paused as he finished chewing on his thick slice of bread, "I've been told that the ship is a brigantine with two masts that stand as straight as a tree. A bowsprit, reaches out over the front of the ship to hold an additional sail. Beneath the bowsprit will be the carving of a mermaid. A mermaid is a maiden with the tail of a fish and bare breasts." John laughed mischievously and his eyes sparkled with adventure.

"John!" his mother growled in admonishment. "We'll have none of that talk at the breakfast table. Maidens that are half fish and have their bosoms exposed, indeed. Surely you stretch the truth!"

"No, mother, just ask father. He's seen mermaids on the bows of ships himself." John looked at his father for support, but his father made no effort to acknowledge this statement. Mr. Doyle, casually sipping at his tea, ignored his son's plea for affirmation and continued enjoying his breakfast.

John went on, "The tallest mast on the ship reaches the sky and at the top is a round platform the sailors call a crows nest. Of course I've never seen a crows nest in trees around these parts big enough to hold a man!" The younger children giggled.

John continued, "A man stands there, in the crows nest, and watches for other ships, whales, and…." John paused, "bare breasted mermaids!" The children, and even Mr. Doyle, all broke into a raucous roar.

"Indeed," scowled his mother, as she fought back the urge to laugh herself. "You just watch yourself, John Doyle. At sixteen years you're still not too big for the switch!" Then, when she could hold herself back no longer, broke out into laughter as well.

Mary, at six months of age, was not accustomed to all this loudness in her world and began to cry loudly protesting this invasion of her peace and tranquility. John jumped up from his bench at the table and stepped quickly to her crib. He gently picked up his youngest sister and cradled her softly in his arms. Lovingly he gave her a small kiss on her forehead.

"Mary, me girl, don't you be crying now. Your big brother is off across the deep blue sea this very day; and as he departs, he wants to remember you smiling like the angel that you are." Mary stopped her crying and John held her out at arms length so he could see her. She smiled at him. "That's me girl. Do you know, Mary, I'm going to pick up a piece of gold as big as me fist just for you. I'm going to buy you the finest dress in all of Ireland and a pony to ride. You'll never need for anything again." He gently hugged his little sister and hummed to her while mimicking a slow dance.

"But, John," complained Michael, "the ship. The Ellen Marie. We want to hear more about the Ellen Marie."

"Ah, Michael, what more can I tell you," John paused in his swaying about the room and turned back to the table. He stood thinking for a moment and then sat back on the bench. He propped Mary on his knee and looked deeply into her blue eyes as he stroked her thin blonde wisps of hair. "The grand ship has a dozen sails to catch the wind. Cannon are lined on the deck ready to fight off pirates or heathens; or anyone else who would seek to steal her cargo."

"What cargo does she carry, John?" Michael asked. "Is it true that she carries a complement of His Majesty's Royal Marines?"

"Aye, I believe so, Michael. With pirates lurking on the high sea, the Royal Marines are a necessary lot. They are there to help protect the cargo, you see." After a pause to kiss his sister on the cheek, John continued, "We sail from Belfast on the morning tide and put in at Liverpool where we pick up ironware for merchants in the West Indies. Then from Liverpool it's off to Wexford in the south of Ireland for grain seed and woolens. When we hoist anchor at Wexford, we shan't set sight on land again until we reach the West Indies."

"Now, John," Mr. Doyle interceded, "Royal Marines aboard a ship flying an American flag? I don't think so, what with all the troubles between the Crown and the colonists."

"And that's where the pirates are, aren't they John?" Kevin interrupted excitedly. "That's where you get to fire the cannons!"

"Tis true, Kevin. Tis true." John sat up straighter and proudly added, "If those pirates come near our ship, we'll blow them right out of the sea!" John flung his free arm in a fast sweeping motion and banged the table with his fist. The sudden movement, loud bang, and his boisterous exclamation caused Mary to fuss once again, but John gently hugged his little sister to calm her.

"Oh, such talk," said his mother. "You've never even seen a cannon up close, John. Just how would you propose to do this brave deed?"

"Captain William Robinson, father's cousin, says that I'll be taught what I need to know." John went on, "When the time comes, our cannons will be aimed at the thieving rascals and 'POW,'" John firmly swung his fist onto the table shaking the cups and dishes, "they're off to see Davy Jones Locker!" Mother grabbed poor shaken Mary from John and held her in her arms to protect her from her wild older brother.

"Now, now, John, lad," said his father jokingly, "you be savin' all that for the pirates. No need to sink me table!" The whole family burst out again in howls of laughter. Little Mary once again loudly voiced her resentment to this disturbance. Mr. Doyle smiled and asked, "And tell us, son, while you're not firing this grand cannon of yours, what will you do aboard the ship?"

"Ah, that's yet to be learned, father. I guess I'll be doing whatever sailors do at sea. Captain Robinson didn't bother to explain those duties to me."

"Well," chuckled Mr. Doyle, "you can bet ye won't be sitting around staring at the sea. There's much to be done aboard a merchant ship. Time during the voyage will pass quickly."

Kevin turned to his father and asked, "Father, will John truly be standing high above the deck in the crows nest?"

"Well, Kevin," his father answered. "I think John will be hard pressed to find a crows nest aboard a brigantine. Only the larger ships have them on their masts." Kevin looked disappointed, but his father quickly added, "A brigantine has a man stand on watch in the tall rigging, and I am sure that John will serve his time high above the deck watching for land or any sails on the horizon."

"Oh, do be careful!" warned Mrs. Doyle. "You were never much of a tree climber, John!"

The children all giggled in agreement with their mother. Mr. Doyle just laughed as John's face flushed in embarrassment.

Mrs. Doyle walked to the fireplace and sat on her rocker where she began feeding Mary. "John, tell us of the fish that can fly," she said mischievously.

"Fish? Fly?" the younger children excitedly responded almost in unison.

"Aye." John told them. "They can fly through the air like a falcon. They leave the sea with a whoosh," he made a flying motion with his hands imitating flying fish. "They sail through the air like a hawk on a hunt. Some seamen say they can fly as high as the tallest mast! Like birds they are. They sail through the air for a league or two with water flashing off their wings making rainbows on the wind. And then splash, it's back into the sea."

John quickly added, "If a seaman's quick enough, he can grab them out of the air and have them for his dinner. Tis a marvel to behold, or so I'm told."

"Father," asked Kevin, "can that be true? Can fish really fly as John says?"

"I've heard sailors say as much, Kevin," his father stated matter-of-factly as he sipped at his tea. "I've never heard the likes of it 'round the Irish seas, but I've heard men say that fish do fly over some of the oceans far, far away. I've also heard from seamen that where the fish fly," his eyes sparkled as they rolled toward his wife, "is where the bare breasted mermaids reside!"

"Mr. Doyle! Please! Your children are full of deviltry as it is," she admonished. Then added, "Don't you be encouraging such behavior in my house!" But she chuckled as she pondered her husband's words, which caused the children to break out into peals of laughter. Mary continued to suckle at her mother's breast and ignored this newest outbreak as she began to drift off to sleep in the security of her mother's arms.

Mr. Doyle calmly tamped his pipe as he continued grinning. Lighting a straw in the fireplace, he sucked in the blue, sweet smelling pipe smoke, which then billowed around his head. Marie, his five-year-old daughter, proudly rushed forward to blow out the straw once her father's pipe was lit.

"When do you get to load the cannon, John?" asked Michael.

"I would guess that as soon as we clear Belfast, we start drilling," John replied as he stood at attention and saluted. "The captain says

33

that within few days out of Wexford, we will all be highly trained
seamen. By the time we reach the West Indies, I'll bet we'll be the
best-trained cannoneers of any merchant ship. Why, we'll sink any
pirate ship that dares to venture near us."

"Then do you sail to America?" Kevin inquired.

"Aye. The Ellen Marie picks up a cargo of rum and sugar in the
West Indies," John responded. "From there we sail to her homeport
of Baltimore. That's where Captain Robinson has a friend, Mr.
George Baylor, who has a position for me in his wagon shop."

John paused, then proudly added, "And once I have coin in me
pockets, it's off to the interior to seek me fortune." John strutted
about the room imitating a rooster.

"You be watchin' all that coin in yer pocket, John," Mr. Doyle
cautioned with a frown. "Scoundrels abound in every port that will
trick a young lad into giving up his coin. Tricks, so say some seamen,
which are slick as a whistle. Cross paths with one of them and yer
coin is gone for good. A man can't be too careful. Be wary, lad."
Growled Mr. Doyle pointing at John with his pipe stem. "Be wary."

"I will, Father," John responded. "Captain Robinson told me of
those rascals and says his friend will show me the ropes. I need all me
coin to go searching for gold, so I'll be alert for those who would have
me parted from me money."

"And John," his father advised. "I wouldn't be too quick to tell
anyone of your plans of seeking gold. Many a man would kill for a
fortune in gold. Keep yer wits about yourself, son."

"Yes, Father," John replied.

"What trade will you learn in Baltimore?" asked Kevin.

"Mr. Baylor, the captain's friend, builds wagons in his shop,"
responded John. "He'll teach me the wheelwright trade."

"Enough talk for now," interrupted mother. "It's time for Mass.
Father Keeler will be saying a special prayer for John and we mustn't
be late!"

For John, the Mass seemed especially long that Sunday. He
couldn't wait for his father and himself to be off on their long walk
to the docks at Belfast. The Ellen Marie lay in wait for him and his

father must report to his job at the Belfast shipyards early Monday morning.

Father Keeler's homily included many references to the "Prodigal Son" and John just knew that the priest was speaking directly to him. Father Keeler also made reference to the fact that the Church choir would miss John's singing and hoped that John would "continue to raise his lovely voice in praise of the Lord." As the Mass ended, the priest said a special prayer for John and asked all in attendance to continue to pray for John's safe return.

After the Mass, Father Keeler embraced John and sternly reminded him not to forget the Church. Friends and neighbors then gathered around John and wished him well on his journey. As the Doyle's departed for home, Father Keeler reminded John once again that there is indeed Mass in America and that he expected John to be true to his faith each Sunday.

It was a tearful mid-afternoon farewell at the Doyle cottage. Mary continued to sleep through John's departure, but he stopped to gently kiss her on the cheek as he headed for the door. Mr. Doyle stood at the gate in front of the cottage with smoke from his pipe swirling about his head. He fought back his tears, as it wasn't a manly thing to let his family see him weep.

Mrs. Doyle tightly hugged her eldest son at the fence for she feared that she might never hold him in her arms again. Tears ran down her cheeks as she stroked his blonde hair and looked deeply into his blue eyes. As they parted she slipped a few coins into his hand from the family sugar jar. She stifled John's protests with another hug. Standing on her tiptoes, she placed a kiss on his forehead and reluctantly loosed her son from her grip. It broke her heart to have him go so far away, but there was simply no work for the young Catholic men in Ireland and the small family farm was ill equipped to feed so many mouths.

"Come, John," his father called gently, but matter-of-factly. "It's a long walk to Belfast and we must be on our way. Your ship sails on the morning tide and waits for no man."

John pried himself from his mother's embrace. He and his father picked up their canvas sacks, threw them over their shoulders, and started their walk toward the city. Tears flowed from her eyes as his mother turned away from her son. Mr. Doyle had told his children that they were not to follow them down the path, but were to stay within the stone fenced yard at the cottage. But that didn't stop them or John from calling back and forth until they could no longer hear each other.

"Goodbye, John!" "Get us some gold, John." "Take care of Mother, Kevin." "Write us of your adventures, John!" "Come back home soon!" "I'll write when I reach America." The words echoed through the valley and were absorbed into the distant mountains.

John's mother, with Mary in her arms and her other eight children surrounding her, stood in front of the cottage waving and watched as the two men disappeared into the distance; not a dry eye amongst them.

Chapter 3

John had gone aboard the Ellen Marie shortly before dark. Captain Robinson had been busy ashore, so the First Officer, Jeremy Martin, greeted him and introduced himself. He had shown John to the crew's quarters where he stowed his gear. John was startled by the limited space allowed for the crew. Due to the low ceiling below deck a man couldn't even stand upright. Mr. Martin had explained that cargo and profit was of supreme importance to the owners. A crewman's comfort came second! John wasn't sure how well he would adapt to sleeping in a swinging hammock after having always slept on a soft straw-stuffed bed.

John was dismayed when Mr. Martin told him that the canvas hammock wasn't his alone. He would share the hammock with another crewman and added that a seaman spent eight hours on watch and eight hours off while under way. The First Officer again emphasized that space was very limited aboard the Ellen Marie.

Mr. Martin gave John a tour of the ship that evening. The first thing that John became aware of was that there wasn't a cannon in sight! The First Officer told him, "Our two swivel cannons are stored in a locker below deck. They are brought to the main deck and placed in the rail mounts when they need to be fired. Some cargo ships do have a few cannons, but only ships of war carry large cannons. We use ours to fire grapeshot. They're mainly for repelling boarders."

He also discovered that the Ellen Marie had no mermaid beneath her bowsprit. John was told that such carvings are only for the large ships at sea and that a ship the size of the Ellen Marie couldn't afford to carry the extra weight of such a frivolous decoration. And, of course, there was the cost of such an item. John began to see that the owners of this cargo ship went to no extra expense for anything that was not a necessity.

As Mr. Martin gave John the quick tour of the Ellen Marie he informed him that she was built at Fells Point in Baltimore. He explained that the Ellen Marie was designed to haul cargo between the British Isles, Nassau and Baltimore. When John asked how fast she was, Mr. Martin explained, "She's wide in the beam and has a shallow draft. This ship was designed to haul cargo into shallow ports, so she isn't very fast. When we get near Baltimore you'll see Baltimore Clippers. Now there is a fast ship. They're built for speed and can easily outrun any privateer attempting to overtake them at sea. But," he added, "they can't take on as much cargo as the Ellen Marie or pass over many reefs surrounding the islands."

Mr. Martin had explained to John, "Most of our crew will be prisoners working off a sentence given by the Crown. The Ellen Marie makes more profit for her owners without a regular paid crew, so we use prisoners from the Crown's debtor's prison. We need a crew for our return trip, so those men are certain to return to Ireland with us. They have a will and reason to pay their debt and get back with their families here in Ireland. In the past one or two have jumped ship on the islands, but it's a rare event as the men are picked because of their family ties here. The captain gives them a few pounds for the voyage, but the bulk of their recompense is paid right to the court and applied to their debt. And, serving aboard a cargo ship is better than sitting idle in a prison cell."

"How many of the crew are prisoners?" John had asked.

"We'll have ten aboard. They'll be along soon. The 'free passage crewmen' are yourself and two other lads. All three of you will be working your way to America. The Ellen Marie has only three permanent crewmen aboard: Su Long, our cook, Captain Robinson, and me. That's the entire crew; and we carry no passengers. No room for them. The Captain and I share the navigator duties. It's a small brigantine, so I bunk with the Captain as only one of us is on watch at a time once we're at sea. Su Long sleeps in the galley. This is a cargo ship built solely for the profit made by her owners."

"Sixteen men to sail a ship this size?" John was incredulous. "How can such a large ship be sailed by so few men?"

Jeremy roared with laughter. "John, lad. This isn't a large ship at all! She's only a hundred and thirty feet from stem to stern at the water line. The Ellen Marie isn't much larger than a coastal sloop. She could be crewed with as little as six men. Just wait until we get to Liverpool. Then you'll see the big cargo ships and even larger ships of the line." Mr. Martin strolled away laughing leaving John to ponder his decision of sailing to America on this little ship.

Not knowing what to do, John went to the rail and watched the hustle and bustle on the dock below. The gas streetlamps were being lit along the dock and nearby streets as darkness approached. There were so many people coming and going it reminded John of an ant colony. He wondered to himself how any one of them could tell where they were going or what they were doing in the dimness of the evening.

He watched as several British sailors staggered arm in arm along the dock singing with wild abandonment. They had tried to encourage other sailors to join them in their celebration, but lacked any takers. They soon disappeared as they slowly staggered into a dimly lit pub.

A few men sat slumped on crates or barrels on the dock near the ship. John realized that they were in various stages of a drunken stupor. Empty whiskey jugs and wine bottles lay all around them. He wondered how a man could allow himself to sink to such depths of disparity.

John's focus had been drawn to laughter and jeering that had arisen from the crowded dock. Peering into the darkened street he had discovered that two guards were escorting a group of men toward the dock. He quickly realized that these men were all chained together at the ankle. Each carried a small sea bag thrown over his shoulder. The crowd had taken pleasure at the discomfort of these chained men. Occasionally a drunken sailor had thrown an empty bottle or jug their way. As the prisoners started up the gangplank, John realized that these must be the crewmen from the debtors' prison. Many on the streets and dock had taken sarcastic delight in the misery of these unfortunate souls.

"Welcome aboard," John heard behind him. A young man had come up beside him and introduced himself, "I'm Patrick Hurley from Antrim. Are you one of the working passage crewman?"

"I am," John had answered as he shook the man's hand. The stranger had a pleasant, sincere smile. Dark brown hair hung over his forehead and almost concealed dark brown eyes, which reflected the fire from the nearby streetlights. The young man seemed to be a few years older than John.

"Well, I'm one as well," Patrick told him. "I have the promise of a position as a printer's devil in Philadelphia. Do you have a position waiting for you in America?"

"Aye, a wheelwright apprenticeship in Baltimore. But that's only until I can make enough money to venture into the interior."

"I envy your daring, John," Patrick responded, "what with all the Indian troubles out in the mountain areas."

"I've not heard that there were…" John's statement had been interrupted by a loud noise that came from the bottom of the gangplank. It was the prisoners' leg chains banging on the wooden gangplank while boarding the ship. Once on deck, the guards unlocked the chains and forcibly lined the men up. Mr. Martin had appeared from below deck and exchanged papers with the guards who wasted no time as they gathered up the loosened chains and scurried down the gangplank. John noted that, with the focus of their earlier sense of amusement being no longer at hand, the crowd on the dock had gone back to doing whatever they were doing before the appearance of the prisoners.

"Attention on deck for the captain," Mr. Martin ordered.

Captain Robinson, a tall, slender, but muscular man, had come up the gangplank and stopped on deck in front of the assembled group of prisoners. He stood for a moment with his hands clasped behind his back then spoke to the men, "I have selected most of you because you have sailed with me before. You know that I can be a fair man and will treat well those who obey orders. Those who resist will face the lash. We sail on the morning tide." He turned to John and Patrick, "You two report to my cabin immediately. Mr. Martin, get these other men settled below deck!" Without further word the captain disappeared through the door to his cabin.

"Come on, John," said Patrick. "I don't think Captain Robinson is a person that likes to be kept waiting!"

Both lads removed their caps and entered the Captain's quarters to find the third free crewman, a short powerful man in his early twenties, already there. His dark black eyes peered out from shaggy black hair. John was amazed at the man's muscular arms. He looked as strong as an ox.

"You three lads will be treated no better than the rest of the crew on this voyage," growled Captain Robinson. "You must learn your responsibilities quickly and your duties at sea are not to be taken lightly. There is danger aplenty once we are at sea. When you are given an order, obey it instantly, whether it comes from Mr. Martin or myself. If any of you give us any trouble, you will face the lash as well as the prisoner crew. We don't have time to give an order a second time. Beginning tonight all three of you will begin rigorous training by Mr. Martin, Su Long, and myself. Any questions?"

"No, Captain," the three answered almost simultaneously.

"Introductions are called for at this point," said Captain Robinson in a much-subdued voice. "You know me and all have met my First Officer, Mr. Martin. Our cook, Su Long, is gathering last minute supplies. Su Long is of Chinese ancestry, but is one of the best cooks at sea. He's sailed with me for over five years. While we are underway rid yourselves of any thoughts of a man's nationality. All my crewmembers are equal as long as they obey their orders. I hope I have made myself perfectly clear."

He gestured toward John as he continued, "John Doyle is from Ballylee; your principal duties will be working for Su Long in the galley. Naturally there will be other work for you, but cooking and cleaning the galley will be your main duty. Patrick Hurley is from Antrim; you will be assigned under Mr. Martin. Jacque Lyons is from Belfast. You'll be assigned under me. Patrick and Jacque will be maintaining the ship and rigging while underway.

"We have ten prisoners from the debtors prison for crew. There's not a hardened criminal amongst them and most have served under my command before. They are all accomplished seamen. While at sea, I expect them to be treated with the same respect any ordinary seaman would receive. Their unfortunate financial woes are no concern of mine and shouldn't be any concern of yours. They all have families back here in Belfast and only want to serve their sentences and receive their freedom."

The captain continued, "Once we sail we each serve eight hours on watch and eight hours off watch. But, while off watch you could be expected to perform any extra duties as required. You just might find yourself not getting much sleep while we are underway. However, if any man is caught sleeping while on watch…well, believe me, you'll regret it! The sea is a hazardous place. You must be prepared for anything at anytime. Any questions?"

"No, Captain," the men all responded.

"Patrick and Jacque report to Mr. Martin on the foredeck. John, remain here for the time being. I want to introduce you to Su Long."

After the two dismissed men departed the cabin Captain Robinson turned to John and told him matter-of-factly, "John, you are my cousin's eldest son, but from this moment on I cease to acknowledge that kinship. I can't show any favoritism while at sea. You are now just any other able-bodied seaman and will be treated accordingly. Do I make myself perfectly clear?"

"Yes, sir."

"Come with me, then. I hear Su Long banging around in the galley."

Captain Robinson took John to the galley and the introduction was brief, as the captain was needed on deck to oversee final preparations. John saw the respect the cook had for his captain as Su Long watched Captain Robinson disappear on deck.

Su Long turned to John and shook his hand. He was a very small man of slender build, but had a strong, powerful handshake. Su Long didn't wear the traditional pigtail that John was familiar with, but in every other respect he was the typical Chinese man that one would see around the dock areas. He dressed in English seaman fashion rather than the "pajamas" that most Chinese seemed to prefer. Su Long, in perfect English, told John, "The captain is a very fair man, but he can be very strict when he must. You and I will get along fine as long as you do as I tell you. We will probably be the two busiest men on the ship because we prepare four meals a day, one every six hours. You may not get much sleep on this trip! You go catch some sleep now. Morning will come quickly and we will have our first meal at sea!"

John went below deck and squeezed his six-foot frame into his assigned hammock; no easy thing for someone accustomed to a flat straw bed. He listened to the noises above him on the main deck and thought he'd never get any sleep with all the thumping and bumping inches above his head. The other five crewmen in the crowded cabin were soon snoring away and without realizing it, he quickly joined them in their slumber.

John was lying back against a tree enjoying the warm summer sun as he watched the sheep that grazed about him. He could hear the creaking of large tree limbs as they swayed in the afternoon breeze. He was suddenly troubled by something tugging at his sleeve. Was it one of the sheep nibbling on his wool jacket? He tried to shake the nuisance away.

"John, John. Get up, lad!" It was Su Long. "It's time to feed those on watch."

John woke up fully and then realized that the noise he had dreamt about was the rigging creaking in the wind. The cabin about him rocked back and forth causing his hammock to swing gently like the pendulum of a clock. It was an odd sensation. He rolled out of the hammock and stood up, but was too late in remembering the low ceiling. He painfully banged his forehead on one of the beams. He staggered to the galley just off the main deck.

Unsympathetic to his plight, Su Long said, "We've been underway for a couple hours. If you're going to get seasick, get it over with."

John was wondering just what Su Long meant when suddenly his stomach flipped upside down. He felt horrible and his belly cramped painfully. He ran to the rail just outside the galley and fed the fish whatever food was left in his stomach from the evening before. He felt pale and shaken by the sensations in his protesting stomach.

Su Long called out from the galley, "We have work to do! Eat some soda crackers. That will help settle your stomach."

John hesitantly nibbled on a soda cracker Su Long handed him. As the spasms eased, he heard laughter and turned angrily to see Patrick standing at the quarterdeck rail above him.

Patrick held his hands up towards John as if to stop him in place. "Hey, take it easy, John. I've already done that several times since we sailed. Just wait a while and you'll have your 'sea legs' as Mr. Martin calls them!"

John looked back up at Patrick and saw a large red welt on his forehead. Simultaneously they each rubbed their sore spots and laughed in mutual understanding.

Then John moaned as his body cramped and tried once again to empty an already empty stomach. Coming to his rescue, Su Long showed up with more soda crackers and said, "You eat these and the sea sickness will be a thing of the past. This happens to many the first couple hours at sea. Come on, we have crew to feed and there is no time for this! Get busy and your stomach will forget the movement of the ship."

It was with great difficulty, caused by his sore midsection and tender forehead, that John carried cups and plates of food to the crew on watch. Several of the crew had given him knowing glances when they saw the red welt across his forehead. For John, it was a new experience, negotiating the deck as it rocked and pitched back and forth as he delivered the meals to the others. He hadn't dared look down at the food on the pewter plates or the liquid sloshing in the mugs he carried! Fortunately, however, his seasickness had passed quickly. Those off watch had gone into the galley to sit at the small table or sat on the deck to eat. But John passed up his first meal at sea as he wasn't sure he could have kept it down.

It wasn't until after all were fed that John realized that the Ellen Marie was actually out to sea. The sun had risen on the portside of the ship and revealed a wisp of land off the starboard rail. He realized at that moment that home was slowly disappearing over the horizon.

The snapping white sails above him had drawn his attention to the rigging and he sharply inhaled the fresh sea air as he looked up at the clear blue sky. He began to feel much better. Mr. Martin had told the three young lads that the ship wouldn't rock around quite so much once they had some cargo in the hold. "When she's empty, the Ellen Marie bobs around like a cork on top of the waves," he advised them in assurance of better days ahead.

John was fascinated by the waves and their white crests. He had seen the ocean from on land, but aboard ship it looked totally different. The sunlight penetrated several feet beneath the waters and he actually saw the many small fish that swam along side the ship. A steady breeze whipped the ocean crests into a gentle foam that slowly disappeared between the rise of each wave. John was stimulated by a strong breeze that blew his hair back and forth as he moved about the ship. On the beach there was always the smell of seaweed mingled in the sea air. He deeply inhaled the clean air and took pleasure in the fresh aroma of its cleanliness.

It had been a quick trip to Liverpool and they soon entered the busy harbor. John was in awe at the sight of King George's ships of the line anchored in the harbor. Each ship was trimmed with bright colors and flew long banners from the tallest masts. Many highly polished brass fittings glistened in the afternoon sun. When they passed the HMS Coronation, John realized that the mizzenmast of the Ellen Marie had barely reached the top-most deck of the large man-of-war. Captain Robinson commented to those standing near him on the deck that the Coronation was heading into retirement after a long and glorious record. "And it's just as well, as I wouldn't want to come under her guns with the current troubles." He had no time to explain himself as he strode off barking orders as the Ellen Marie neared the dock.

None of the crew were allowed ashore. The Ellen Marie was to be at dock for only a few hours to load cargo, then immediately sail for Wexford. John had been so busy helping load crates into the central hold that he didn't have time to give the port a good once over. He did note that there seemed to be a lot of military activity going on with many soldiers moving around the docks in formation to the beat of a drum. Even that didn't seem so unusual at the time, as England was at war with France.

It wasn't until they were well underway that Mr. Martin said to John and Jacque that he was glad to be out of Liverpool before there was any trouble. "Some people in England don't take favor to a ship flying the American flag taking on cargo at English ports these days."

"What trouble is that?" Jacque had quizzed him.

In response, Mr. Martin grumbled, "English bureaucrats want all the shipping business to themselves. More coin in their pockets! And I guess they're still agitated about losing control over the Colonies and the profit from all the taxes they imposed."

John hoped he was going to get a lesson in politics, but as usual, there were shipboard duties to be performed. He quickly learned that Mr. Martin and Captain Robinson didn't express their opinions on their political thoughts. After all, there were many English subjects aboard who only wanted be get back home to their families.

Wexford, in southern Ireland, was another short stopover. John went with Su Long into the town to purchase supplies for the next leg of the voyage. When they returned to the Ellen Marie, they found that the cargo, bound for Nassau in the West Indies, was all loaded and Captain Robinson was anxious to set sail. There seemed to be some sort of trouble brewing in the busy port and the captain wanted to be quickly at sea.

"It's all politics," said Su Long as he walked away shaking his head. That statement had left John even more confused. Little did John know about the troubles at sea between the United States and England.

To gain best advantage of the trade winds, Captain Robinson took the Ellen Marie south toward the northern coast of Africa before heading west. As they entered the warmer waters of the Atlantic Ocean the sea had come alive with fish. Earlier in the voyage Su Long taught John how to catch pilchards by dragging a net behind the ship. When fried the fish had a fairly decent taste, but they were small and very bony. In the warmer tropical waters Su Long threw several hooked lines over the side and immediately caught two tuna. They were hard to pull aboard and the lines cut John's hands as he helped pull on the strong cord. These were the largest fish John or Jacque had ever seen. Their flesh was red, almost like beef, but had a distinctive taste once they were filleted and fried in hot lard. John decided that he liked tuna much better than pilchards. They also caught a few mackerel, but John found their meat to be oily. In addition, any mackerel they caught had to be eaten the same day as the meat spoiled quickly in the heat and began to have a most undesirable odor.

Flying fish were of great interest to John. He had suspected that the tales he heard back home were not true. Something sailors told just to draw you into their fanciful yarns. But as they entered warmer waters fish did indeed fly from the sea and glide for long periods alongside the Ellen Marie. Every once in a while a flying fish would soar above deck level and land with a plop on the deck. John asked Su Long about cooking them, but was told that they were as bony as the pilchards in the northern sea. "Why eat flying fish when we can have tuna or mackerel?"

Some sunny days silver flashes in the water had drawn the attention of the crew. Mr. Martin told John and Patrick that the silver flashes indicated that Blue Bonita were swimming alongside the Ellen Marie. Try as he may, Su Long had no luck catching any. He told John that he was disappointed as they are a very tasty fish.

The occasional fin cutting the waters around the ship was also spotted. "Sharks have learned to follow ships," Su Long told John. "They know we throw garbage overboard and sharks are opportunistic eaters. Don't fall overboard, Lad," he told him as he laughed. "They'll eat anything that falls into the sea!"

A month into their journey, the Ellen Marie came across a raging storm. Both Captain Robinson and Mr. Martin were called to deck by the watch. As soon as he realized the ship couldn't sail around the huge storm, the captain ordered everything battened down and the hatches checked for tightness.

"This will be a bad one," Mr. Martin advised John. "Get below and wake everyone. We've got to drop some sail before the winds pick up."

John had only been below deck a few minutes when the winds began to howl and whistle through the rigging. Several men were ordered to the topmast. The topsails were pulled in and lashed tightly to the spar. The Ellen Marie would sail through the storm with only her two main sails.

As the small ship pitched furiously back and forth, waves crashed over her bow soaking everyone on deck. John and most of the crew were ordered below once their duties were completed. Patrick, the captain and two others remained at the helm. The pitching soon became so erratic that it took two men to control the wheel. Captain Robinson, his voice barely heard over the howling winds, ordered all on deck to be secured with safety lines around their waist, the opposite ends tethered to the rail.

Only minutes after the order was obeyed an enormous wave hit the bow of the Ellen Marie and she lunged to port and quickly swerved to starboard. Her entire hull moaned at the extreme force of the wave. Patrick, at the helm, lost his grip on the wheel and was washed over the side. Quick action by the other men on watch saved him as he was pulled back aboard sputtering and gasping as his lungs emptied of seawater.

Captain Robinson ordered Jacque to the helm as Patrick was carried below. Once inside the galley, Su Long discovered a long gash on the side of Patrick's head. When he went over the side he had struck a rigging stanchion on the rail. With the ship pitching so wildly around, all Su Long could do was tie a cloth around his head to stop the bleeding. Patrick wasn't unconscious, but was stunned by the blow. He lay on the floor of the galley as seawater sloshed back and forth across his limp body. There wasn't much else any one could do for him until the storm abated.

The storm raged on for several hours. Then the sea became strangely peaceful.

Su Long took the opportunity to sew up the three-inch gash in Patrick's head with fishing line. John grimaced as he held Patrick's head while the stitches were sewn in, but Patrick just groaned unaware of the needle that was piercing his skin. He seemed to be still stunned by the initial blow to his head.

John and Su Long went up on deck to a strange sight. The sea was calm, but all around them was a wall of dark gray clouds and mist. Su Long pointed upward, which drew John's attention to the sky. There, high above the Ellen Marie, the gray clouds formed a tight circle. In the middle the sky was a clear, eggshell blue. An eerie silence lay all about the ship. The sea had become ominously still and calm.

John noticed that two crewmen had begun manning a pump amidships. As each man pumped up and down, a stream of water was removed from the hull of the Ellen Marie and returned to the sea. Other hands got busy securing lines and sails that had come loose during the storm. John had been puzzled by the urgency of the crew since the storm seemed to be over.

"We're in the middle of a hurricane," Su Long explained. "It's called the eye. In a few minutes the storm will once again overtake us. We better go check below and be sure everything is tied down."

Su Long was correct and shortly the strong winds struck the ship once again. John began to think that the Ellen Marie would last no longer in the continuing tempest. He felt like the storm would tear her in half. However, as suddenly as the hurricane had returned it slipped off over the far horizon. Under a clear blue sky, a gentle breeze arose and sent the battered ship back on her course toward Nassau. The only remainder of the storm was a few wispy clouds passing peacefully overhead.

A few days later, as they neared the American continent, a few whale pods had been spotted splashing and spouting in the distance. John was fascinated by the size of them. Captain Robinson let John look through his telescope, but the whales were too far away to give any size comparison. He had seen drawings of whales in books back home and wished he could have seen them up close.

Occasionally a porpoise or two would play in the bow wave created by the Ellen Marie. They were fun to watch as they jumped in and out of the water. Much to Captain Robinson's relief, no pirates were sighted as they neared the Caribbean.

The daily routine had become almost boring to John. It seemed that just as the clean up from one meal was completed another was being prepared. He even gave up going to his hammock below deck and slept on some cargo crates in the galley. Su Long laughed at him for sleeping on the hard surface, but John's youth allowed him to sleep peacefully in such an uncomfortable place, blocking out the noises of crewmen passing in and out of the galley as he slept.

John and Jacque developed a friendship during the trip. They spent many hours talking and discussing the Ellen Marie and the sea. Jacque also took pleasure in fishing when the opportunity arose. Patrick was recovering from his injury and had returned to some of his duties. It was rare that the three had time to spend together as Patrick was on a different watch than John and Jacque.

About three nights out of the Port of Nassau the Ellen Marie gave a lurch when it bumped something large while sailing on a calm sea. The bump was enough to awaken the off watch sailors. Lanterns were suspended over the side, but other than the foam caused by the wake of the Ellen Marie, nothing was sighted in the darkness. Some of the crew had gone below to check the integrity of the hull at the bow, but there was no damage. The Captain assumed that they had made contact with a whale. "Sometimes that happens," he mumbled to those nearby.

Everyone was relieved as the islands of the Bahamas finally came into view. The lush, distant hills grew higher and higher as the ship neared land. To John, the island seemed to climb magically right out of the sea. The Ellen Marie had been at sea several months and John was glad that his voyage would soon be over. A few more weeks, he thought to himself, and he would plant his feet on land for good. He looked forward to the day the Ellen Marie arrived in Baltimore. He and Jacque decided that a life at sea was not for them.

As the Ellen Marie neared the island the ocean waters became clearer. John could look down and see the coral reefs as they passed over them. The reefs were like mountains looming up from the kelp beds. The water was blue-green and many colorful fish could now be seen as they swam beside the ship. The multitude of colors and shapes of the fish around the reefs had surprised him.

Captain Robinson was startled to find several British warships at anchor as the Ellen Marie neared the British port of Nassau. The war between Britain and France had kept most British warships on the far side of the Atlantic Ocean. While it was not unusual to see ships flying the Union Jack in these waters it seemed unusual to find so many here. Aboard the Ellen Marie there was much speculation, as none could understand why so many ships of war were needed in the southern West Indies.

As the Ellen Marie slowly began to enter the harbor a long boat filled with British sailors and Marines approached her. When the long boat drew alongside, several sailors and armed Royal Marines boarded the Ellen Marie. A naval officer held up a scroll and read it to Captain Robinson, "By order of his Majesty, your ship and its cargo are hereby commandeered by the Royal Navy."

Captain Robinson was shocked by this order. "That's piracy!" He protested as he accepted the scroll from the officer. He scanned the document before handing it back.

But his complaints had fallen on deaf ears. The British sailors took over the helm and guided the Ellen Marie dockside. As Captain Robinson and his crew stood helplessly on deck, their ship was secured to the dock. Captain Robinson was immediately escorted away by two Royal Marines. The Marine guard ordered the remaining crew to leave the ship. The men from the debtors prison were gathered up by Marines and escorted away. The remaining five crewmen stood on the dock in indignation over these events as they watched their "pirated" cargo unloaded.

Captain Robinson returned shortly to the dock. He was angrier than when he had departed. "The Ellen Marie has been taken by the Royal Navy! War has been declared between King George and the United States," he growled. "Our prisoner crew is being sent back to England and at any moment we may be conscripted into the British Navy. Let's not stand about here. I don't think this is a safe place to be."

The six men departed the dock as the evening shadows began to fall. As they were heading down a dimly lit street of the town, they glanced back and saw the Ellen Marie being moved to a mooring out in the bay.

Just as they passed a darkened pub a man beckoned to them, "Here, lads, come in here out of harms way."

The six stepped into the dim pub. Only a few smoky candles illuminated the interior. It took a moment or two for John's eyes to become accustomed to the darkness after the brighter light of the warm Caribbean evening. His attention was drawn toward the bar where a very heavy woman of indescribable age stood loudly laughing as a drunken British sailor amused himself by plunging his hand into the bodice of her dirty, ragged dress. The sailor was trying to kiss her on the heavy wrinkles on her neck and she giggled lewdly at his attempts, but still encouraged him on.

The stranger led the men to a table in a darkened corner. The heavy-set woman that had stood at the bar came to the table and draped her ample bosom over Patrick's shoulder. Sweat trickled down her heavy jowls and into the crevice between her huge breasts. She smelled as if she never bathed.

With a big grin, she asked, "What will it be, Lads?"

Captain Robinson said, "Rum all around."

The men felt relieved when she quickly departed the table. However, she soon returned with seven mugs of warm rum, foam dripping sloppily down onto her meaty hands. She grinned at them with a mouth that was missing several teeth and laughed aloud while reaching over to gather up the few coins Captain Robinson threw upon the dingy table. The men drew back as her breath was even worse than her body odor.

John sipped at the warm rum and found it bitter. He had only tasted rum a few times back in Ireland. This liquid was obviously a poor, watered down substitute. None of the other men made comment, but sipped at their mugs, so John didn't say a word.

Once she departed, the stranger had peered cautiously about the pub and then waved the six men closer. "My name is Mike Handshaw. My ship was commandeered ten days ago and the Brits conscripted all my crewmates. While my mates were being gathered up I slipped over the side of our ship and swam to the dock in the dark. I've been hiding out waiting for a chance to get back to New York."

"What can we do for you?" Captain Robinson asked cautiously.

"Your ship is only a few hundred feet out in the bay," Mike responded. "I suggest we swim out there tonight, take the ship and sail out of here."

The crew all looked at him with astonishment. After a long pause, Captain Robinson responded, "Are you mad? It's bad enough to be pressed into service in the Royal Navy, but to take our ship back would be considered piracy. We could all be hung!"

"Men have been conscripted by the Brits and never heard from again." Mike whispered. "Would that be any better than being hung? Conscripts are nothing better than slaves and are treated so. I have a wife and three small children waiting for me. If the Brits take me I may never see my family again. At least taking your ship back and sailing for home offers some chance; some hope."

After a pause to let these men think about what he just told them, Mike continued. "Your ship could be gone tomorrow. We must act fast. There will be a sliver of a moon tonight. We can swim out to your ship in the darkness. The guards are very lax about their duties and only two or three marines will be aboard. We can probably catch them sleeping at their posts. We slip aboard, tie them up, cut the mooring rope and set only one sail. As sleepy as this garrison is they won't notice a small ship slowly moving across the bay."

"And how do you propose we pass the Man-of-War anchored near the harbor entrance?" inquired Captain Robinson. "They surely will notice even a small ship passing by."

"Small local fishing craft come and go at all hours. The tide and wind will be with us after midnight. I've spent the past week watching the harbor all night waiting for a chance to climb aboard one of those boats. But British loyalists, who would certainly capture me, have manned them all. I needed Americans to help me overpower a ship. And then God sent your ship and crew to answer my prayers!"

"Naturally, the British Navy will simply let us sail away!" Mr. Martin mumbled.

"Once outside the harbor entrance we set full sail. If we steer to the west there is a reef that no Man-of-War can cross. Your ship is empty of cargo. She sits high in the water and being light she can out sail any other ship on the morning winds. We will have several hours head start on any pursuer. Tacking around the reef will take the war ships an additional six or seven hours. By the time the Brits know what's happening we can be over the horizon and start north for home."

"How do we know that you're correct in your facts?" asked Captain Robinson.

"I was the first officer on my ship, the Genevieve. We ran cargo between New York and Nassau for many years. I know the tides, the reefs and phases of the moon. I do know what I am talking about," Mike Handshaw responded desperately. "We've only got one chance to escape the Brits. Now that there are several American seamen in port, the marines will begin a intensive search for all of us. You are all lucky that you are not in prison now."

"It's an awfully dangerous undertaking, but the plan sounds feasible." Captain Robinson responded. After a pause, he turned to his men and asked, "What do you lads think?"

The seven men sat murmuring for a long time pausing their conversation each time someone neared their table. What a risk to take! This man seemed to know what he was talking about. They all could be much worse off being pressed into the British Navy. The plan sounded well thought out, but...What to do?

Chapter 4

At midnight, the seven men had silently slipped into the warm waters of Nassau Bay. It was a crystal clear night and the town was almost silent at that hour. A few distant windows were seen dimly lit by the occasional candle or lantern. The Marine guards lolled at their posts on the docks sleepily snuggling their muskets to their chests. In the distance, an occasional barking dog was the only sound louder than the lapping of the water on the rocky embankment. It almost seemed too quiet and the hairs on John's neck stood up with the fear of discovery. At any moment he had expected to hear a shot ring out and feel the searing pain of a bullet tearing into his flesh.

The seven men slowly swam toward mid-bay creating barely a ripple in the calm waters. They moved determinedly toward the Ellen Marie and while the swim was only a few hundred feet it seemed like a mile in the darkness. The warm waters had cooled as the men reached the deeper portion of the bay. Barely a sound was heard as the men cautiously approached the Ellen Marie. The ship appeared before them as a darkened shadow in the dim light from the sliver of the new moon. A million stars had twinkled above, but offered very little light to brighten the dark night. Not a lamp was lit aboard their ship.

As they neared the Ellen Marie, only one marine was visible. He had removed his coat. His white blouse now seemed to glow in the minimal moonlight making his frame standout from the darkened objects on the deck. He was slumped over his musket as he sat on a hatch near the mizzenmast. John almost chuckled when he realized that he could hear the man's snoring fifty feet away from the ship.

The feel of her wooden hull against their fingertips reassured the men that they had finally reached the Ellen Marie. They groped around the side of the hull until they reached a rope amidships that had been left carelessly dangling by the British sailors when the ship was moved from the dock to the mooring.

Slowly and silently the anxious men eased themselves up the rope and over the rail onto the deck. Keeping in a low crouch, they floated stealthily like ghosts across the deck not making the least bit of noise. The trickle of water that dripped from their clothing was muted by the gentle whisper of the almost calm waves that lapped on the planking of the Ellen Marie. The dozing guard had heard not a sound.

Mike was right in his estimate about the two marines aboard the Ellen Marie. The guard John had seen on deck, and heard snoring, sat on a hatch leaning against the mast. His head dropped to his chest. An empty bottle of rum had lain on the deck nearby. His loud snoring was annoying, but appreciated, as it told the approaching men that the guard was unaware of their presence. Patrick and Jeremy softly eased their way aft to silence the dozing man. Jeremy grabbed him from behind clamping a firm hand over his mouth. Just as his musket slid toward the deck, Patrick caught it and gently lowered it without a sound. The guard, who barely stirred from his sleep, was quickly subdued. Only a slight rustling sound was heard as they bound him.

John and Jacque found the other guard a few seconds later sprawled out, asleep, in one of the crew hammocks. He held a piece of partially eaten biscuit in one hand and a half empty bottle of rum in the other. He had obviously been gorging himself on their stores of food. In his drunken state, he hadn't wakened as he was bound and gagged. Both guards were locked in the galley storeroom. The Captain left Su Long to stand guard over the Marines, with his trusty meat cleaver, lest they wake and make any sound.

John was amazed how quiet they had been at hoisting the small staysail. By sprinkling grease on the halyard, the men were able to muffle the top pulleys as they slowly heaved the sail into place. Even the pulleys seemed to understand the pending danger and had quietly allowed the sail to be raised without complaint. A slight tug on the sail line told the men that even nature was cooperating. The gentle winds were, as Mike had promised, blowing toward the open sea. As Patrick cut the mooring line, the Ellen Marie nudged softly forward heading for freedom. The star filled night seemed brighter to John, but the sleepy town didn't notice the little ship as it slipped farther and farther away from peril.

It seemed an eternity, but within an hour they neared the looming Man-of-War anchored at the harbor entrance. They were pleased to find that gun ports had all been closed and the entire ship seemed to sleep peacefully in the warmth of the tropical night. The few deck lanterns aboard dimly revealed a handful of marines and sailors on watch. Two marines had been idly chatting beneath one lantern at the nearby port rail. It seemed to John that if he had cast a stone at the two Marines, he could have easily hit one of them. As the Ellen Marie silently passed by, one of the marines did look their way, seemingly straining as he peered into the darkness at a sound he thought he heard. After a moments pause, he went back to his animated discussion with the other marine who had his back to them. In the clear night air John could have almost understood their muted words as the Ellen Marie drifted by them without a sound.

Shortly after passing the Man-of-War the small ship neared the mouth of the bay. Captain Robinson told the crew to quietly load the two captured marines into the long boat and put them over the side. Mike mumbled that he'd rather cut their throats and drop them overboard at sea, but the captain quietly replied, "In the eyes of the Crown we may be pirates stealing a ship, but if we become murderers we'll carry a bounty on our heads the rest of our lives. Do as I say. In their drunken state it will take them hours to untie themselves. By then we'll be safely at sea." The long boat was stealthily launched and had quietly entered the waters of the bay. Without delay the two sleeping marines were sent into the night on a soundless cruise.

The Ellen Marie finally reached the breakwater and it was time to set all her sails. The winds were stronger here and the surf loud enough to swallow any sounds that the crew might make as they unfurled the remainder of her sails. The men worked as quietly as possible, but the Ellen Marie had held her silence as long as she could. As her mainsail opened there was a loud snap of canvas as the wind filled the large sail placing a weighty strain on the lines. The mainmast had groaned and squeaked loudly with the heavy load. Far behind, in the darkness, someone yelled, "Ahoy, who goes there?"

Just as the topsails were set, a commotion was heard aboard the Man-of-War as she came alive. More lanterns lit up the darkness as the ship bell frantically clanged. Bellowing orders were now heard echoing across the waters of the bay. Doors banged open and shut on the warship in her hasty arousal from a quiet nights sleep. By this time the Ellen Marie was a full half-mile away and flying like the wind onto the open sea. Captain Robinson spun the helm and the Ellen Marie, in answer, had gone hard to port. Without hesitation she headed out over the dangerous reef that lay just below the foaming ocean waters. Every man aboard could feel the joy that the Ellen Marie felt with her new found freedom!

The officers aboard the British warship could do little more than watch in disbelief as the small cargo ship slipped around a point of land and disappeared rapidly into the night.

As Mike Handshaw had suggested, Captain Robinson kept their heading to the west until almost midday. Any ships in pursuit would likely assume that the escaping ship would immediately head due north for a safe port in American waters. During the day a few sails were spotted heading toward Nassau, but not a sail was seen following the Ellen Marie. Once he felt she was out of harms way,

Captain Robinson changed her helm to the north and the security of home!

A quick inventory of their supplies revealed that the store of rum had been almost completely consumed by the British sailors and marines. Her armory was devoid of its two small cannons, muskets and gunpowder. The small safe in the captain's cabin had been discovered in its hiding location and the door had been jimmied open. Except for the ships log, the contents were gone. Obviously lining some British sailor's pockets.

Only a few bottles of rum remained untouched and the water supply was too low for a long, non-stop trip to Baltimore. However, the good news was that her dry food stores were almost untouched. They had more than enough to last them the next several weeks. Fresh fruits and vegetables would be a welcome addition, but were not as serious as the lack of fresh water. After a trip across the Atlantic, the small amount of water remaining in her kegs was becoming fouled.

While the captain's cabin was found to be in complete disarray, John, Patrick and Jacque were pleased to discover that the Brits had not ransacked the crew's quarters. Most of their personal belongings were untouched. While the men had taken few possessions along on this trip, what little they did take meant a lot to them. A lock of hair from a loved one, a hand written love note, or a locket with a tiny portrait was a very important memoir. To have a British sailor steal these items would have been devastating. John found the coins his mother had given to him still safely hidden behind a bulkhead. He was much relieved at their safety.

Once the Ellen Marie had cleared land, Captain Robinson assembled the men at the helm. "Mr. Martin, set our course to the Berry Islands. We will take on fresh water near Whale Cay. There's not much there of interest to the British Navy and, with luck, we will not see any war ships. We have almost enough food aboard to get us to our homeport without rationing, but we'll take on any fresh fruits and vegetables we stumble across. Let's just hope that the

British Navy has spread itself so thin that it can't protect all these small islands."

"What's this all about?" Jacque had asked. "I thought the British had a peace treaty with the colonists."

"Apparently the peace is over." As he shook his head in disbelief, Captain Robinson explained, "The British have decided to halt all trade and take control of the shipping between America and Europe. American ships are being taken as prizes and their crews pressed into service aboard British war ships. It was fortunate for us that there was an oversight by the Port Commander and we were not immediately conscripted. We could have been imprisoned or taken aboard a British war ship."

Looking out to the horizon, he added, "The Ellen Marie is going to get back to Baltimore as quickly as we can sail her. I want to find out what's going on and I don't trust stopping at any other ports and have her, or any of us, fall into British hands. We were very lucky to get out of Nassau before the Ellen Marie was sent off on some military mission."

Captain Robinson turned to Mike Handshaw and shook his hand as he told him, "We owe a deep gratitude to you for your audacious plan of escape. I don't think any of us would have thought of attempting such a bold venture without your help."

The following evening they arrived at Whale Cay. As they frequently sounded the bottom for any treacherous reefs, the men slowly and cautiously guided the Ellen Marie through the unfamiliar waters. The long boat would have made things simpler, but it was gone. The captain knew that the Ellen Marie would be hidden inside the cove in the event a British ship happened to pass by. By nightfall the ship was safely anchored close to shore. A raft had been quickly assembled to carry barrels, filled with fresh water, back to the ship.

The men found a spring a short way inland and carried several kegs of precious water back to the ship under the cover of darkness. The island also offered many fruits and nuts ripe for the picking. John and Su Long filled and carried several baskets back to the ship while the rest of the men transported the water. In the darkness of a new moon it had been difficult work, but the less they were seen, the safer they were from watchful eyes. Captain Robinson had told the others, that at this time he didn't know where the British might have ships or troops.

During the night several fires had been spotted along the shore several miles from the cove. The captain surmised that the fires were islanders, but to be on the safe side they took turns on guard throughout the night. The distant fires died down around midnight and no one was seen or heard while they were anchored in the cove. The captain was also pleased that no ships' lights were seen at sea during the darkened hours.

The crew hoisted anchor just as the red glow of the sun began to light up the eastern horizon. However, it was still quite dim in the small bay when they departed. Leaving the Cay over the hazardous reefs in the early morning light was dangerous, but the tide was high offering a deeper crossing over the reefs than when they arrived. The orange ball of sunlight was just showing itself on the horizon when the Ellen Marie returned to the open sea.

Captain Robinson felt they were safer on the open sea where distance offered some protection. There was no way to know if the British Navy was bothering to search for them. A few triangular sails were spotted in the distance while they were leaving Whale Cay, but none of them seemed to be interested in a small cargo ship passing through the area. The sails they spotted were assumed to be local fishermen.

Keeping the coast a good distance off to her portside, the Ellen Marie rapidly put the West Indies behind her. Captain Robinson decided to keep as close to the coast as possible in the event a Man-of-War should spot them. He knew that the Ellen Marie could sail over shallow reefs where the larger war ships could not give chase. His ploy was to stay far away from the shore, and avoid identification, but still be close enough to use the reefs to his best advantage.

On the open sea a careful watch was kept. The men took turns standing in the upper rigging during the daylight hours watching for other ships. If any sail was spotted, the Ellen Marie would steer slightly off course to avoid any contact with the other vessel. At night the captain forbid lanterns or fires in the galley to be lit. This prolonged the trip, but was the safest course to follow.

The Ellen Marie began sailing closer to shore as they neared the mainland in hope that most shipping would be further out on the regular sea-lanes. They had spotted a few distant sails near the Carolinas, but no one approached them. This area of the coast did cause some concern for the crew, as it was well known for pirate activities, and they were completely unarmed. Good fortune still sailed with them.

The Ellen Marie arrived at the entrance to the Chesapeake Bay in the very early hours of the morning. After searching the southern shore with his telescope, Captain Robinson ordered the men to take her into the bay keeping close to the northern shore at Cape Charles. No sails had been seen at the entrance to the bay, but he reasoned that by this time the large port at Norfolk could have fallen into enemy hands. And, while no activity was seen around the southern coast, he felt that if any warships were in the area, they might be close to the port at Norfolk. The captain also had expressed his concern that there were no sails near the mouth of the Chesapeake. In this normally busy sea-lane there certainly should have been some activity.

They were doing well until they reached the entrance to the Rappahannock River. There they had discovered two small British warships at anchor. The Ellen Marie was signaled to 'Heave to,' but she continued sailing north under full sail. A cannon ball, which barely missed the top fore rigging, whistled through the air. There was a large explosion just off her starboard bow that sprayed the deck with little more than water. She shuddered from the shock wave, but kept foraging north into the heart of the Chesapeake Bay. Because the first warning had been ignored, another round had exploded just off her stern. But, by now they were out of range of the

British cannons. Her sails filled with wind, the Ellen Marie flew across the tops of the waves and laughed at the danger.

"They'll never stop us now," grinned Mr. Martin, just as the Captain appeared on deck. "By the time they hoist anchor we'll be half way to Tangier Island. We'll use the shallow draft of the Ellen Marie to avoid them should they give chase."

The two British ships raised sail and clumsily began pursuit, but the Ellen Marie had a good wind and had rapidly left them in her wake. Another cannon ball did explode well aft of her, but by then she was well clear of any peril.

Near Tangier Island a small cutter, flying the Union Jack, was spotted in the distance. In the evening mist, the crew on the cutter apparently did not spot them. The bright, late day sun, setting low in the west, also protected the Ellen Marie with a protective glare that reflected off the waters between the two ships.

Captain Robinson did not like the idea of sailing through the shallow bay at night under full sail, but he did agree with Mr. Martin that without cargo the Ellen Marie sat high enough in the water to avoid most sandbars or reefs. Time was of the essence, but it was still a risk sailing these waters at a higher speed. Something was wrong with all these British warships inside the Chesapeake Bay. Captain Robinson yearned for the safety of his homeport at Fells Point.

Due of the danger of warships and other obstacles in the water none of the men slept that night. The moon was almost full and the sky was clear of any clouds. The sails of the Ellen Marie seemed to glow in the moonlight as if to say, "Hey, here I am!" Thus, the crew had kept a watchful eye for British ships.

Sailing under full sail all night brought them to the entrance of the Patapsco River early the next morning. As they neared the entrance to the river, they discovered a British man-of-war anchored near Sparrow's Point. During the night, Captain Robinson wisely ordered removal of any item on deck that identified them as an American ship, but his ploy didn't work. As they came within range of the British ship two of her cannons had fired without warning. The balls screeched as they passed dangerously overhead, one passing through the topmost rigging. The second flew aft of the Ellen Marie. Fortunately both balls had missed striking sail or mast. They both exploded twenty yards off the port beam showering the Ellen Marie with an angry spray of muddy water.

Mr. Martin instinctively spun the wheel and headed for a fog bank off to the port helm. The Ellen Marie reached the protective mist just as two more cannon balls exploded near the aft starboard rail and shook the entire ship. A pillar of water, mud and oyster shells soared into the air revealing just how shallow the bay was in this area. However, once again only muddy water had splashed over the deck. It had soaked the men at the helm, but missed the Ellen Marie. As they disappeared deeper into the fog bank, the captain ordered that all but the staysail be taken down. It was difficult to do quickly with such a small crew, but they managed to slow down the pace of the Ellen Marie as she headed for even shallower water.

Slowly drifting, she hid in the morning mist. A slight morning breeze would keep the Ellen Marie within the fog for a long period of time. Another explosion was heard aft of their location, but then all became quiet except the lapping of water on her hull. The light breeze through her rigging was barely detectable as her sail began to gently flap. However, the Ellen Marie still crawled along pushed by the incoming tide.

Captain Robinson called a quick meeting with all on board. "The morning mist grows this time of day. We need some speed. With only one sail set her helm will be unresponsive. We'll raise another sail or two and try to proceed slowly in this fog. We must add more canvas, but still keep her speed down.

"I think if we sail very slowly along a northwest route, we can pass by that warship unseen and enter the harbor. It's a big risk as the bay is very shallow here. The Ellen Marie drafts eight feet in the water laden. I would guess she drafts at about five or six feet empty. If she hangs up on the bottom and the fog clears...well..." He paused as he shook his head. "The only other option is to abandon ship and swim to Rock Creek. I don't know what we might find there. The

British obviously haven't taken Baltimore yet or they wouldn't bother blocking the entrance to the harbor."

"Well, Captain," Mr. Martin smiled as he replied, "I prefer to walk down the ramp and onto the dock in a gentlemanly manor in Baltimore. The insect infested swamps around Rock Creek are not very inviting. I vote we go on to Baltimore."

All the others agreed. They had placed their complete trust in the capabilities of the captain and Mr. Martin.

"Mr. Martin, tighten the fore mainsail and set just the spritsail for now. We'll use them to pull us along. If the bow sits lower when we hit the bottom, we have a better chance of pulling ourselves free. Take us north-northwest once again for a short time, then north. And, men," he added, "say a prayer this works!"

Twice the crew had heard an eerie groan as the bow ground onto the bottom. But luck was with them as the Ellen Marie proceeded on her way after a slight shudder each time she scraped mud and seaweed loose from the floor of the bay. The crew could do little but watch the muddy waters swirl up as the keel plowed up the occasional sandbar.

As Captain Robinson had guessed, the Maryland fog held fast as they slowly sailed north toward Baltimore. Late in the morning, as the fog began to dissipate, distant landmasses gradually appeared. The Ellen Marie was right where the captain had predicted she would be. As she broke out of the last wisp of fog, and entered Northwest Harbor, the crew spotted Locust Point.

Captain Robinson ordered Patrick to raise the ships flag, which unfurled just as they approached the guns of Fort McHenry. A huge American flag above the fort was a welcomed sight to all aboard. When the ship finally rounded the point of land at Locust Point, Fells Point was spotted only a mile away. The Ellen Marie was home at last!

A great commotion had arisen as the Ellen Marie neared the dock. People began to realize that an American ship was arriving at their port, the first in many weeks. As she entered the Fells Point

Dock cheering was heard. Many thought that the arrival of this ship meant that the British blockade was now over.

A large crowd stood on the dock as the Ellen Marie was secured. Everyone had questions about the British blockade. A hush fell over the crowd as Captain Robinson briefly advised them of their encounters inside the Chesapeake Bay. The crowd began to drift away in disbelief as the news had sunk in. In fact, current events were no better than they were the day before.

A Naval officer soon arrived to inquire as to how the Ellen Marie avoided the British blockade. Captain Robinson took him to his cabin to brief him about their encounters. There was much dismay along the docks of Baltimore, but aboard the Ellen Marie the crew breathed a sigh of relief!

Chapter 5

Mr. Ellsworth, one of the owners, boarded the Ellen Marie shortly after her arrival at Fells Point. He had shown a great deal of displeasure in finding her holds empty of cargo, but relieved that the ship came home intact. While he waited for the captain to appear, Mr. Ellsworth advised the crew that war had broken out adding that the United States had declared war on Britain on June 18, 1812.

He explained that it had all begun much earlier with a British Navy blockade of American shipping on the Atlantic. The British had captured several ships and taken their crews to be pressed into service aboard British warships. He remarked assuredly that, "The Ellen Marie is indeed fortunate to have made it through the blockade unscathed!"

Captain Robinson finally returned on deck and escorted the Navy officer from the ship. The captain and Mr. Ellsworth then had a lengthy discussion. The men on deck had tried to listen to their conversation, but couldn't hear what was being said. After Mr. Ellsworth had finally departed the ship, the captain told the crew that he had a meeting with the Navy Commander at noon. He told them that he would discuss the situation with them upon his return.

In the mid-morning, Captain Robinson and John departed the Ellen Marie and headed to the home and shop of the captain's friend, George Baylor. Vendors could be heard as they hawked their goods loudly. John could smell the delightful aroma of freshly baked breads and other baked goods as they passed through the market square near the dock. The delightful smell of fish and meats, as they were cooked on open fires, filled the morning air. Carts filled with fresh produce were parked along the road as farmers hawked their wares to the citizens of Baltimore. Large wagons, filled with fresh straw for bedding, intended for either man or beast, lumbered along the cobblestone road pulled by enormous oxen.

Several men were locked in a pillory at the far end of the green. John noticed many townspeople who took great pleasure in stopping by to throw rotten fruits and vegetables at them. The incarcerated men who were suffering this barrage looked very miserable at the indignity of these actions. An effigy of a British soldier in full red-coated uniform hanging from a nearby tree limb caught the men's attention. As the straw figure swung back and forth, children were having a great game of attacking it with sticks and stones, encouraged on by the gathered crowd.

As they left the village green John noted the many shops offering wares such as pottery, pewter, linens and fine glassware. Men and women, of obvious gentry, mingled in and out of the various shops. Some gentlemen were dressed in fine suits with elegant tri-cornered hats. A few of the men sported a large, billowing feather on their hats.

Ladies decked out in their finest attire giggled as they tried on hats at the local millinery shops or dabbed samples of perfume on their wrists and necks. Several, John noted, exposed much more of their bosom than what would ever be permitted on the streets of Ballylee. Whirling their lacy parasols to chase away pesky flies, the ladies daintily strolled along the streets of Fells Point.

Several blocks from the dock, John and the captain rounded a corner to find a disastrous sight! Only ashes and burnt, smoldering timbers remained where a thriving business and home once stood. Captain Robinson spotted a woman who was hanging out her laundry near the Baylor home. "Would you be so kind as to tell me what happened here?" he asked.

"Ah, those Baylors!" she sneered. "British sympathizers, they were. A mob burnt them out two days ago and ran them right out of town! And good riddance to them, as well, what with the Brits pirating our ships and taking good American men to work as slaves on their own ships!"

"I didn't realize where the Baylor's sympathies lay, Mum," the Captain responded. "We've just arrived this morning from the West Indies. The British attacked us within the waters of the Chesapeake Bay. That's American territory! We had no warning that American shipping was in jeopardy." He purposely avoided mention of the sordid business at Nassau.

"Lucky for you," the woman snapped back. "My husband and his brother, along with their crew, were taken by the Brits a fortnight ago near Saint Michaels. I don't know what has become of them, but their skipjack was spotted several days ago flying the Union Jack. That's piracy, it is!"

Their attention was drawn to a man who ran wildly along the street shouting, "The British Army has landed south of here! They're going to attack and burn Baltimore!" Startled gasps were heard all along the crowded street. Many rumors abounded. Uncertainty was taking over the citizens of the city. It all made John feel extremely distressed over his lot. Here he was in a strange place with no position waiting for him and in a city under siege.

Without hesitation the two men headed back to the Ellen Marie. Passing the village green, John noticed that the effigy had been changed from a British soldier to a straw figure dressed in a green tunic and white wig. A sign around his neck read, "King George." The poor British soldier effigy was slowly being torn apart by several dogs that were having great fun at a tug of war with several children. To the relief of the men in the pillory, the throng was no longer tossing rotten produce in their direction. The cheering crowd had become too busy enjoying their new endeavor of encouraging the dogs and children in their disemboweling of the straw soldier.

Captain Robinson and John quickly headed toward the Ellen Marie where the remainder of the crew had waited impatiently for the latest news. As the men approached the docks there was a continuous loud clamor of confusion. Some men were shouting about fighting the approaching British Army and some said they were packing their goods and heading out of the city. But most of the crowd just wandered about in forlorn rejection not certain what action to take.

As they departed the green, and crossed Thames Street, they noticed that a hooded man hung by his neck from a lamppost by the edge the wharf. It was a grotesque scene as the wild mob below took great glee in yanking on the dead man's legs attempting to see how far they could make his body swing back and forth. Each sway of his body brought joyful cheers from the crowd that watched the mob's actions. Not wanting to become involved with the mob gathered there, Captain Robinson and John moved quickly past the scene. The captain commented to John that the current situation in Baltimore demanded immediate attention by the local authorities.

Captain Robinson called the men together on the aft deck to discuss what he and John had seen and learned about the crisis in Baltimore. "My intention is to offer my services to the American Navy," Captain Robinson firmly stated. "I feel my talents can be put to best advantage by serving my country at sea." Mr. Martin spoke up and said that he would go along with the Captain's thoughts and join him in his venture.

"If it's all the same to you lads," Mike Handshaw spoke up, "I'll be heading for New York. My family will be wondering what happened to me and I must share the bad news with the families of my shipmates. With the Captain's permission, I'll take along some of the ships food for my trek."

Captain Robinson nodded in agreement. The men all wished him well on his journey and watched as he disappeared below deck to gather some food for his long trek.

Captain Robinson turned to the other men still on the deck. "I have a meeting with the Baltimore Navy Commander at noon. I don't know what each of you plan to do, but if you wait until that meeting is concluded we can make plans for our future. Patrick, you have a position waiting for you in Philadelphia. If you want to be on your way I wouldn't blame you for wanting to put these troubles behind you."

"Thank you, Captain," replied Patrick. "I think I'll join Mike on his way north. He said he'd be walking close to Philadelphia on his way to New York. I think it will be safer if we travel together."

"Fine," the captain answered. "I suggest you gather some food for the trip as well. If indeed a British invasion is underway food may be scarce throughout the countryside. I'm sorry I can't offer you any money. The ships safe was robbed in Nassau. We wish you well on your venture." Without another word, the captain turned and headed down the gangplank on his way to his appointment with the American Navy. He quickly disappeared in the swarm of confusion on the dock.

There wasn't much for the remaining four men to do until they heard from the captain. Su Long went off to the galley to make something for them to eat while Mr. Martin went off to inspect the ship.

John was in a dilemma and couldn't seem to get his thoughts together. His position had literally gone up in smoke. Here he was finally in America, in the middle of a war and without any means of support. He stood gloomily at the rail staring down into the murky waters of the bay thinking of the warmth of the fireside at home in Ballylee. He could almost smell his mother's cooking emanating from the large, cast iron pot suspended above the peat fire.

Jacque walked up and stood quietly beside John. After several moments he said, "What a mess we have here. I didn't have a position waiting for me in this country, but I felt sure that something would arise. It was bad enough in Belfast dealing with the Brits. I thought I was free of that. Now here I am facing the same enemy. I hope that Captain Robinson returns with some encouraging news."

Their conversation was suddenly interrupted as a mob of men on the dock dragged a screaming man down Thames Street and headed for a nearby lamppost. His arms were tied behind his back and a noose hung loosely about his neck, which told the intent of the mob. John and Jacque turned away from the scene not wanting to witness another hanging. There was no way they could know the man's crime, but the madness of the mobs in the city seemed to demand immediate justice. They walked to the leeward side of the Ellen Marie and watched several gulls as they swooped low over the murky waters of the bay. A cheer rose from the massed crowd as the screams of the desperate man were abruptly silenced.

John and Jacque both felt concern about the actions of the mobs. Each shared an uncertainty as to where the mob's hatred was directed. They anxiously stood on deck until Su Long called them to the galley. The four men ate in silence while the uproar and confusion continued to echo from the mayhem on the crowded dock beyond. The unsettling noise reverberated throughout the wooden bulkheads of the ship.

It was almost two hours later before Captain Robinson returned to the Ellen Marie. He seemed more upbeat and full of news. "There are many rumors at hand, but the important thing is that the British Army has not landed and is not on its way to invade Baltimore. It seems to be just a naval blockade. There are, however, battles going on at our border with Canada."

As he grabbed a quick bite to eat he continued to explain the situation, "The Navy has procured the Ellen Marie. She'll be outfitted with cannon and her rigging modified for more speed. I have been offered, and accepted, the position as her Captain. A crew of regular Navy will man her. The Ellen Marie will become an inner coastal gunboat with a mission to harass the British Navy in the Chesapeake area."

He looked at Mr. Martin and said, "Jeremy, you've already expressed the desire to join me in this undertaking. Now that you know what's planned are you still with me? I can assure you a position as my second in command aboard the Ellen Marie."

"Aye, Captain," Mr. Martin quickly responded. "Just tell me where to sign my name and I'm with you all the way."

"Su Long, this is not your battle. Have you given it some thought?" the captain inquired.

"Well, I've sailed with you for many years," replied Su Long. Then with a big smile added, "I can't have someone else cook your food. They might accidentally poison you! I'm with you and the Ellen Marie wherever you two go, Captain!"

The men all chuckled at Su Long's amusing response.

"Thank you, men. John and Jacque take your time and think this over. You can join the Navy, but will be aboard another ship. Or you can find work somewhere here in Baltimore. It's a big decision to make. You certainly didn't come to this country to fight a war. I was told the shipyards are shorthanded with so many men leaving to join this fight. With a war commencing, fast ships will be greatly needed by the Navy and many will be built here in Baltimore."

John thought to himself for a few moments and then told the captain, "Since I can't be aboard the Ellen Marie with you Captain, I think I'll try to get work here in the shipyards. I've had enough of the sea for a long, long time."

"John," Jacque spoke up, "I think you expressed my thoughts as well. Let's go build some ships!" He slapped John on the back and all the men laughed as the tension of the moment was relieved.

"Modifications to the Ellen Marie will begin first thing tomorrow," the captain advised. "You two can stay aboard ship tonight and find other arrangements in the morning."

The captain turned to the other two men and said, "Well, gentlemen, let's head to the Navy Office and get sworn in!" John and Jacque watched the three men as they headed down the gangplank and disappeared into the swarming crowd on Thames Street.

Shortly thereafter, John and Jacque headed for the nearest shipyard, that of Thomas Kemp, and were hired on the spot. Many men had indeed left the shipyard to join the Army or the Navy. Manpower was greatly needed for the ever-increasing demand for ships. Both lads were pleased to discover that they would be working on building Baltimore Clippers. These ships were considered the finest and fastest on the sea and able to outrun any of the lumbering British warships.

Later that evening John and Jacque sat on a hatch aboard the Ellen Marie. By the time the nearby streetlamps were lit, the streets and docks had emptied. Sanity had finally returned as level heads took command. A hush slowly prevailed over Fells Point and the city of Baltimore. Now that an invasion wasn't imminent, people began to return to their normal lives. The lines of men at the hastily assembled enlistment booths dissipated with most of the men heading for nearby pubs to discuss current events.

John and Jacque had found a small attic room above the nearby Ox and Plow Tavern. However, they were not pleased that their rope bed, topped by a dirty, straw-stuffed mattress, was to be shared with two other men, several lice and a multitude of bedbugs. Only the rats seemed to avoid their third story accommodations. Upon inspecting their new lodging, it occurred to them that a swinging hammock aboard the Ellen Marie was much more enticing. And they would certainly miss Su Long's cooking, as they now had to eat their meals in the crowded, dingy pub. It was not an arrangement they liked, but for the time being it was the best the dock area had to offer.

They sat joking about their lodging arrangements, but deep down neither man was pleased with the accommodations. As they watched the last orange remnants of sunset disappear on the horizon, John asked Jacque, "Do you miss home?"

"Well, there is no real home for me," Jacque sighed. "I was born in France, and my mother died when I was born. When I was quite young my father went off to war and was never heard from again. He just disappeared. My father's parents lived near Paris and took me in, but when my grandfather died a few years later, my grandmother moved to Belfast, the place of her birth. I have spent most of my life in Ireland.

"Grandmother became quite sick five years ago and died. I lived on the street doing whatever odd job I could find. Sleeping wherever it was dry. I had to hide my French ancestry while we lived in

Ireland. Grandmother wasn't sure what the Brits would do if they discovered that I was French born. Ireland wasn't really home. Home is where I hang my hat. So, now I guess Baltimore is my home!"

"I guess I didn't realize how much I would miss home and my family," John mused. "For a Catholic lad there isn't much opportunity to be found in Belfast. The Protestants take all the good paying positions. I was determined to make a purse quickly in Baltimore and then travel west in search of gold."

"Gold?" Jacque raised his eyebrows. "I was told that there were lots of opportunities here in America, but no one said that there was gold to be found. I would be pleased if I found a good position, but just where is this gold?"

"In the mountains to the west," John responded. "But first you must have a purse. There are supplies you need before venturing into the wilderness. A good musket, powder and shot are vital as there are unfriendly Indians and wild animals to contend with. Then there are other supplies that are needed. I planned to work for George Baylor for a year or so and then head west. Now that position is gone up in smoke and the shipyard certainly doesn't pay a laborer as well..." John's voice trailed off in almost the same fashion as his dream seemed to be slipping away.

"I'd be interested in such a venture," Jacque interjected. "No man would be foolish enough to turn down a chance for gold and wealth!"

"I'd be pleased to join up with you on this venture," John told him. "The only problem is that it may take years to gather enough money for the endeavor."

"I know I was given a better paying job at the shipyard than you, but I did have more experience to offer them" Jacque told John. "However, if we pooled our money we may have a large enough purse sooner."

"Yes," agreed John. "But as an ordinary laborer I don't make much more than the cost of my living expenses."

"But the shipyard is only a start," Jacque interceded optimistically. "You certainly don't expect to work as a laborer for long. You could become a carpenter or blacksmith at the shipyard. Those positions offer much better pay. And this country has lots of opportunities. The shipyard is only a foothold."

"This war with King George may also have some affect on my plans," John mumbled. "I don't know how this war will turn out, but I don't like the sounds of it."

"Aw, buck up, lad," said Jacque as he slapped John on the back. "Let's go have a pint and get a good nights sleep. The hammocks aboard the Ellen Marie offer a better nights sleep than the pub lodging promises tomorrow night." They both laughed as they headed down the gangplank to the now empty dock.

Chapter 6

Fells Point in Baltimore had been an important shipbuilding locale for many decades before the War of 1812. The speedy cargo ships known as Baltimore Clippers were a totally new design and were the envy of many sea captains and ship owners. At sea, time was of the essence as the competition for cargo was not limited to ships flying the American flag. Ships from many countries vied for the cargos hauled between Europe, the Far East and the Americas. The fastest ships received the most lucrative contracts. With its unlimited supply of wood, shipbuilding was booming in the United States. Shipyards sprang up all along the coast, but the Chesapeake Bay offered something more — a safe harbor from coastal storms. Thus, Baltimore became a major player in the shipbuilding industry.

Then war broke out between the United States and Great Britain, who was already deeply involved in a war with France. The Baltimore Clipper now had another very valuable asset that other cargo ships did not — speed. The design of the lightly armed Baltimore Clipper allowed their captains to outrun any British warship patrolling the Atlantic waters. The demand for Baltimore Clippers skyrocketed almost overnight.

From the logging areas in the northern mountains of Pennsylvania, trees were felled, stripped of their branches and dragged by teams of oxen to the Susquehanna River. Once in the river, the huge logs were strapped together into enormous floats and guided by men with poles down the river to the Chesapeake Bay. Boats then guided the floats across the bay and up the Patapsco River and into the harbor at Baltimore where the floats were separated and sent on to the many shipyards.

At Thomas Kemp's shipyard the individual logs were then dragged by horse teams onto the shore for the drying process. After a lengthy drying period, the horse teams pulled the individual logs to the shipyard cutting area to be parted into boards, planks, or beams for the ship-builders. As each log was dragged to the sawpits, men used pikes to roll it onto supporting beams over a long sawpit.

Jacque, being a very muscular man, was chosen for the sawpit. He didn't object, as it paid much more than the common laborer received. The sawpit was hazardous work and required great physical strength. Once a log was set in place, one man entered the long pit below as another stood upon the log itself. A two-man cross-saw was used to cut the log lengthwise to create the required type of lumber. The six or eight foot long saw was pulled and pushed up-and-down until the board was separated from the log. Laborers quickly removed the separated board and another cut was started. It was a long and arduous undertaking. If the log slipped loose from one of the several mountings, the man in the pit below could be crushed to death. Many men working in the pit had also lost arms or legs in this dangerous task. A young boy was paid a pittance to sit upon the log and keep the saw blade lubricated with animal fats dripped from a bucket. Many a youthful finger dropped into the pit below as an inattentive, screaming child put his hand too close to the saw blade while performing his duties. It was a dangerous job for both man and child.

John began working as an unskilled laborer at the shipyard. His main task was carrying cut lumber from the saw area to the dry dock where the ships were being assembled. Most of the beams and boards were so heavy it took two or three men to carry each one to the carpenters' work area. The carpenters cut the board to the correct length, then shaped and drilled each piece for a proper fit.

John and the other laborers would then carry each piece to the dry dock and hoist each part into place while the boards or beams were bolted, pegged, or nailed onto the frame of the ship. Like a line of ants scrambling along the ground, the men constantly moved the lumber from the sawpit to the carpentry area then onto the dry dock as each sailing ship was born in the backwaters of the Chesapeake Bay.

In the first few hours of the day John's muscles ached from the strain, but he didn't let the others know of his anguish. He kept silently working as his body adjusted to the strenuous task. Toward the end of his first day the blisters on his hands had burst open and some bled leaving red stains on the wood. Digging splinters from his hands became a daily chore. John, following the advice of others, regularly soaked his hands in the salty waters of the bay to help close the wounds. And he kept working. Working so he could achieve his dream of searching for the treasure that lay to the west. By the end of the first week the rough lumber and salt-water soaks began to form hardened calluses. His youthful muscles slowly adjusted to the strain of long hours of work.

Jacque's hands were already quite calloused by the time he reached Baltimore. He had worked various jobs back in Belfast. Jobs that toughened his hands and body. Blistered hands were the least of the problems for the men who worked in the sawpits. Their biggest complaint was the constant rain of animal fat and sawdust falling onto their heads and shoulders during their turn in the pit. At the end of the day they would be coated with a slimy mixture that stuck in their hair and to their clothing. As each workday ended the men headed for the cold waters of the bay to wash and rid themselves of this offensive blend. Jacque never quite accustomed himself to the daily cold-water baths, especially in the winter months, but the pay was good.

In early fall John read in the newspapers that during the previous August the American Frigate *Constitution* captured two British brigs off the New England coast. They took the crews prisoner and burned the ships. Shortly after that engagement the *Constitution* recaptured an American brig the British had taken earlier. The Baltimore newspapers also reported that the same American warship captured the prized British frigate *Guerriere*. The citizens of Baltimore happily celebrated the news of these American victories. A few weeks later the newspaper noted that during the sea battle British cannon balls were seen bouncing off the thick oak sides of the *Constitution*. The American sailors thus adopted the endearing name "*Old Ironsides*" for the frigate.

News arrived almost daily throughout the fall of battles along the Canadian border. Not all the war news reported in the newspaper was good. There were some devastating losses as well. John began to grasp the magnitude of the War with Great Britain. Along the docks there were daily reports of American cargo ships being taken captive by the British Navy and their crews conscripted. Events seemed to worsen for the United States as the weeks passed into early winter.

One morning a news report had stated that several American coastal cutters had survived an attack on a British Man-of-War off the coast of Virginia. The Ellen Marie was one of those attacking ships and had survived the battle with minor damage. Little else was said about her. Jacque and John wondered how much damage the British ship suffered from the Ellen Marie before she sailed away to safety. Nothing was mentioned about the crews.

The pace of work in the shipyards began to pick up as the demand for new ships increased. John and Jacque helped build several of the ships that were launched at Fells Point. They took pride in watching each hull slowly slide into the bay. The birth of each new cutter was cause for celebration in the shipyards.

The months dragged on and the two young men slowly fell into the daily routine of the thriving city of Baltimore. Each day brought updated news of the war, good and bad. Some reports were rumors and some were fact. John chose to depend on the daily newspapers for his information. Listening to other workers at the shipyard and people on the streets of the city didn't always reveal what was actually going on in the war.

Enthusiastic crowds, seeking the latest news from their homeland, would meet each ship as it arrived from across the Atlantic. Baltimore was a melting pot for various countrymen and the war was deeply affecting many residents of the city.

In the evenings, John spent his time whittling near the fireside. He had always enjoyed carving wood back home and this was a way to pass the time. Scrap pieces of wood from the shipyard were plentiful. Selling the toys, geegaws, and novelties he created brought him some additional money for his savings account. Jacque was not one to sit around, but rather found his pleasure in the wild life of the local pubs. John didn't care for that lifestyle.

John never missed Mass at the local Catholic Church on Sundays. The pastor soon discovered that John had an excellent singing voice and encouraged him to join the church choir. John enjoyed the music and the companionship as it reminded him of home. He wrote his parents often telling them about the church, marveling on the size and splendor of the building itself. John had found comfort being with these parishioners each week as he was welcomed and treated as one of the fold.

Try as he may, John could never encourage Jacque to attend Mass with him. Jacque had other adventures in mind; adventures that held little interest for John. To him, it seemed that Jacque was wild and unrestrained, but he still liked him as a friend. As different as they were in character, their friendship suffered no ill will.

In spring and summer, after Mass, John would often go to the village green at Fells Point and relax on the grass and watch the many activities that took place. There was never a dull moment as the area was often crowded with gentlemen and ladies dressed in their finest out to soak in the afternoon sun. Street vendors sold every imaginable item, imported from all over the world. Ethnic foods were cooked and sold along the village green. John found the aromas delectable. He would watch as entertainers performed with the hope of a coin or two from onlookers. John took pleasure in all these goings-on. It had been a satisfying way to pass a Sunday afternoon.

During cooler weather he walked several miles from the city into the countryside. He studied the local forested areas and talked to those who resided in the woods. He was constantly thinking of the day he would venture away from civilization and head west into the mountainous areas of Virginia. He felt in his heart that he would find his fortune in the rich gold fields there. John was determined that destiny was waiting for him in those distant mountains.

Both young men usually finished work at the same time of the day and headed to the Ox and Plow Pub for dinner together. However, one fateful night in October, Jacque had a prior arrangement elsewhere. John headed back to their lodging alone. It was late in the evening and John was aware of the dangers that lurked along the docks. Many unscrupulous individuals skulked about in the dim areas waiting to pounce on some unwary soul in search of bounty.

As John passed a darkened alley he heard a man call to him from the shadows. John cautiously stepped farther into the street to avoid an ambush. Another man, with his collar pulled up high about his face, was coming down the sidewalk from the opposite direction. As John stepped further into the street to avoid them both, the man on the sidewalk threw a handful of dirt into John's face. The action caught John off guard and temporarily blinded him.

Just as he reached for the knife in his belt, the shadowy figure in the alley quickly stepped up behind John with a large club in his right hand and struck him forcefully on the back of his head. The severe blow dropped John to his knees and his knife clattered to the cobblestones. John struggled to rise, but another blow struck him in the same spot. As numbness tingled throughout his arms and legs, a soft blackness obscured his vision and he collapsed on the spot. Darkness fell upon him as he passed into unconsciousness.

The night was dark and foggy when John slowly awoke. He was chilled and shivering profusely from the slight drizzle that fell from the sky. He then realized that a dark figure had crouched over him. But John was so immobilized with pain he couldn't move. A female voice asked, "Sir, are you alright? I saw what those men did. They've run off now."

Her warm hand touched his arm as she tried to ease John's pain. The action was dreamlike and he wasn't fully aware of the reality of her soft touch.

Awareness was slow to return to John. He discovered that his boots, coat and cap were gone; his shirt and trousers were torn to shreds. He was almost naked lying on the cold cobblestone street. In embarrassment he pulled what little of his clothing he could onto his cold, wet body. He then remembered the earlier events and realized that he had been robbed. He tried to stand, but his legs were rubbery and refused to cooperate.

"Wait here," the concerned female voice told him. "I'll get help."

She was only gone a moment or two and reappeared with another woman in tow. "Help me get him into my room," the first voice said.

The two women struggled to get John to his feet, but his legs just wouldn't support him as they should. Grunting with the effort, the two women half dragged him a short distance down the street where the first woman unlocked and opened a door. They helped him inside the darkened room and sat him down on a bed. He was vaguely aware of an oil lamp being lit. The first woman gasped as she held the lantern above his head, "Oh, my. They did you an evil deed. You're bleeding badly."

She disappeared for a moment and returned with a basin of cold water. With a clean rag she gently dabbed the back of John's head. The second woman picked up a towel and began carefully drying his back and chest. The water in the basin turned red as the wound on his head was cleansed. The pain was immense and caused him to wince each time she lightly touched the back of his head.

He heard the second woman say, "Why do you want to bother with the likes of him? He's probably some ignorant sailor what got way-laid!"

"Hush," the first woman hissed. "Look at him. He's a beautiful, young lad. He belongs to someone somewhere and there just might be a reward for helping him."

Shivering profoundly, John drifted off once again into blissful unconsciousness and fell backward onto the bed.

He awakened slowly and realized that daylight was streaming through a small window. His head throbbed and his vision wasn't very clear. Outside the window he heard gulls screaming at each other as they fought over a morsel of food. Gradually he became more aware of his surroundings. With a start he realized that he wasn't alone in this strange bed. A woman lay beside him. When he struggled to sit up she woke and asked him, "Are you alright? You shouldn't move too much."

She sat up and leaned over John looking at his head. "You have a nasty head wound. You've been unconscious for two days."

John was too stunned to answer. Then he realized that he wore no clothing under the single blanket. He became alarmed when he suddenly realized that this unknown woman was undressed, wearing only her undergarments. He had tried to get out of the bed, but couldn't stand because the room was spinning so wildly. He sat partially up, his mouth gaping, but words wouldn't form.

She sat up in the bed and studied his face. "You took quite a beating. That gang worked you over right royally and they stole everything you own. I guess if they hadn't ripped your shirt and trousers, they would have taken them as well."

The words slowly sunk in to John, but he still sat there in bewildered silence. A sharp pain on the back of his head throbbed. He reached back to touch the spot. Just his gentle touch was a scream to his senses and he almost passed out again. He felt cold and shivered profusely.

She touched his arm to steady him. "I had to warm you in the night or you would have frozen to death. I lay beside you to share my body heat. You were in a sorry state when my friend, Lily, and I brought you here. Do you know where you are?"

Words just wouldn't form in John's mouth. The room had been an unfamiliar place and at that moment he wasn't quite sure who he was and what had happened. He was aware of the bed, the table and chairs and the rays from the sun shining in the window. But, that's all his stunned mind would allow.

"Who are you? What's your name?" she prodded.

"…don't…know…" was all he could mumble, startled by his own reply.

"Well, you just rest. I'll go get us a bite to eat. Be back shortly, Love," she said as she stood and slipped back into her dress. Putting on her cape and bonnet she picked up a small market basket and disappeared out the only door into the morning mist.

John hadn't even realized that he had fallen back to sleep, but suddenly she was there beside him trying to pour a small spoonful of a warm fluid between his lips. He coughed a bit, but managed to get several spoonfuls down. The warmth of the weak soup had slowly warmed him.

The room was now well lit by the bright sunshine beyond the single window. He studied the face of his rescuer. She was much older than John, almost as old as his mother. She had a kind, but rugged face. The woman's auburn hair, interwoven with occasional gray strands, surrounded a face filled with concern for him. He found her eyes soft, understanding and caring. John began to feel at ease in her presence.

As he thought of his mother, the hazy cobwebs seemed to be slowly clearing from his memory. "Where am I?" he managed to murmur.

"This is my place," She replied. "And it's also my place of business! So, you can't stay here much longer." She brashly added.

John was confused by her response at first, but when he realized what her statement meant, he felt embarrassment that a woman of the streets had saved his life. He tried to rise, but still didn't have the strength to stand. She helped him lay back and the sunlight drifted away into darkness as he fell asleep again.

John had awakened to find the sunlight outside the window dimming. Outside the small window he could see that the oil streetlamps were being lit. He was alone in the room. Slowly his memory began to return as he lay back upon the bed.

"I've been robbed," he mumbled aloud to himself. John began to remember the events that had brought him to this place. He was thankful that his wages were safely deposited in the nearby bank. And he was also thankful that he had secretly hidden the few coins, which his mother had slipped into his hand the day he left home, beneath a floorboard in his room at the Ox and Plow Tavern. Those few coins were his closest connection to his family in Ireland.

How long had he been here? What about his job? He must get word to Jacque. He tried to rise, but he still couldn't seem to stand. His legs didn't respond to his brains command to move. Near the hearth, John noticed his tattered clothing lying across a chair back where they had been placed to dry beside the small fire. Confusion reigned as his clothing certainly looked dry. How long had he slept? Slowly darkness approached his thoughts and he drifted off into oblivion.

John woke to feel someone beside him. The woman who had saved him was back. She once again lay beside him. In the darkness he listened to the slow rhythm of her deep breathing as she slept peacefully. He tried to rise once again and that slowly aroused the woman.

"Relax, Love. Roxie will take care of you," she whispered to him. Her words were very slurred. Her response had also brought a repulsively strong smell of whiskey on her breath.

Roxie rolled onto her side and slid under the blanket with John. It was with apprehension that he felt her warm, soft naked body against his. Her squirming about under the blanket made him nervous. With a jolt he realized that she had reached between his legs and was touching his manhood. John had been too startled to move. No one had ever touched him there before. He lay there paralyzed with uncertainty as she gently started to stroke him. In profound embarrassment, John realized that his body began to respond to this woman's gentle caressing.

In short order, John had reached full arousal. Roxie straddled him and, reaching down between their bodies, guided him inside her. John was mortified. This was against all his teachings and religious beliefs, but he had been too traumatized to stop the copulating. She leaned forward and drunkenly kissed him as she began undulating on top of him. Normally the strong smell of whiskey on her breath would have sickened him, but the rising passions within him were far too distracting.

John was perplexed by his body's reaction to her movements. He wanted the pleasurable sensations to stop because he knew this was a sin, but the animalistic ache mounted within his loins and they begged for more. Without command, his hips gradually began to respond. Faster and faster he thrust upward seeking an end to the driving carnal lust that was slowly reaching a crescendo. It was over in a few moments.

John wasn't sure what had happened until it was over. Then the humiliation of the act sunk in and he quickly shoved her aside. Roxie never woke up. Her snoring told him that she was deep in a drunken stupor. The alarm he felt over the incident gave John the strength to rise quickly from her bed. He found the remnants of his clothing and quickly donned them. He had quietly slipped out the door and staggered barefoot into the cold, wet night. With a throbbing head, he headed for the Ox and Plow.

John was too embarrassed about the situation to tell Jacque what had occurred, other than the robbery. He avoided Jacque's questions of his whereabouts for the past three days. Jacque told John that he had worried about him fretfully. He knew John wouldn't leave without a word and added that their friends had searched all around the dock area asking many people of his whereabouts. No one had any idea where he was. John had simply disappeared.

His supervisor at Kemp's shipyard was sympathetic once he saw the wound on the back of John's head. He also knew that John was a good worker and didn't take to drink, as did many of the other workers. Thus, John didn't lose his position.

At confession the following Sunday he told the priest that he feared for his soul, but the priest assured him that since he didn't initiate the action, John would be forgiven.

Jacque never went to mass, or any church, so John didn't know what his religious beliefs were. Because of that, John resisted the temptation to tell Jacque all the details for John still felt that he had sinned. It took a day or two for John to completely recover, but finally the incident was put into his past.

John worried for some time that someday he might run into Roxie on the street or in a pub. He felt a deep gratitude for her saving him and nursing him back to health, but what she had done to him had been such an embarrassment. He also worried that someone else may discover that he had a liaison with a common prostitute. However, fate saw to it that they never met again.

Chapter 7

By the spring of 1813 John's supervisor was so impressed with his diligent work that he decided to make John a carpenter's apprentice. One big advantage for John's employer was that John could read and write. Educated men were hard to find amongst the pioneer stock of the new country.

John made more money as a carpenter's apprentice. Thus he entered a new phase in his life where his dream could possibly come true. In spite of all those who had scoffed at finding easy wealth in the western hills, John still held the hope that someday he could send his promised treasure back to his family in Ballylee. He stubbornly refused to give up that vision.

John was assigned to Frank Moss, who taught him the correct use of the many different tools used in the carpentry trade. While a bit of a stern man, Mr. Moss was friendly and patient. John quickly discovered that Mr. Moss took his craft seriously. He was meticulous about maintaining his tools and spent extra time cleaning and honing the various edges to keep them sharp. John was extremely pleased to be able to use such fine tools. At home he had made trinkets and a few pieces of small furniture, but was forced to work only with his knife. A well-made knife was hard to come by for a young lad in Ireland and John was lucky that his father had given him a good one.

Mr. Moss and his team worked within the hull of the ship on the final components of each cabin. The detailed work fascinated John. Mr. Moss taught his men to work with all types of wood working tools; tools that created finely crafted cuts, joints, and grooves. Each cut, John learned, had to be accomplished expediently and without waste because only wood of superior quality went into Mr. Kemp's cabins. These woods were too expensive to waste with mistakes. John learned to build cabinets, doors and furniture that would bestow any sea captain with great pride and pleasure. Kemp ships were famous for their extra little touches of excellence.

For Mr. Moss, working with the excellent hardwoods that went into the building of the Baltimore Clippers, was almost his religion. He trained his apprentices to take pride in their work and produce the ultimate in quality. Of all the carpenters in the yard, the Moss crew was unequaled in craftsmanship. All the master carpenters at the Kemp Shipyard were noted for their expertise, but Mr. Moss was the most respected.

This expert carpenter worked a piece of wood and then gently caressed the finished object with his hands as he marveled at the silken feel of the grains. John couldn't have been assigned to a better mentor and slowly began to appreciate the point that Mr. Moss was making as he diligently worked to finish each project with perfection.

With his increase in wages, John was able to move to better lodgings. The third floor attic above the pub had not been the most desirable accommodation. Even though Jacque could have afforded better lodging, he had stayed with John at the Ox and Plow all these months. But John had quickly discovered that Jacque preferred to spend his money on ale and loose women. Surprisingly, it hadn't taken much persuading from John to convince Jacque to move into a small cottage several blocks from the docks.

The two-room cottage was in a cleaner, more virtuous neighborhood away from the rowdy noise of the docks and pubs. They no longer would have to share their bed with two men and the lice and fleas above the noisy pub. Many nights John had lain in bed listening to the fighting and yelling inside the pub and outside on the docks of Fells Point. This would be a pleasant change. The new lodgings were even good for Jacque as he began spending less time in the pubs drinking himself senseless.

Jacque occasionally brought a girl back to the cottage with him for the night. The grunting and moaning coming from the bedroom embarrassed John. But at least at the cottage John could sleep in the other room on a straw mat and give Jacque some privacy. After all, he reasoned, it hadn't occurred that often. Jacque tried to interest John in some of these loose women, and even brought two girls home one night, but John had resisted. His upbringing had taught him to wait for that one special girl; the one he would someday wed. John respected Jacque's needs, but was not pleased with such trysts.

John moved his mother's precious coins from under the floor of their room in the pub to a hiding spot behind a hearthstone in the cottage. He had loosened a stone on the side of the hearth and dug out a small hole behind it. While he trusted Jacque with his life, he wasn't sure about some of Jacque's friends and lady acquaintances. Thus, he didn't tell Jacque about his new hiding spot. John continued to deposit most of his wages at the small bank on Washington Street. He had a goal and spending his hard earned money carelessly would not help him attain it.

John had also begun to have doubts about Jacque joining him in his quest for wealth. Jacque had constantly spent his money without any regard for his future. John hinted to Jacque that if he wanted be a partner in their joint venture, he should put a portion of his pay in the bank. Jacque had laughed at the suggestion.

When a cargo ship, flying an independent flag, managed to slip past the British blockade at sea, John received the occasional letter from home. In the same fashion, he was also able to send letters back to his family. But a letter from his mother that summer brought bad news. His younger brother Kevin had been shanghaied on a street in Belfast where he was seeking employment. The letter arrived six months after Kevin's disappearance. John's parents had no idea of Kevin's whereabouts. Many suspected the British Navy, as they were in dire need of sailors to man the ships fighting the wars with France and the United States.

Mr. Doyle had approached the British Admiralty Office in Belfast and they vowed that they would not, under any circumstance, abduct an Irish youth off the streets. However, there was doubt as to the words of the Admiralty. Shortly after Mr. Doyle's inquiry, several people reported that they had witnessed kidnapping incidents. They reported that the abductors were British sailors in uniform. Kevin had simply vanished.

The British attempt at a total blockade of the American coast continued throughout the winter. But in Baltimore, for the time being, the war seemed to be far away. There were reports of sea battles all over the Atlantic Ocean and in the Saint Lawrence Seaway, but the Chesapeake Bay remarkably had little activity. The American Navy was reported to do well with sea battles, but there were failures during the land battles on the Canadian border and the northwest frontier. In spite of the invasion of Canada by American troops, the British seemed to be getting the upper hand in the north. More and more men left the shipyards and joined the Army or Navy as the fighting intensified. John and Jacque agreed that ships were needed and that's where they stayed during the early war years.

The spring of 1814 brought bad news to the United States. The French and British had reached an accord after the abdication of Napoleon Bonaparte. This allowed Great Britain to move many more troops to the American continent and the outlook for winning the war began to look dismal. Then news reached Baltimore that a squadron of British ships had entered the Chesapeake Bay and were attacking small ports and shipping from Norfolk, at the southern end of the bay, to Havre de Grace, at the northern end.

Early in the summer of 1814 John and Jacque were saddened by the news that the Ellen Marie had been sunk during a battle in the Patuxent River. The newspaper article had no details about the battle or the fate of her crew. Both men felt downcast at the loss of the ship that had brought them to America and they had become concerned about their friends who were aboard at the time of her final destruction.

August brought even more distressful news to the citizens of Baltimore. This time the newspaper reports were factual and verified by the military. Many British ships had landed British Army troops near Annapolis and the army was marching west to invade Washington, D.C.

In Baltimore and the surrounding areas, volunteers were called to arms and immediately began training to defend the city. Baltimore, being a prosperous seaport and shipbuilding center, would be a great prize for the British. The crown realized its capture would greatly aid the British Isles in winning the war. John and Jacque felt that the time had come to join the many others in protecting the city they now called home.

The first week of their training was barely over when word was received that Washington had been taken and most public buildings had been burned. The defending militia from the city had performed poorly on the Bladensburg battlefield against the professionally trained British Army. President and Mrs. Madison had barely escaped into Virginia with their lives. Panic gripped the streets of Baltimore and morale dipped to an all time low. Training intensified as the volunteer militiamen of Baltimore learned to quickly load and fire their newly issued muskets.

News soon arrived that British ships loaded with troops had been discovered heading for North Point, to the east of Baltimore. The volunteer militia was spurred into action. The resident defenders made a dash to North Point, just in time, to unite with the American Army that had assembled on the battlefield. As the American militia took defensive positions, they saw the British unloading troops and supplies in preparation for the invasion.

Defensive ditches were quickly dug. The militia stacked logs, farm wagons and anything else that would offer some safety from the British musket and cannon balls. The brave, determined defenders then settled in for the night and waited for the invaders impending attack on the following day.

John and Jacque huddled around the small campfire with the other men assigned to their defensive location. One of the men brought out a concertina and began playing Irish songs familiar to John. When he played "Danny Boy" John began singing along and the sweet music drifted across the glen and drew more listeners. A fiddler had shown up during the evening and several more singers joined in singing songs from Ireland and America. The music chased away any fears the men might have shown about the battle that would begin the following morning. But, beneath their resilient posture, each man harbored a concern over the upcoming battle.

Around midnight, as the fires began to burn low, the men slowly dispersed to their individual sleeping areas to settle in for the night. The music took John's thoughts to Ballylee as he wrapped himself in his blanket. He drifted off with pleasant thoughts of home and family.

Someone nudged John as the first dim light of the new day began filling the distant horizon. John in turn nudged Jacque who was snoring away without a care in the world. John had spent a restless night waking to every little sound in the campsite.

Each man had quickly arisen as the camp stirred to life. Breakfast offered water, a little dried jerky and some fresh bread that had been brought to the battlefield during the night. Obviously, John thought, someone back in Baltimore had spent a busy night at their ovens thinking of the defenders.

John and Jacque shook hands, and after wishing each other luck, headed to their assigned spots. John settled in behind a huge oak tree that had been toppled for use as a protective barrier. He had peered out upon the mist-covered field that lay between him and the enemy lines. A few yards away he saw something move and realized that it was a doe and her two fawns. She was casually nibbling at new grown grass as her fawns took turns nursing. It was a surreal scene. It was difficult to believe that soon a fierce battle would take place where she grazed.

The morning's serenity had been short lived. From far away, through the morning mist, bagpipes and bugles called the British troops to formation. The noise of the pipes sounded raspy and loud across the open field between the two armies. John thought back to home and the sweeter, gentler tone of the Irish Élan pipes. To John, that day, the Scottish bagpipes had been menacing and aggressive.

Shortly thereafter the beat of many drums added to the din of the pipes and bugles announcing the advance of the British army as they began to press forward toward the American lines. The enemy had gradually emerged from the low fog, which slowly evaporated from the field of combat. The rows of red coats seemed to go on forever, but the Baltimore militia and regular Army were ready. They were resolute that Baltimore would not fall into British hands.

Shortly after the advance began, the British cannons commenced firing. The distant horizon was filled with flashes of fire and smoke as the cannons belched forth their deadly missiles. Smoke rings drifted lazily upward from the ground fog as cannon balls whistled through the air high above the defenders. The massive explosions shook the ground as the artillery rounds returned to the earth. A few of the cannon balls failed to explode as they landed behind the line of the defenders and were seen bouncing crazily, almost comically across the open fields behind them.

The British readjusted the cannons for the proper range and another volley screeched across the open land this time hitting within the American lines. Explosions tore open defensive positions and defenders alike. Many proud Americans died in the bombardment, but the defenders stood fast. John felt as if the gates of hell had opened and belched fire and brimstone. As he felt the raw chill of fear rise up along his spine, he tightly clasped his hands on his musket to stop them from trembling.

The front lines of the attackers drew closer. The drums, bagpipes, and bugles became louder and louder as they enemy neared. The tramping of the advancing army shook the very ground under the American defenders, but all bravely stood their ground. And then it was time for the American Army cannons to respond. From behind the defenders came a furious roar of cannon fire. Cannon balls filled the air and fell upon the British Army exploding just in front of the rows of red and white uniforms. American cannon fire was being returned to the British and exploded with an equal vengeance.

Many Redcoats fell from this onslaught, but their line continued to advance. The next barrage from the American Army cannons brought more accuracy and more death and destruction to the British troops. But still they advanced to the drumbeat as red-coated soldiers from the rear ranks filled the gaps left by the dead and dying. The shrill of the bagpipes had become deafening as they neared John's concealed position.

John had been assigned a defensive position, with several other volunteers, behind a large oak tree that had been quickly felled. Fifty feet to his left he saw Jacque crouched behind a tipped-over farm wagon loaded with freshly cut straw. A deeper, sharper chill ran down John's spine as he watched the red coated line draw nearer and nearer. The stomping of their black, high-topped leather boots was like thunder on a stormy day.

When the British Army had approached so close John could make out a man's face, the advancement suddenly stopped. From the British Officer came the order, "Ready!" The front line dropped to one knee. "Aim!" and a thousand muskets clattered as they aimed at the Americans. John and the others instantly crouched down even lower behind their protective barriers as the command was given to "Fire!"

The roar had been deafening! John's world shook with a vengeance. Smoke and fire billowed toward the defenders as a thousand musket balls emerged from the confusion to deliver a mighty blow to the Americans. The huge oak tree in front of John reverberated as hundreds of the balls burrowed deeply within the entire length of its tightly woven fibers.

Then it was the defenders turn to answer the British outrage. Muskets and long rifles appeared from their hidden positions and responded to the challenge. John took aim at a kneeling red-coated soldier a hundred feet away who was loading his musket. John squeezed the trigger and fired. With all the smoke and confusion on the battlefield, John never knew if he hit his target. The minute the ball left the barrel of his musket, John reloaded and then fired again. This action was repeated many times, over and over.

Throughout the morning the British Army attempted to reach the American defenses, but the Americans held fast causing the aggressors to finally retreat back toward the bay. The British withdrew from the battlefield leaving scattered dead or dying red-coated soldiers. Wounded men had been dragged unceremoniously back by the survivors in a desperate attempt to save their lives and escape the fury of the American muskets and riflemen. Even though they finally reached safety, by being out of range of the defenders' muskets, American riflemen had continued to punish the British ranks with their highly accurate long-range rifles. Cannon fire from both sides continued the occasional harassment for another half hour as explosions rocked the ground.

Then suddenly, a strange silence had fallen upon the bloody arena save the moans of dying men. John had been so focused on the approaching army, and keeping up a constant barrage of fire, that he hadn't stopped to look about him. He finally took a deep breath and took time to study the defenders that had shared this battle with him. Several men near him lay wounded. One had died from a bullet striking him in the head just above his right ear. The back of his head had split open like a ripe melon. John looked toward the hay wagon for his friend Jacque so he could let him know that he had survived the battle. A horrified tremor suddenly ran through his entire body. Jacque laid spread eagle on the ground, a gaping wound in his chest. The white shirt he wore was soaked red with his blood.

As John jumped up to rush to Jacque's side he felt a deep stabbing pain in his left side just below the ribs. Looking down, he had found the hem of his shirt covered with blood. Opening his shirt, he had expected to find a wound caused by a British musket ball, but what he saw was a large oak splinter, as thick as his finger, protruding from the skin.

A nearby fellow defender was at his side in a flash to aid him. "What luck you have today," the man spoke with amazement as he peered at the wound. "The wood is just under the skin and not deep at all."

Deftly, the man had taken his knife from his belt, made a slit in John's skin and removed the six-inch long debris that had apparently come off the oak log. John felt no pain at all until the man poured some liquid from a flask over the open wound. John gasped at the shock of the searing, burning sensation.

"There," the man told him. "A little whiskey will clean that out just fine and you'll be fit as a fiddle! You need a drink?" he asked, as he offered the small flask to John.

"No thank you," John mumbled. He felt relief that it was such a minor wound.

John laid his musket against the oak log and, in a few short strides, reached the hay wagon where Jacque's body lay. Even before he had reached his friend's side he could tell by the immense wound in Jacque's chest that he was dead. In spite of the fact that he had seen men dying all morning from the battle that had taken place, John had been shaken and tears trickled down his cheeks. He felt sad that Jacque had no relatives to mourn his passing. What a sad day it was. But there was only time for a moments pause when a shout was heard, "They're rallying again!"

As John rushed back to his position he was startled to see a gray squirrel sitting atop the felled oak tree beside his musket. The squirrel shook his tail and chattered his disapproval that someone would be in his territory. As the men all returned to the oaken barricade, the squirrel rushed up a nearby tree and noisily chattered away at the men below. As the first sounds of battle began the squirrel had wisely disappeared.

The sounds of the bugles were heard once again and a slow drum roll began as the British formed up for another attempt at removing the Americans from their defensive positions. John quickly loaded his musket and watched in disbelief as once again the long lines of red-coated men began their slow advance across the field before him. The bleating pipes had started their threatening whine as well, but there weren't as many pipers as there had been during the first attack. John thought that during this second attack the pipes had sounded almost woeful rather than the fierce outrageous peril they warned of earlier in the day.

Before the attackers had taken ten steps, the American riflemen began to take their long-distance toll. Individual British soldiers could be seen falling as the line advanced. Cannons on both sides commenced spitting death and destruction, and men on both sides once again were torn apart by horrendous orange and red explosions. During the second attack, the volunteer militiamen were now battle hardened and more resolute than ever in stopping the British intruders. The number of dead redcoats on the battlefield before them was proof of their resoluteness.

Amidst the dead bodies that already littered the battlefield from the earlier battle, the entire scenario was again repeated as the British advanced to within a hundred feet of the immovable American defenses. The command to "Fire" wasn't as intimidating the second time as it had been earlier in the morning. The volunteer Army knew what came next and were well prepared.

The roar of gunfire from the advancing Army removed a few American defenders as they crouched behind protective barriers, but the response was more deadly for the British because they stood erect and in formation out upon the open field. More and more red uniforms littered the battlefield in a shameful waste of young manhood.

During the second attack, the British cannons were not as loud. The American artillery, as well as the accuracy of the American long rifle, silenced many of the enemy gun positions. To John, that day, it seemed tragic to watch so many men die for the whim of one king.

The afternoon bore on for John. Fire-load-fire-load — again and again. The smoke and confusion of the battlefield hadn't allowed anyone to be certain that he actually killed any one man. There was really no time for any of the defenders to watch as their musket balls traveled across the short distance to strike its intended target. But many dead British soldiers now littered the battlefield. The scene had been madness as so many of those brave British soldiers died for their king and country.

Late in the afternoon, the British generals decided on one last attempt to oust these insolent defenders. On the third attack, the British soldiers were given the order to fix bayonets and a contemptible demand given for the "Charge!" Their steady yell rose up to a loud bellow as the remaining redcoats charged the American positions. It had been a fearsome sight as hundreds of red-coated men dashed across the remaining battlefield jumping over their dead comrades. Their long, shiny bayonets had protruded far ahead of them, determined to take a life.

When the attackers drew near, John stood up behind his secure position, aimed at a red-coated soldier charging him, and fired. As the bluish-gray smoke cleared in front of him, John saw that the young man lay dying only a few yards away. He didn't look to be much older than John himself. Blood gushed from his chest onto the ground as the soldier gurgled his last breath. The battle was over for this young soldier.

The British army retreated from that field of death in defeat. The American defenses had held. Baltimore was saved.

As the British Army fled the battlefield the American riflemen had continued firing. John watched as a crying young boy, with a bloodied arm, was trying to drag his splintered drum along as he fled for safety. As John watched, a dark red spot suddenly opened on the side of the boy's head and he fell to the ground draped across his prized instrument. The war was over for him, too. In England a mother would cry for the loss of her loving son, a child too young to die in this manner.

John sat upon the oak log in exhaustion and looked at the motionless young soldier that lay before him. He felt no emotion. This could have been the very man that took the life of his friend, Jacque. John also remembered the mistreatment that his countrymen had suffered under British rule back home and felt no remorse in the taking of this life. He thought of Kevin who might have been kidnapped by the British to serve in their Army or Navy.

John vowed then not to look back upon this day just as he vowed not to look back on the unfortunate incident with the prostitute. Neither occurrence was a result of an event he had initiated. John felt at peace with himself.

A few days later Baltimore seemed to return to normal. John returned to the shipyard to discover that many men who worked with him had been wounded. A few had died in the battle, but the number of deaths on the American side, during the battle, had been remarkably low. Mr. Moss, the carpenter who was guiding John through his apprenticeship, had suffered a burn on the right side of his face from a misfire in his flintlock during the battle at North Point. Mr. Moss was thankful that it wasn't worse and that he hadn't lost an eye. His brother-in-law had lost an arm to a British musket ball in the same battle and would no longer be able to work in the family's carpentry business in Baltimore. Mr. Moss told John that he was leaving the shipyard at the end of the month to take over the family's cabinetry business.

Shortly after the British lost the battle for Baltimore, a flotilla of British war ships began a major blockade of the Chesapeake Bay. However, construction of Baltimore Clippers optimistically continued. The fast clippers could still outrun any British blockade ship and once the blockade was over there would still be a great demand for ships of this design.

Only a week into September word was received that the British flotilla was advancing on Baltimore. The American Army increased the number of soldiers stationed at Fort McHenry located at the harbor entrance. The British commenced firing on the fort in mid-September. Both sides exchanged fire for a full day and night.

That evening John had sat, with many others, on the docks at Fells Point where they watched the battle two miles away. It had been a gloomy, rainy night and the clouds had burst forth with a myriad of colors as explosions rocked the city of Baltimore. Many citizens fled the city in panic, but those who worked in the area knew that the harbor was impenetrable. A large chain and recently sunken ships blocked the entrance to the harbor. The British assault was thwarted. The thick walls of the fort stood up to the pounding and the following day the British flotilla sailed away.

Fall ran into winter and then in January of 1815 news was received in Baltimore of a major defeat of the British Army in New Orleans and the consequent treaty between the two countries. The treaty had been signed late in December 1814, but word hadn't reach the combatants until after the battle. The war was finally over and the busy seaport of Baltimore returned to its pre-war business as usual.

In March, as John was leaving the shipyard, he saw a familiar face on the dock. The man was just leaving the Ellsworth Shipping Office. It was Captain Robinson! He ran to greet his father's cousin relieved that the captain had survived the sinking of the Ellen Marie. Captain Robinson told John that he had arrived on the stagecoach from New York City the day before.

Captain Robinson invited John to accompany him back to his home a half-mile away. There he introduced him to his wife and two young daughters. The two men sat long into the night beside the fireplace as they brought each other up-to-date on their adventures. John told the captain of the battle of North Point and the sad loss of his good friend, Jacque Lyons. He also related the strange tranquility before the battle as a doe and her fawns casually grazed upon the open field.

He told the captain about the battle of Fort McHenry; how he and others sat on the docks and watched the battle between the British warships and the American fortress. And John told Captain Robinson of a poem a lawyer had written that had been published in *The Baltimore Patriot* newspaper describing the battle. John carried a copy of that poem and proudly shared it with his father's cousin.

Captain Robinson told John that the Ellen Marie had suffered a cannon ball below the waterline during a raid on a British frigate near Norfolk. All attempts to save her were futile. The crew of the British frigate that sank them plucked the crew from the waters of the Chesapeake Bay. They were then taken prisoner and sent to Bermuda where they sat in a British prison for many long months.

The captain told John that once they had all been released at the port of New York, Su Long decided to give up his career at sea and open a restaurant in New York City. Mr. Martin chose to go to New England and sign on to a whaling ship, as he wanted to see the Pacific Ocean.

Upon his return to Baltimore, Mr. Ellsworth was pleased to hire Captain Robinson as the captain of a cargo ship with runs between American seaports. The captain told John that he no longer wanted to travel on the open sea to other countries. He wanted to be with his wife and two young daughters as much as possible, but couldn't totally give up the sea.

John reminded Captain Robinson of his dream of finding wealth in the mountains to the west and bringing prosperity to his family back in Ballylee. John told him of all the plans and preparations he had made for this journey. The Captain was skeptical of this young man's dream, but said nothing to dissuade him.

John worried about the small leather purse containing the coins his mother had slipped into his hand as he departed Ballylee on his adventure. He asked Captain Robinson if he would hold them in safe keeping while he was away. In the back of the family storeroom Captain Robinson had loosened a floorboard to bury some family valuables in the dirt. Not telling John the exact location, he told him that he could hide Mrs. Doyle's precious gift with the family's valuables. It would be safe in that secret spot as only the captain and his wife knew of the location.

The two men parted late in the night and John promised to write. They agreed to meet again someday soon. Both men looked forward to their new ventures.

John's daily routine didn't change much during the winter of 1815. However, the spring of 1816 brought a change to the shipbuilding industry in Baltimore. The fast Baltimore Clippers were no longer in demand as there were no longer British warships to outrun. The blockade was now history. The emphasis now was on larger ships that could haul more cargo more profitably.

Thomas Kemp's dry-dock was geared to build the smaller clippers and not ready for such a major change so quickly. John was almost at the end of his third year as a carpenter's apprentice when the shipyard cut back on manpower. John lost his position shortly before he had completed his apprenticeship.

That's when he decided to head west and search for the wealth for which he yearned. The mountains of the Virginias beckoned to him. He had saved his money for almost three years and decided he had enough to strike out in search of his fortune.

He bought a used flintlock rifle that was still in good condition and after firing a few test rounds he was amazed at the accuracy. The rifling within the barrel made the weapon far more accurate than the musket he had carried onto the battlefield at North Point. He bargained for a powder horn, powder, extra flint and a mold to make his own rifle balls from the same man and was pleased with his purchase. Lead would be a precious commodity in the wilderness, so each shot fired would be melted down and remolded to be used again.

The past two years had not been wasted for John, as he had not idly allowed the time to pass. He had asked a lot of questions of those who had already traveled into the mountains and earnestly listened to their advice. These men spoke of the fur trapping business and trade with the local Indians as being a most lucrative venture.

At times John had to separate the tall tale from the truth, but felt confident that he had his facts right. One lesson he learned from others was of the multitude of thistles and briars along the old Indian trails and knew he would need a good set of buckskin breeches to protect his legs from scratches and cuts.

John spent time studying the clothing that these trappers and traders wore. He also took an interest in the uniform that the American Army adopted during the battles along the Canadian border. John discovered that those men copied the Indian method of dress as well. A linen or flaxen shirt was best in warm weather. Bear or buckskin shirts and coats chased the winter chill. The last two items would be obtained, when the weather demanded a change by killing a deer or a bear.

Thus John learned the practice of skinning an animal, tanning the pelt and using sinew to assemble any needed garment. To perfect his endeavor John set traps for squirrels and rabbits in nearby wooded areas. He stretched and dried the pelts then assembled hats and mittens, which he sold to friends and acquaintances. At times the walls of his small cabin would be covered with pelts drying by the heat of the small fire on the hearth. His nightly fire was also adorned with tiny strips of squirrel and rabbit as he accumulated jerky for his journey.

There was much for a young lad to learn before heading into the wilds. A man had to live off the land. Gaining knowledge of what plants and roots were safe to eat was imperative. Learning what could be eaten uncooked was also important, for he had been told that there would be times when a fire in the forest could only draw the attention of undesirable visitors.

John had cautiously not mentioned searching for gold to anyone, as these were times of peril for those carrying items of value on their person. He had certainly learned his lesson a few years earlier when he was accosted by the two thugs near the docks at Fells Point.

By mid May 1816 John felt that he was prepared. He planned his departure from Baltimore the first week in June. His attire would include a flaxen shirt, breechcloth, buckskin breeches, Indian moccasins and a good wool hat. John would carry his meager supplies in a backpack made from the pelt of a large fox that he had trapped.

"Travel light," he was warned, as he would never know when he might have to outrun hostile Indians. He heard many tales telling how the Indians along the mountains almost made it a game to run down a white man and kill him. Like a cat pursuing a mouse the Indians would chase a man, slightly wound him and let him escape so they could continue the chase. John didn't know if this was fact or fiction, but would use extreme care while in the distant mountains.

He bid farewell to the Robinson family and his other friends, then early one morning John started west leaving the smoke shrouded city of Baltimore behind him. He never looked back.

Chapter 8

It had taken John three days to reach the town of Front Royal at the foot of the Shenandoah Mountain range. There he was surprised to find a busy, bustling village that had been established a century earlier by trappers and farmers.

At a store in town he learned that years of hunting and trapping had reduced the quantity of game in the area. But he still had hope in his heart as he started up the steep climb at the northern end of the mountain. What he found was no Indian trail, but a road wide enough for wagons to pass each other. The timber industry had truly taken over the area and many trees had been removed over the years. The mountain was more scrub brush than forest. The rutted road also revealed that many wagons and carts had traveled this way over the years taking lumber down the mountain for the growing population in the valley below.

Day after day John pushed on deeper and deeper along the Shenandoah mountain range, but the wilderness he sought was not there. Not an hour went by that John didn't meet someone along the winding road. Doubt formed in his mind of acquiring any fortune in the mountains of northern Virginia.

He was not alone on the mountain. Every night he shared a roaring campfire with others. But, John listened intently to the tales they told. He became disheartened that there was never the mention of gold. Mostly the hunters and trappers talked about the way things were in previous years with plenty of game in the forests. They speculated about going west where beaver, deer, and bear were abundant, but the fear of the Indians seemed to be what held them back. John was told tale after tale of the ferocity of the Indians and their hostilities toward the encroaching pioneers. It was difficult for him to separate fact from fiction. These mountainmen liked their tall tales!

The Shenandoah Mountain Range was not going to be the source of prosperity John had envisioned. If prosperity were to be found, this was not the place. People he met on the mountain barely survived day-to-day living.

After two weeks of meandering along the mountain range, John had had enough. He found no bear or deer and was only lucky enough to trap the occasional rabbit or squirrel for his meals. From the little he learned at the nightly campfires, he decided to descend the mountain on the western slope and head further west into the mountains of West Virginia. There he hoped to at least find a more secluded forest to hunt and trap while not encountering hostile Indians.

He came down the mountain and entered the town of Shenandoah. Once again he found a prosperous village that catered to the local farming community. Many businesses thrived in the fast growing town.

John had spent almost all his funds equipping for this journey and was well aware that he soon find some means of replenishing them. But the Shenandoah Valley did have something to offer him for the time being. The town lay beside the Shenandoah River and there was a great deal of commerce involving the movement of supplies along the waterway by stern oared barges. Experienced carpenters were needed to build the barges. Putting his dream of finding instant wealth on temporary hold, John took a position as a carpenter at the Valley Boatyard.

He located a small log cabin for rent beside the river and settled in. Month after month he worked at the boatyard constructing barges and boats for use on the nearby Shenandoah River. But, his dream still persisted. His venture west was delayed, but the job paid well and the boatyard was kept very busy with the ever-growing population. Every penny he could spare went into the Shenandoah Valley Bank in preparation of his continued search for wealth.

John was pleased when he discovered that the local Cherokee Indians were not hostile; in fact they were downright friendly and he made many Cherokee friends. One craft he learned from them was carving bowls, spoons and other utensils from wood. Many of the items they made were of excellent quality. John had been a great whittler back in Ireland and was good with a knife. The Indians used small chisels and knives to produce superior wooden bowls and small storage boxes. He shared many evening fires with his new Indian friends and watched as they carefully produced their wooden products. He quickly learned a new craft and paid close attention to their stories of life and survival in the forests.

The bowls, spoons and boxes sold quite well at the Indian trading posts, but no one in town made or sold them. There just wasn't enough profit for the townspeople to be bothered with such a trivial undertaking. John decided that this was another sideline that could bring in a few extra dollars. At night, as he sat beside his hearth, he began carving oak and walnut bowls from blocks of wood. These wood blocks were plentiful as they were unused pieces from the Valley Boatyard. His employer threw the unused blocks of wood on a pile for people to take. They, in turn, used the excess pieces for their evening fire. There was no expense for wood in John's undertaking, but there was a profit. Soon, his bowls became in great demand by the villagers.

Whenever he had time to spare, John would head into the forests in search of game. His Indian friends had taught him alternative methods of trapping and various ways of treating pelts to produce softer furs. Fur was still a desired commodity by the local residents and some small game could still be found in the local forests. The problem was that the bear and deer had all but disappeared from the region. For years the Indians and trappers had gleaned most of the large game from the local forests in satisfying the fur market for the growing population. So John went back to trapping raccoon, fox, squirrel and rabbit. There was a good profit to be made in the sale of mittens and hats. His account at the bank slowly grew.

Working at the boatyard kept him busy and his evenings were spent either carving wooden items for his customers or tanning furs for the upcoming winter weather. His small cabin became a popular place for the townspeople to purchase wood products, mittens and hats. There were also requests for the occasional piece of small furniture that John did his best to fulfill.

Watching his Indian friends spear fishing in the Shenandoah River gave him an idea for another source of income. Carving several spears, he purchased barbed iron tips and began spear fishing when time permitted. His salted trout sold the best and the clear waters of the Shenandoah River offered some very large, tasty fish. Many customers requested fresh fish, but with John's busy schedule, he could not always oblige. Each of his businesses were doing quite well.

In the early fall of 1816 John was spear fishing when he noticed something shiny on the bottom of the riverbed near the shore. He reached down into the water and retrieved a small shiny stone. Holding his hand open he discovered a tiny gold nugget.

"GOLD!" It shouted inside his head. He couldn't believe it. No one ever mentioned that gold could be found in this part of Virginia. Was it a well-kept secret? John had found his wealth. His heart pounded wildly and his breathing became shallow and difficult.

Quickly he looked around to see if anyone had seen him holding this precious article, but the nearest people had been many hundreds of yards away. Before anyone could notice his find, he instantly stuck the nugget in his pocket. Slowly his composure returned and he began searching the riverbed for other nuggets. And there were several to be found amongst the river pebbles that he stirred about. With trembling hands he anxiously gathered up all he could find and stuffed them in his pocket. Soon his pocket was full of tiny golden nuggets. He couldn't believe his good fortune.

John gave up fishing for the evening and quickly returned to his cabin. He had a sleepless night as he dreamt about what he would do with his newfound wealth. Naturally, he would send money home so his parents could move into a larger house of their own. He would buy a new dress for his mother to wear to Mass. The poor woman only had one nice dress that she wore on special occasions. John would see to it that she had the finest dress in Ballylee and his father would now proudly sport a new suit on his way to Mass. In the wee hours of the morning he finally dozed as he planned his return to the riverbank where he would resume his search for more of the tiny nuggets. He dreamt of returning to Baltimore, his pockets bulging with money. Morning couldn't come quickly enough.

The Shenandoah Bank opened promptly at nine that morning and John was at the door waiting. He was as animated as a young boy on Christmas morning. His exhilaration was difficult to hide as he waited for Mr. Duggan to open the teller window.

With an enormous grin, John opened a small leather bag and spilled his fortune on the counter in front of Mr. Duggan.

"And what would you have me do with these?" asked Mr. Duggan.

"I want to trade these for dollars and have the money placed in my account," John smugly announced.

By then, several other customers had entered the bank. They began looking over John's shoulder watching with great curiosity and listening to this conversation.

Mr. Duggan roared with laughter, "John, my friend, you have been had by someone. This is Fools Gold. It's not gold at all, but iron pyrite! Why you can pull hands full of it out of the river any day of the week."

Mr. Duggan's laughter stirred the others in the bank into laughter as well. Many passed the joke on to those nearby on the wooden sidewalk outside the bank. In John's opinion, the situation was an embarrassing joke shared by far too many.

His heart sunk deep down into the soles of his boots. Fighting back tears of frustration he stumbled blindly from the bank. His humiliation seemed as large as the looming Shenandoah Mountains. It was as if everyone in town had laughed at him that day.

He returned to his cabin under a huge, black cloud where he slunk down at his table beside the hearth. He should have been at work at the boatyard that very minute, but there he sat seemingly the object of humor for the whole valley. In his soul he heard everyone laughing at him. In his confusion, he couldn't begin to think about his next course of action.

After a short time there was a tap at his door. He opened the door and found Mr. Campbell, a neighbor, standing there.

"John, may I come in?" Mr. Campbell asked.

"Are ye here to laugh at me as well?" he snapped at his neighbor. That was very out of character for John who was usually the politest and most humble person in town. Mr. Campbell entered and John slammed the cabin door behind him.

"No, John," Mr. Campbell responded as he held his hands up in defense. "I came to sympathize with you. You see, I moved here about twenty years ago and found gold nuggets in the river. I was so excited that I went to the Deer Run Pub and ordered up several rounds of drinks for anyone that was there. Well, when folks heard I had found gold and was buying drinks, a lot of men showed up and consumed a lot of whiskey and beer. I ran up an enormous bill."

Listening to this story, John calmed down and sat on the edge of the table. He gestured for Mr. Campbell to sit in the cabins only chair.

Mr. Campbell continued his story, "After a couple hours, and I was quite drunk by then, the barkeep demanded some payment. I reached in my pocket and proudly poured a handful of gold nuggets on the table in payment.

"Well, what a commotion that caused. It seems everyone in town knew about the iron pyrite. It was a big joke on me. They were drinking all that whiskey and knew the entire time that what I had discovered wasn't really gold."

He paused and bowed his head as he recalled the incident, then added, "It took me months to pay off that debt. My wife was furious with me. I was lucky that the pub owner was indulgent of my plight or I could have ended up in jail. I was the joke of the entire town for a long time. Since that day several other men have fallen victim to the Fools Gold in the river."

"I appreciate your coming to me and telling me your story," John replied. "I don't think I could stay in town another day if I thought I would be the center of cruel entertainment for the whole valley. The stuff certainly looks like gold," he added.

"Many a man has thought so, John," Mr. Campbell explained. "That's why it got the name Fools Gold. It certainly made fools of you and me and many, many others."

Shortly after Mr. Campbell departed, Mr. Duggan approached John's cabin. "John, I'm sorry for my actions," he apologized. "I should have known better. You are a respected customer of the bank and that was a terrible thing I did to you.

"Your big smile caught me off guard at the bank," he continued to explain. "I thought you were just pulling a joke on me because I assumed that everyone around here knew about the pyrite being in the river. It's been years since anyone found the nuggets and thought they were real gold."

He shook John's hand as he added, "I hope you will forgive me."

Typical of John's character, he took the man's hand in friendship and accepted Mr. Duggan's apology. And because of John's friendships in the town there wasn't much said about the episode afterwards. A few kidded him in a friendly manner thereafter, but John was able to laugh along with them never revealing the heartbreak he had truly suffered. John's dreams of wealth were once again put on hold. This was one incident that he never mentioned when writing home to his parents.

The winter of 1816-17 was unusually cold. That meant business was good for John. He sold many fur items, his salted fish sales were good, wooden bowls were in demand and he was fully accepted in the village as a businessman. The frozen Shenandoah River slowed the pace of barge building, which gave John more time to hunt and trap. Big game was still scare, but he did manage to bring down two deer. Their hides and the meat sold well. John's account at the bank began to show a nice balance. He was pleased.

In the spring, as his twenty-second birthday neared, he decided he would settle down in this lovely town. He liked the quietness of the Shenandoah Valley. He had a good business going and enjoyed his work at the small boatyard. Even though there was no instant wealth, he indeed had found prosperity. Occasionally he had been able to send a little money to his parents. With all his new friends, his life was really very rewarding.

On a warm July day in 1817, he was spearfishing in a remote area up stream from the town. Following Indian fashion, he had worn a breechcloth in the water. Standing quietly in waist deep water he heard giggling from the nearby bank. John turned and found three girls watching him. Being in waist deep water he must have given the appearance of being nude which caused the girls to openly snicker.

One of the young ladies caught John's eye. Her long hair, draped over her shoulder, was the color of gold and glistened in the afternoon sun. Her eyes were as blue as the sky and sparkled as she laughed. Even with her hand over her mouth he could see she was the prettiest girl he had seen in a long time. The distraction caused him to lose his footing and he fell backward into the water. Peals of laughter greeted him as he rose from beneath the water. Shaking the water from his blond hair he laughed as well, but the three girls had vanished back into the forest as quickly as they had appeared.

He rushed through the water to the bank, but could find no trace of the girls. They left no footprints on the stony bank. John searched in vain in the nearby woods, but like a dream, they had simply vanished.

He was stymied. This fair-haired maiden had appeared like a delicate sprite on the riverbank and disappeared just as quickly. A strong yearning arose within his soul. His rapidly beating heart told him that this was love at first sight and he vowed he would discover this nymph's identity.

When he returned to town he made subtle inquiries and soon discovered that she was Katherine Smythe, the daughter of the Presbyterian minister. Being a good Catholic, he was torn, but he was absolutely infatuated with this girl and wanted to meet her. The following Sunday he attended her father's church service with the intent of catching her eye. And he did. She shared an all too brief exchange of glances with him and then went back to her concentration on the hymnal she held in her dainty hands. But John knew that she had seen him watching her because her cheeks became as flushed as a newly opened rose. However, after the service she was nowhere to be found.

The following Sunday, he again attended services at the Presbyterian Church and steeled his nerve with determination to speak to her. But, unfortunately. the opportunity for him to do so never arose. Katherine stood beside her father after the service as the pastor greeted the departing members. She stood with her arms wrapped tightly about her father's left arm. Unlike the day he found her openly laughing at him from the riverbank, she was coy and bashful that day.

As John spoke briefly to her father at the church door, he glanced surreptitiously toward Katherine and noticed her cheeks flush once again as he caught her studying him. Katherine quickly looked down and away when she saw him look her way. But John knew then that she shared his interest in becoming acquainted. A special magic had sparked within each of them when their eyes met during that enchanted moment.

The following Sunday the Presbyterian Church was holding a fundraising event. A "Picnic Basket" auction would be held. This was a chance for John to introduce himself to Katherine, for included with the picnic basket was lunch shared with the creator of the delicious contents. As the minister's daughter, John was sure that Katherine would be one of the contributors and he was determined that he would have the winning bid for her basket.

When it came her turn to be "auctioned off,' she stood proudly beside the auctioneer in a dark blue skirt with a white bodice. A gray shawl was thrown properly over her shoulders. Her blond hair had been pulled back and tied tightly with a blue ribbon at the nape of her neck. When her basket was put up for bid, she coquettishly looked down at her picnic basket. John noted that the basket was tied with a blue ribbon, matching the one in her hair. As the bidding began, her eyes turned gently toward John bashfully hoping to catch his interest. Their eyes briefly met and as a rosy glow filled her cheeks, she demurely looked down again.

Many other hopeful young men in the crowd were also interested in Katherine's basket, for many wished the attentions of this comely young woman. The bidding rose quickly and the last few bids caused a gasp of surprise from the gathered parishioners. A murmur passed among the onlookers as many wondered which one of these daring young men was so brashly raising the bid. All eyes turned toward John as he continued to recklessly raise the value on the basket held by their pastor's daughter. After several long, agonizing minutes he won his prize paying far more than what was deemed reasonable.

Throughout the bidding process the pastor's wife kept a wary eye on John and sought his identity from those about her. Since this young man lived at the opposite end of town, and was new in the congregation, he was unknown by most church members. Some had seen him in town, but were not too sure who he was or where he came from.

John's heart beat uncontrollably swollen with pride as he carried Katherine's basket to the church picnic grove beside a gently, bubbling brook. They strolled in mutual silence past a crowd of admiring onlookers. With trembling fingers he set her basket upon the soft grass in a cool, shady spot under a large, spreading willow tree. From her basket, Katherine spread a checkered blanket on the grass. She gracefully sat down as he sat on the opposite side of her basket. Other couples sat around them, but John's attention was firmly on this vision of beauty. He was indeed the envy of all the young men that day.

"My name is John Doyle," he had spoken with a wavering voice.

"I am pleased to meet you, Mr. Doyle." Katherine timidly replied in a soft voice. "My name is…"

"Katherine Smythe," John interrupted with a smile. "The pastor's daughter. And what a lovely daughter he has." His lilting Irish accent certainly captured her attention.

Katherine blushed and looked demurely down as she ran the fingertips of her right hand daintily along the handle of the picnic basket. Her hand had almost brushed against John's, which still rested on the basket handle, but then she pulled her hand back just before their fingers touched.

"And how do you know my name?" she asked warily, but with a tease in her voice. Her mouth, however, gave her away as it showed the hint of a slight smile. John didn't miss the small dimples as they formed at the edge of her lips.

"Oh, I saw you laughing at me when I fell into the river. From that moment I had to know who you were, so I was determined to learn the name of my sprite from the forest. But, please, you must call me John."

"You are so forward, John." She tilted her head as she smiled at him. "I don't know if I should like such a brash young man." But her interest in John had already given her away by her deep blue eyes.

After a long pause she added, "And now we must have our lunch. You certainly paid dearly for this basket, John." She gently, but teasingly laughed. "Do you think the food within will be that good?" It was one of those questions that needed no answer.

Her blue eyes had sparkled at John as she tilted her head back the least bit. The white skin on her neck vibrated with her laughter and it was all John could do not to reach over and place his lips on that most sensitive spot. But, above all, John had been taught by his mother to be the perfect gentleman. He would do nothing to frighten this petite fawn from his grasp.

Katherine delicately opened a napkin revealing a ham sandwich made with thick homemade bread. "I made the bread myself," she proudly announced. "The ham was seasoned in my father's smoke house with apple wood. And if you eat it all like a good boy, I have an apple pie in my picnic basket that I made as well."

John took half of the sandwich gesturing for her to take the other half. "And if you eat the other half," John teased, "There just might be a kiss on the cheek for you!"

"Oh, from my father, I suppose," she laughed at her light battle of wits with John.

John thrilled at her laughter. He felt cold and hot flashes vibrate throughout his entire being. His mind flashed a thousand thoughts. Her laughter was like a cool summer breeze; a warm breath of fresh air on a wintry day. He was in ecstasy.

John nibbled at the sandwich as Katherine poured them each a small glass of wine, but his eyes never left her face for a moment. "This wine was made by my father. The grapes come from a small vineyard he has behind our house. This valley produces the finest wine in all of Virginia." She proudly proclaimed as she handed him a glass. Their fingers touched as he took the wine and an electric charge ran through his fingertips, up his arm and plunged deeply into his heart. John was love-struck.

The sensation was not wasted on Katherine either. The small hairs on the back of her neck stood up and she shivered from the pleasant sensation. She struggled to hide the rising passion within her heart.

With a trembling hand, he held his glass up to her as in a toast and remarked, "And the prettiest girls!"

Katherine blushed anew as they both nervously sipped their wine.

The afternoon passed far too quickly for John and Katherine. While others had played games and sat in groups talking, the young couple sat quietly for the most part, just looking into each other's eyes. They both felt an equal attraction growing within their hearts. There was magic in the air, magic that only young lovers can know.

Pastor Smythe had not been oblivious of the attraction this young man and his daughter shared. He had never seen his daughter so infatuated with any other young man in the Shenandoah Valley. Attempting not to be too obvious about his investigation, Pastor Smythe had cautiously questioned others about this bold, young man. He didn't discover much in his exploration of this man's past, for John seemed to be a solitary man. Many knew of John Doyle, as he had lived in the area for over a year now. Several knew that he was from Ireland, but that had been obvious by his accent. Several parishioners had purchased fur goods or wooden items from John, but knew little else about him. And a handful were aware that John had fought the British at Baltimore during the last big war, but the pastor ascertained no further details.

Pastor Smythe and his wife cautiously decided that Katherine was not in any danger of starting a courtship with an undesirable individual. But as vigilant parents, they didn't let their guard down for a moment. They decided they would watch this young man's attentions closely with the utmost concern shared by many a young girl's parents. The Smythes stood united, ready to step in at a moment's notice, to protect their daughter's virtues.

At the end of the day John approached Pastor Smythe to ask for his permission to call on Katherine. While the pastor was still hesitant, he consented. There was a church dance scheduled the upcoming Saturday night and John boldly asked Katherine's father if he could escort her to the dance. Since the social hall was next door to the Smythe's house, this request seemed almost humorous to John, but protocol of the times required such tact. The pastor again cautiously gave his blessing.

Mrs. Smythe was not in full agreement with her husband's decision to allow the couple to continue seeing each other. She strongly protested the continued relationship. But the pastor calmed her fears and advised that they would keep a close eye on the courtship. He reasoned with his wife that their daughter was of age and she could do worse. "Whatever that means!" demanded Mrs. Smythe.

The week painfully drifted slowly by for John. He concentrated on his work at hand and counted the hours until he could be with the girl of his dreams once again. The Church was on the opposite end of town from the Valley Boatyard and John's cabin, thus he didn't see Katherine the entire week.

Of course in the village, all eyes were on John and Katherine. The small town reverberated with the rumors of the new courtship. Both young people were well liked by everyone and most hoped for a happy union, but there were those who scoffed at the couple's chances of surviving Mrs. Smythe's scrutiny.

Saturday finally arrived. As soon as his workday was completed, John rushed to his cabin to prepare for the evening. He thoroughly washed, shaved, brushed his hair several times, and donned his only suit. With a bouquet of wild flowers for his fair maiden, he departed his cabin and headed for the church grounds.

Pastor Smythe greeted John at the door. Behind him stood Katherine, a vision of splendor, dressed in a dark gray skirt topped by a light gray bodice. She wore a crimson ribbon tied about her slender neck closed in the front with a small silver pin. Her blonde hair draped down over her slender back, falling lightly upon a black shawl that lay gently upon her shoulders. The couple walked the short distance to the social hall with Katherine's mother closely in tow as she kept a critical eye on her daughter.

John's attempt at light conversation with Mrs. Smythe was in vain for she was much more critical of this young suitor than was the pastor. John could tell by the look in her eye that he did not hold favor with her! He decided then and there that he would do everything he could to win over Katherine's mother!

That night he briefly held Katherine in his arms while dancing. Most dances of the day allowed only occasional touching of one's partner, but on the few occasions their hands touched both could feel the warmth and magic of the moment. After a few dances John escorted Katherine to the large punch bowl for refreshment. He gently placed his hand on her waist to guide her along, but Mrs. Smythe came from out of nowhere to remove the offending limb.

However, in that brief moment that John touched Katherine, he felt her warmth and softness, which caused a momentary sensation of dizziness to pass throughout his body. While Katherine seemed not to respond to his touch, he felt her quiver under his fingertips.

When the festivities of the evening were over, John walked Katherine back to her home under a full moon as a thousand stars twinkled above the young lovers. Mrs. Smythe stood by as John bid Katherine goodnight and even allowed a brief handshake. It all seemed far too formal to both, but each shared a gentle squeeze of their hands as they parted. John's feet sailed over the dirt road as he dreamily returned to his cabin.

In spite of Mrs. Smythe's objections, the romance grew over the next few months. John was becoming a regular at the Presbyterian Church. He and Katherine spent more and more time together, but always with Mrs. Smythe or the pastor in tow. They enjoyed church picnics together, the monthly dance, and the rare stroll together, all three of them, along the banks of the river.

Katherine's maternal grandfather was the local doctor, Dr. Ward Patrick. The doctor had been born in County Cork, Ireland, and immigrated as a young man. Dr. Patrick was John's closest ally in his courtship with Katherine, for the doctor viewed John as a fine upstanding young man and a potential grandson-in-law. The two spent many hours in discussion about Ireland and their newly adopted country. John related facts about his coming to this country and his years in Baltimore. However, he purposely omitted a few of the darker moments. A great fondness grew between them.

Dr. Patrick's penchant for John gave him cause to appeal his case to the highest court in the land, his daughter, Mrs. Smythe. He begged his daughter to give John and Katherine a chance for a normal courtship. In time Mrs. Smythe began to weaken her stance against John, but still kept a wary eye on the couple.

The doctor loved fast horses and had bought a pair of black horses that had once been winners at county fair racetracks. He teamed them up to pull his surrey while out visiting patients. On the rare occasion that someone challenged him to a race, the doctor was quick to respond. His team won every race in the valley. Dr. Patrick's reputation for having the finest, fastest team in Virginia spread. His wife often complained that, "He loves those horses more than he loves me!"

Dr. Patrick's shiny black carriage, with its red cushions, was the envy of the town. But the doctor thought so much of John that he allowed John to take Katherine for a ride in the country one day. Of course, a team of roan horses, rather than the doctor's prize team, pulled the carriage. Mrs. Smythe sat on the uncomfortable rumble seat of the surrey as they drove slowly along a shady lane. John's leg had secretly rubbed Katherine's on occasion and if Mrs. Smythe had been aware of this contact, she ignored this mild show of affection. By this time the couple were well into their romance and Katherine's mother was accepting the inevitable.

While visiting a family with a sick child in March of 1818, the doctor had been consulting the father of the child while standing next to the oxen used for plowing. One of the oxen suddenly swung his head back in answer to a biting horsefly. His huge horn struck Dr. Patrick in the back of his head and sent him crashing to the ground. The farmer was horrified when he realized that the blow had crushed the doctor's skull and killed him instantly.

Everyone in the area was stunned. Dr. Patrick was so well loved by all. When a family couldn't afford to pay him he accepted chickens, vegetables or fruits as payment. He never pressured a family for payment. Rainy, windswept nights never kept Dr. Patrick from his medical duties. In the dead of winter people would hear his sleigh bells in the distance and know that he was off to deliver a baby, set a broken limb or ease the pain of an elderly patient. Dr. Ward Patrick was always there for the people of Shenandoah.

In Dr. Patrick's will he had stipulated that he wanted his coffin delivered to the cemetery by his black stallions, for he loved his team of horses. Almost everyone in town attended the funeral service held for Dr. Patrick. His son-in-law, Pastor Smythe, conducted the service at his church. The doctor's coffin was then gently placed in the back of the black hearse. As his body was slowly driven from the church, the procession made its way to the cemetery high on a hill a few blocks away. Mrs. Patrick, her daughter, and Katherine followed behind the hearse with the congregation trailing behind. John walked beside Katherine as the solemn parade took the doctor to his final resting place. It was the largest turnout the town had ever seen.

As the hearse entered the cemetery, and began to climb a short embankment, a gun shot from a hunter in a nearby forest shattered the silence of the morning. The high-spirited team bolted up the hill, the hearse doors flew open, the coffin slid out onto the road, the coffin lid popped open, and Dr. Patrick's body rolled down the hill stopping at the feet of the shocked congregation. As extremely disconcerting as this was to the family, Dr. Patrick's funeral was the talk of the town for many, many years.

During the winter months John decided to leave his job at the boatyard and begin his own business. He started building small sheds and barns, but then began building houses. The citizens of Shenandoah were improving their living style by tearing down the old log cabins and erecting more substantial, formal houses. His construction business steadily grew, so John hired several workers to help build the houses. When word of his expertise as a carpenter began to spread through the area, people of the town requested that John also make furniture for them. The Doyle Carpentry Company began to build frame houses in the daylight hours and John built furniture in the evenings.

John procured two horses for the Doyle Carpentry Company and opened his own lumber mill along the foothills of the Shenandoah Mountain. Through the winter and spring both businesses prospered.

On a cool April evening John approached Pastor and Mrs. Smythe and requested Katherine's hand in marriage. The Smythes were so impressed with him that there was an immediate nod of approval from both parents. John now knew for certain that he had finally gained Mrs. Smythe's favor.

Katherine, standing unseen at the top of the stairs, let out a very unladylike squeal, which caused the three in the parlor to break forth in peals of laughter. In the joy of the moment the Smythes forgave their daughter's breech of etiquette.

Mr. and Mrs. Smythe retired to the kitchen and let the young couple have the solitude of the parlor. Naturally they remained within earshot distance lest the ecstasy of the moment get out of hand. Katherine sat on the settee as John dropped to one knee, took her hand, and haltingly asked for her hand in marriage.

"Oh, yes, John," she whispered through her tears of joy.

John stood and with powerful arms swept Katherine up into his embrace and kissed her. It was their very first kiss and they both regaled with the intensity of the sensation. John found her lips moist and soft, tasting like the sweetest wine in the valley. A shiver ran down his spine as, for the first time, he held her tightly in his arms. He thrilled at the feel of her soft body against his. Their kiss lingered and lingered until there was a loud, "Hrrmmm" from Mr. Smythe in the kitchen. From afar he asked, "Would either of you like tea?"

The four all met in the parlor and spent the evening making plans for a June wedding. Mr. and Mrs. Smythe relished this moment and took delight in their daughter's happiness. The remainder of the spring would be busy at the Smythe house with all the preparations for the upcoming nuptials.

As the first flowers of spring blossomed forth, John and Katherine's love blossomed even more. The engaged couple were allowed occasional private moments together, but not too far from a chaperon at any time. They shared a tender kiss one evening on the porch of her parent's house when Mrs. Smythe went inside for some yarn. The taste of Katherine's lips stuck with John for days afterward. In his mind he compared her lips to the taste of a fresh, ripe strawberry dipped into honey and placed lightly against his lips. There were also other times for a quick kiss or two, a squeeze of the hand, or the occasional hug. The young lovers yearned for each other and their love grew stronger with the passing of each day.

John purchased a lot near the church and began the construction of their first home. They planned it to be a small cottage with a parlor, dining room, kitchen and two bedrooms upstairs. Late into the night the eager couple would sit in her father's parlor drawing up sketches and making plans for their future home. She wanted a white picket fence around the yard, but because of the expense John told her that she would have to wait until the following spring.

Katherine decided to put a small garden in back of the house where she could grow vegetables for their table. An apple tree already grew there and she told John she would make apple pies and other apple treats for him.

They talked about children in the near future and John dreamed of a son that would join him in his lumber and carpentry business. Everyday brought new dreams for the couple and dreaming together made it a special event for the young lovers.

It was the last week of May. John was working at his lumber mill three miles away, near Grindstone Mountain, when a horseman was seen riding at full gallop up the road. The rider was off his horse before it came to a complete stop and, in a cloud of dust, ran quickly to John. Tears streamed down the rider's dusty cheeks as he grabbed John by the shoulders in desperation.

"Katherine, Katherine," he sputtered. "She's been hurt, John! There was a shooting..." his voice fell away as he wept uncontrollably.

John mounted the man's horse and was off in an instant. Kicking the sweating beast to action, it snorted and headed back to town.

A crowd stood around the steps of the Presbyterian Church as John rode onto the scene. As he jumped off his horse the crowd parted and revealed Katherine laying on the church steps, a large red stain billowed out on her white blouse just above her heart.

Pastor Smythe wept as he tenderly held his daughter's lifeless body. Mrs. Smythe, in the arms of a neighbor, shook uncontrollably in her sorrow. John bent down and gently held Katherine in his arms. She felt so cold and small. He bent down and kissed her unresponsive lips. Life itself was torn from his very soul.

"What happened?" he screamed out as he sobbed.

The sheriff stepped forward and told him, "There was a robbery at the bank, John. As the man left the bank he fired a shot at someone in the street, but the bullet struck Katherine instead."

In rage, John bellowed, "Where is this man?"

The crowd slowly parted. In the nearby grove of trees John saw the lifeless body of a man hanging at the end of a rope from the very Willow tree where he and Katherine had shared her picnic basket the day they first met. The man's head was twisted harshly to one side, his purple tongue grotesquely protruding from the side of his mouth.

"It was an angry mob that killed him, John," the sheriff answered without waiting for the question. "When he stopped to reload his gun, several men grabbed him. He was dragged up on that limb and was dead by the time I got there."

John tenderly picked up Katherine's lifeless form and carried her up the church steps. He took her inside and kissed her cold lips again as he lay her gently on the altar. He then stood silently for a moment with his tightly clenched fists held high above his head. John wiped his tears and, without a word, departed the church.

Marching angrily through the town he swiftly arrived at his cabin. He threw a saddle on one of his horses; gathered up a few possessions and strapped them on the other horse. John rode west leaving everything else behind.

Chapter 9

For several hours John had ridden hard with little regard for his well being or that of his horses. A fierce burning hatred in his heart obscured any common logic. With a snort, his mount decided that enough was enough and dropped to her knees. She rolled onto her side and let out a groan. His packhorse staggered nearby and shuddered with exhaustion. Both animals wore a thick coat of frothy, sweaty lather. John was not the type man to treat any animal in such a manner. The incident was enough to bring John to his senses. His whole body trembled as he took a deep breath and realized his stupidity.

With a cupped hand beneath the downed horse's mouth, he poured water from a leather bag so the animal could lap at the moisture. He then attended to his packhorse. After a few minutes, he had a sensation of relief as his mount once again struggled to her feet. He felt pity for these animals that he had pushed so cruelly. After both animals calmed, and their breathing returned to normal, he fed them a few oats and brushed each down with calming strokes. John spoke to them softly and vowed to never again take his hatred out on any animal. Once the horses began grazing on freshly grown grasses beside the trail, he knew that they would mend from the mistreatment they had just received.

He took no food that first day. The loss of Katherine and the mistreatment of his horses had robbed him of any appetite. Deep in a pine forest he made camp the first night. After hobbling the horses, he lay on his blanket beside a small fire. A gentle wind whispered through the pines and he drifted off to sleep as a multitude of stars twinkled above him between pine limbs that seemed to wave away all care. The horses snorted quietly showing their content with the peacefulness of the night.

Late that night Katherine came to John dressed in a gauzy white gown with an emerald green flowing sash. She had smiled as she pulled her veil aside and knelt down beside him. She had leaned down to kiss John, her golden tresses tickling and teasing as they fell across his face and chest. He could feel the warmth of her breath as she pressed her warm, soft lips on his. John rejoiced with the taste of her delightfully sweet, tender kiss. Her lips were as sweet as a fresh strawberry, dipped delicately in honey and then placed gently upon his lips. But when he had reached up to pull Katherine closer, she vanished. Desperately grasping at the empty air, he awoke sobbing loudly. It was as if the grief in his heart would never end.

Once he had taken control of his emotions, he glanced over at the horses and saw them looking over their shoulders questioningly at him. But it was almost as if they understood the misery he suffered because they hadn't made a sound. They had stared at this broken figure of a man briefly then turned away and resumed dreaming of whatever it is that horses dream about.

The next few months were a blur to John. His sorrow slowly ebbed, but Katherine never left his mind for a moment. Katherine repeatedly came to him in the night, but the dreams became farther and farther apart. John was a broken man. He ceased shaving and cutting his hair, choosing to let his grooming go the way of a mountainman. A reddish beard grew on his face and his blonde hair grew long falling over his shoulders as the months wore on.

John went out of his way to avoid contact with other people. He skirted around towns and farming areas. He had chosen to stay in the heavily forested areas, alone, occasionally hunting and fishing.

He lacked any pattern to his life. Sometimes he just sat for hours staring off in the distance, not thinking about anything in particular. Much of the time he didn't know where he was and didn't really care. John had lost all goals. He no longer had plans for any sort of future. He felt that all hope had been lost back in the Shenandoah Valley.

There were occasional stops at trading posts where he traded furs for basic necessities and oats. While there he avoided any type of conversation and only mumbled in response to questions by others he met. As he meandered across mountain range after mountain range John kept slowly pushing further west, never too certain what it was that he was seeking.

One frosty morning he awoke to hear geese honking as they sought their way to the south. The early morning sky had been filled with the dark specks of geese flying in enormous vee formations. He sat and watched them for a long time as he marveled at the power of nature. It was a sure sign that winter would follow closely behind. He must find safe winter quarters for himself and his horses.

A few days later he found himself on the edge of the Ohio River just east of Louisville. The smell of winter was strong on the November wind. John hesitantly entered the city. He and his horses needed the local ferry to cross the icy cold waters of the Ohio. No one took particular notice to him. He had been just another crusty mountainman passing through the busy streets of Louisville.

Aboard the ferry John had overheard local trappers casually discussing where the best trapping was in Indiana. One trapper had mentioned a remote, mountainous area in the southwestern area of the state. John never said anything to any of them, but decided to explore those areas. In the wilderness he could build a small log cabin and spend the winter. There would be solitude in the tree-shrouded mountains that were described. For the present time, that is what he most desired.

Once he placed the Ohio River behind him, John followed a trail to the northwest. It led him to a distant mountain range. Many farms lay along the edge of the river, but the farther northwest he traveled, the more remote he found the countryside. After a days travel, he left the trail and headed cross-country toward a mountain he spotted in the distance. It just might be what he sought.

A day later, while passing by a narrow gorge, he discovered the secluded spot he had wished for. A wide stream cut through the gorge. Entering the chasm, he did some quick exploring, which revealed a quarter mile long cut into a hillock at the base of a higher rise. As he continued on, following the stream, the chasm narrowed and then came to an abrupt end. There a waterfall spilled into a deep, secluded pond. He found fish abundant in the pool of water as well as the stream.

Halfway into the gorge, John had noticed a narrow ledge that gradually angled up to an open area about twenty feet above the narrow stream. He returned to the spot and began cautiously edging up the side of the cliff. He was halted many times by overgrown foliage and was forced to hack his way through to continue the climb. He discovered that the ledge was not too steep, thus the horses would be able to climb to the area single file. An open area at the top of the incline was just large enough to hold a lean-to and a small corral. At the far end of this area he discovered a cave opening behind some bushes and fallen trees.

Making a torch, John explored inside hoping to find the cave of some use. The opening into the cave was large enough for a horse to pass through between the narrow sidewalls. He discovered that the cave had a large, oval room — as big as a small barn. The ceiling of the cave was about twenty feet above the fairly level floor. This was far more than he had hoped for. Once the incline was cleared, this would be an ideal location for the three of them to spend the winter.

He noticed that the smoke from his torch disappeared upward into a narrow, twelve-foot long crack in the ceiling. At one end of this crack, at the deepest end of the cave, a trickle of water formed a small, basin-sized pond. He felt quite pleased with his discovery. The cave would be better than a lean-to or log cabin.

John set about splitting logs and erected a corral for his horses outside the entrance to the cave. It would keep them from accidentally falling down into the gorge. Upon completion of the corral, he returned to the floor of the chasm and led each horse, one at a time, up the incline to the corral.

He gathered enough firewood for several days and, within a ring of rocks he set in place inside the cave, he lit a small fire. Outside, he climbed up the side of the steep bank and arrived at the area above the cave. He was quite pleased that the smoke did indeed pass completely through the crack, but still dissipated enough that it was barely perceptible from the area above the cave. Over that spot he built up branches and rocks to further disperse the smoke. There was no sense in attracting unwanted attention.

John spent the next week making the cave his home. He framed the entrance with logs filling the cracks with a mud and moss mixture. A door was crafted with birch saplings and woven reeds. He completed the opening with a deer hide stretched over the inside of the saplings and woven reeds. It made an acceptable door that kept out the winter wind. With birch and bark he made a raised platform so he wouldn't sleep on the cold, damp floor of the cave. Rushes from the stream below made a makeshift mattress. Stacking stones, he created a waist high wall that would separate his living quarters from the horse stalls. To contain the heat from his fire, he spread reeds from the stream around the cave floor. His next project was a more substantial fireplace and chimney to direct the smoke out through the crack in the cave roof. Two stalls were added on one side of the room and would shelter the horses from winters worst.

The first time John went hunting, he shot a deer only a few yards from the chasm. Unlike the Shenandoah Mountain area where over-hunting had gone on for years, he found game plentiful near the cave. In only a few days he had slain a fair sized bear and two more deer. He was thankful that he was able to obtain such fine pelts before the coldest months of the winter arrived. It was fortunate that he had purchased plenty of salt at the last Trading Post he passed. With the hides salted and stretched, strips of salted meat cured on sapling racks before a gentle fire. He saved the brains of the animals to tan and soften the hides at a later time. The pelts would be necessary for the wintry days that would soon be upon him. Wrapped in a warm bearskin, he would keep out the chill of the coldest wintry night as he sat by the fire.

John made and set traps for raccoon, fox, squirrel and rabbits. This game was numerous near the cave, so his efforts were not in vain. Roots, tubers and nuts were added to his provisions, but he also would need a large stockpile of feed for the horses during the winter months. At the last trading post, he had traded several pelts for a large bag of oats, but they would not last the entire winter. He collected wild oats, rice and grasses for fodder storing them in a crib he built beside the stalls. There the fodder would dry safely off the damp cave floor.

By the end of the first week John was pleased with his new home. As the first flakes of snow began to fall he knew he was ready for the worst of the winter weather. He had a warm, safe shelter and the forest offered plenty of game. He felt his hoard of food, for both man and beast, was sufficient until the end of winter. In the spring it would be time to move on again.

The first storm of winter hit a few weeks later. John moved the horses inside the cave as the sky darkened. The winds began to howl with wrath and the snow started to come down so hard that he couldn't see much beyond the door to his shelter. Wrapped in his bearskin beside a cozy fire, he whittled small game traps. The fury of the winter storm shook the door to the cave, but it didn't allow any wind or snow within. While nature did its worst, he was thankful that he had prepared so well for anything that the blustery winter weather would blow his way.

The following day he had awakened to find the outside of his cave entrance completely covered in snow. Once the door was removed, it took some time to clear the snow away. Then he spent a number of hours clearing several feet of snow off the ledge outside the entrance to the cave. The snow was packed so tightly that he broke two of the wooden shovels he had crafted. He was thankful that he had had the foresight to make several wooden shovels.

Most of the morning had been spent making a narrow trail along the incline by stomping down the thigh deep snow with his feet. It made no sense to clear the entire width, as the horses were not of much use in this deep snow. Also, a narrow path down the incline would not draw the attention of any one that might have passed by the base of the chasm.

In the early afternoon he finally reached the bottom of the chasm. There the snow was not quite so deep as the winds had blown the looser flakes away. Several trees had been blown over during the fierce storm. John had gone a short distance from the trail to investigate just how much damage had been done to the surrounding forest.

He was suddenly stopped by something large and black in a nearby tree. In the crotch of an oak tree, about ten feet off the ground, a large black bear slept soundly. John felt relieved that the bear had not spotted him first. He had slowly backed away from the enormous animal as a chill of fear ran down his spine. Breathing heavily, he returned to the cave and retrieved his flintlock. How could he have been so foolish as to venture into the forest with nothing but a hunting knife? This had been his first mistake and it could have been fatal. In the future, he decided, he would use more caution when leaving the security of the cave.

Slowly, being as quiet as possible in the crunching snow, he crept back down the incline. The bear was still asleep when he returned to the spot where he had first discovered it. John quietly pulled back the hammer on his rifle, but the clicking of the cold metal loudly echoed throughout the nearby chasm. As luck would have it the bear did not stir. He took great care as he aimed at the bear's huge head and fired.

The bullet left the barrel of his rifle with an explosion that shook the forest and sent loose snow falling from nearby branches. When the gun smoke cleared, he realized that the bear had not budged. Startled to reality, he quickly reloaded his flintlock with anxious, trembling hands wondering why this bear was still asleep. The noise of the gunshot should have awakened the beast. John was close enough to the target. Could he have missed?

Struck with curiosity, John approached the tree constantly aiming at his target. He wondered why there was no blood dripping from the bear. As he went around the far side of the tree, his question was answered. During the storm, another tree had blown over and into the crotch of the tree in which the bear slept. A branch from the falling tree had impaled the bear and the creature had frozen solid in the frigid night air.

Laughing aloud for the first time in many months, he spent the remainder of the day freeing the frozen bear from its trap. Another warm bearskin was added to his cache and this pelt was easily twice the size of the first one.

The winter of 1818 began with the ferocity of that first storm, but then wore on with much lighter snows. John busied himself with his traps and occasional hunting trips within a mile of his cave. Game had been so plentiful that ventures further away had not been needed. Although he built a functional chair and small table, some days were spent whittling just to pass the time.

He started to find himself in somewhat better spirits and sang to pass the time. He sang songs his mother had taught him and he often thought of home. Remembering his parents and siblings had given him pause to ponder, but most of all, Katherine was constantly on his mind. He wasn't as dispirited as he had been the previous months, and the anger within his soul had subsided, but he spent many hours thinking of what could have been if the tragic catastrophe had not occurred. His search for wealth seemed unimportant now. It was no longer what John sought.

Late in November, while on a short hunting excursion, not too far from his cave, he heard an animal making an odd sound in a shallow gully. Thinking it could be the low, guttural growl of a mountain lion he dropped cautiously to his hands and knees. He crawled to the edge and peered below. The white snow revealed a few red splotches of what appeared to be blood. Obviously an animal had been injured and had hidden in the brush at the lowest part of the gully.

Realizing that an injured mountain lion could be dangerous, John slowly turned and began cautiously retreating from his vantage point. But suddenly he was stopped in his tracks. He was certain that the whines he had heard now turned into mumbled words. The muted sounds were not comprehensible, but they certainly had sounded human.

Vigilantly he descended into the gully and, with rifle at the ready, eased his way to a pile of undergrowth at the far end where he had first seen the red spots in the snow. That's when he spotted a moccasin covered foot protruding from beneath the brush. His attention was then drawn to a small blood covered hand that stuck motionlessly out from beneath a log.

"Who's there," John queried.

There was no reply other than a moan. Carefully he reached forward and pulled back the bush. A young face had peered back at him from under a rabbit skin hat. He saw that it was a young Indian boy. The boy suddenly realized, at the same time, that it was a white man that had found him. With his left hand, he awkwardly reached for the knife in his belt, but John grabbed his arm before the boy could withdraw the weapon. The minor exertion from this action caused the weakened boy to pass out.

John cautiously searched the immediate vicinity, but no one else seemed to be around. Other than his own footprints, the only other set of tracks in the snow apparently belonged to the Indian boy. John felt certain that he and the boy were the only ones in this section of the forest.

He carefully removed the remaining undergrowth and studied the boy. The feathered end of an arrow protruded from the boy's front right shoulder, the point stuck out behind the boy. The shaft of the arrow had barely missed his shoulder bone.

The boy was dressed in buckskins and wore a rabbit skin vest. A leather belt held his hunting knife. John reasoned that the boy must have been hunting as his bow and quiver of arrows lay nearby along with a small sack containing a dead rabbit and two squirrels. John wondered what other Indian would have shot him and left him to die? One question he had held in the back of his mind, since his arrival to this mountain, was answered. This boy proved for certain that there were Indians living in the area.

Thankful that the Indian had passed out, he cut and snapped off the pointed end of the arrow. He grabbed the feathered end and pulled the arrow out of the boy's shoulder. The unconscious youth had moaned in pain, but didn't awaken from his stupor.

John stuffed wet moss into the boy's two wounds to stop the bleeding. Easily hoisting up the youngster, he threw him over his shoulder. He picked up his rifle and headed back to the cave leaving the bow and arrows behind to retrieve later.

The horses were very nervous when John entered the cave. He didn't know if it was the smell of the Indian or the scent of blood that unnerved them. John gently laid the boy on his bed and took a few seconds to calm the horses.

As he warmed a pot of water on the fire, John placed his knife directly on the hot coals. To stop the bleeding, he had to cauterize the wounds. He removed the boy's vest and buckskin shirt, and then began cleansing the wounds with the warm water. He was thankful that the boy was unconscious as he seared both wounds with the tip of his knife. The bleeding immediately ceased. He quickly smeared bear fat on the cauterized areas, covered them with fresh moss, and placed his bearskin blanket over the boy.

It was almost two hours later before the boy woke with a start and sat up in the bed. John held his hands up trying to let the boy know he would come to no harm, but the boy was clearly alarmed that he was alone in the presence of a white man.

"You're alright now," John spoke with soft words, trying to comfort the boy. "Can you speak English?"

All John got in response was a cold stare from the boy's black eyes. When he took a step toward the boy, the Indian instinctively reached for the knife in his belt, except it was no longer there. Frantically the boy searched around the bed for his weapon. John picked it up from beside the hearth and handed it to the boy hilt first.

Grabbing the knife with his left hand, the boy pointed it at him in a threatening manner.

John sat back down hoping that his action would ease the tension of their encounter. The boy cocked his head to one side as if questioning this move and slowly dropped his arm. John reached over to the fire, picked up a cooked rabbit leg and held it out to the boy.

A look of curiosity came over the boy's face and he cautiously laid the knife aside. He reached out, grabbed the rabbit leg, and attacked the meat like a starving animal.

As the hours passed, the boy seemed to become more composed, but still kept a watchful eye on this white man. John tried to communicate with the boy several more times to no avail. Obviously the boy couldn't understand him. They shared the remainder of the rabbit, but the Indian refused any other food that was offered.

At nightfall, John spread a deerskin on the floor beside the fire and lay down to sleep. The boy stretched out on the bed, pulled the bearskin over him and lay there a long time keeping a wary watch, his knife firmly in his left hand.

A horse whinnied and woke John as the first light of the day entered the cave. He sat up to discover his bed empty. A quick look around the cave revealed that he and the horses were alone. Stepping outside the cave entrance, into a lightly falling snow, he spotted footprints leading down the ledge. He slipped on his bearskin coat, picked up his rifle and went outside to follow the trail. The tracks headed into the forest beyond the chasm. John followed the footprints until they disappeared under the newly falling snow. He returned to the cave.

For several days he worried that the boy might lead other Indians to his cave. He carried several large logs into the cave and barricaded the entrance at night, but he never saw the boy or any other Indians after that day.

Time passed slowly in the cave. Other than hunting and fishing through the ice, there hadn't been much to do to pass the time. He often wished he had thought to bring some books to read, but he wasn't thinking too clearly when he had so hastily departed Shenandoah. He decided the next break in the weather he would go down the mountain to the trading post and see if perhaps they might have a book or two they would trade for some of his furs. That thought gave him something to look forward to.

One morning, after a few inches of snow had fallen in the night, John awoke with the realization that it must be Christmas Day. Well, he had been pretty sure it was Christmas Day at the time. The days had slipped by so quickly that he wasn't positive of the date, but he was fairly certain that it was the right day. His thoughts went back to his home in Ireland. Thinking of Christmas at home with his family made him downcast. He whispered out loud, "What am I doing here?" He had become a recluse living in the middle of nowhere; living off the land without human contact. He hadn't written home for months and months. He was concerned about giving his mother so much worry. But here in the wilderness, in the middle of winter, there was no way he could write his mother and tell her all that had happened. He promised himself to do so at the first opportunity.

He cut down a small pine tree and erected it near his hearth. He spent the morning decorating it with bits and pieces of sinew and thread from his haversack. Small pinecones and bits of moss finished the decorating. He sat back and marveled at his creation. After a quick bite for lunch he sat by his fire and sang as many Christmas carols as he could remember. The horses stood in their stalls and whinnied contentedly at the sound of his soothing voice. As he sang, John planned for the Christmas feast that he would have that evening.

After a Christmas dinner of rabbit, grouse, acorns and wild tubers, he dozed off. Katherine came to him dressed in her gauzy white wedding gown. She smiled at him as she knelt down and pulled her veil aside. Her golden tresses fell teasingly on his face and chest as she bent down and pressed her warm, soft lips on his. But John no longer could taste their sweetness. He had forgotten how sweet her kiss had been. In desperation he reached up to pull Katherine closer so he could place his lips on hers once again, but in a flash she was gone. He bolted awake sobbing loudly. His body was wracked with his crying. He lay there a long time thinking of Katherine, Baltimore, and home. Then he dozed off once again. The rest of the night he slept peacefully, dreaming of the green hills of Ballylee. The aroma of his father's pipe permeated the air and his mother held him tenderly in the warmth of her arms.

By the end of February John began to yearn for human contact once again. It had been nine months since he had allowed himself the company of others. He talked to his horses, but they wouldn't answer. He craved human contact. He decided he must begin exploring further out from his cave to see what lay beyond the heavily wooded forest. He wanted to be with people once again. It was time to seek out civilization.

A visit to the trading post was out of the question. That was a full days travel by horseback. The snow was too deep for the horses to safely negotiate the trail down the mountainside. And it was too far a journey on foot with the weather this time of the year being so unpredictable. Wherever he decided to explore, it would have to be nearby and probably on foot.

Several days later he had gone to the pond below the now frozen waterfall to fish. As he broke through the ice on the pond with a rock, he saw his reflection in the water. John was startled by what he saw. Peering back was an old mountain man with a dirty face covered with matted hair. He looked frightening! No wonder the Indian boy had been afraid of him. The boy must have thought John was an animal or evil spirit. John laughed loudly at that thought.

Quickly returning to the cave, he lathered up his face with a mixture of bear fat and ash. He honed his hunting knife to the sharpest it had ever been and removed his red beard. The long blonde strands of hair hanging over his shoulder were next. He trimmed them even with the collar on his buckskin shirt. Using the same soapy mixture, John returned to the pond, broke a larger hole through the ice and, taking a big breath, plunged fully dressed into the icy waters. With a gasping whoop that echoed throughout the chasm, he rose quickly from beneath the frigid water and began quickly soaping himself and his buckskins thoroughly. He quickly decided that he didn't want to be in these icy waters for very long!

By the time he was done with this wintry bath John was shivering from head to toe and hastily retreated back to his cave. Wrapped in his bearskin, the fire quickly warmed him as he dried his buckskin clothing on a willow rack. "Tomorrow," he told the horses aloud, "I will explore beyond the forest to the north." The horses completely ignored his remark. He slept peacefully that night and dreamt of gently sailing on a warm, calm sea aboard the Ellen Marie as flying fish sailed nearby.

In the morning there was a fresh coating of snow and the ground beneath was frozen hard with icy patches. As he prepared for his exploration of the area, John decided not to take a horse for he feared that it could fall on an icy patch and injure itself. Donning his bearskin coat, he grabbed his rifle and started out on foot heading north from the top of the falls. He had already gone in that direction during his hunting treks, but decided he wanted to see what lay beyond a high rise about three miles away. The ice and thick foliage slowed his pace. He was thankful for the warm coat the bear had accidentally given him.

Icy puffs of his breath followed him in the frosty air as he trudged slowly for over hour before he came to the top of the rise. Topping the ridge he discovered a group of buildings in a glen about two miles down the other side. Smoke streamed out from one building telling him that it must be occupied. He slowly eased down that side of the ridge and made his way to the clearing.

John stepped out of the thick forest and into the middle of a clearing. Before him were the buildings he had seen earlier. Smoke emanated from a log cabin with a sod roof. The other two buildings in the clearing were a barn made of slab board and a small log building obviously built for storage. From the barn he heard the occasional lowing of a cow. As his crunching footsteps approached the cabin a dog began barking.

He stopped and called out, "Hello, the cabin." The sound of his own voice in the stillness of the icy morning startled him momentarily.

A small window opened up and the barrel of a rifle was poked through. A woman's voice called back, "Who are you? What do you want?"

John stopped about 50 feet away from the cabin and removed his rabbit fur cap. "I live in the next valley. I just wanted to see who my neighbors might be and say 'Hello.'"

After a long pause the rifle was withdrawn and the window slammed shut. Several long minutes later the door slowly creaked open. The same voice called to him from the dimly lit entrance, "Come on in and warm yourself by the fire, neighbor."

John cautiously entered the cabin. The dog kept up his barking and sounded angry. Inside, once his eyes adjusted to the light of the hearth, he found the dog being held by a young boy. A small woman stood watching him, rifle at the ready. It had been almost a comical scene as the rifle was so large, and the woman so small, it was a wonder she could hold it in a horizontal position. John slowly closed the heavy log door.

"You can't be too careful now a days," she explained as she eased the hammer down and hung the rifle back on the pegs above the fireplace. "There are Indian troubles hereabouts. You looked like one of them redskins from the distance in yer buckskins and bear, but when I seen yer yeller hair I know'd you wasn't one." She walked to the door behind John and dropped a heavy latch into its cradle barricading the door once again.

It was comfortably warm in the cabin, so John removed his heavy bearskin coat. "I live five miles south of here. I saw your smoke and was wondering who lived here."

"Shut that dog up, Jeff!" She turned back to John, "Me and my husband been here 'bout five years and didn't know nobody lived up there. We ain't never seen you before," she replied.

"My name is John Doyle. I just built a place up there this winter," John answered her. He was not too sure he wanted anyone to know just where his 'place' was located. Not until he knew more about these people at any rate.

"I'm Ann Cooper and this is my son Jeff. My husband, Jim, and our daughter are in town on business. Be back any day now."

"I just got lonesome up on the mountain and was hoping to find a town nearby," John explained.

"I'm pleased you stopped by to visit us. You didn't happen to see my husband and daughter on your way here, did ya?" Mrs. Cooper asked hopefully.

"No, Maam," John replied. "I didn't see any tracks anywhere along the way. How far away is the nearest town?"

"Nearest town is a days walk northeast of here. Brownstown is just a small place. Ain't much there. Me and the boy are just gettin' ready to have a bite to eat. Sit yerself down and join us," said Mrs. Cooper as she turned to her fireplace and, using her apron, took a pot off the fire and carried it to the table. "Got some beef stew today. Taters and carrots weren't too bad this year. Makes a meal that'll stick to yer ribs." John's mouth watered as she continued, "Yer in luck. I just baked bread yesterday and it ain't too hard if ya dip it in the stew."

"Maam, this is the best meal I've had in months!" The aromas that surrounded John were like a heady perfume as his nose soaked up the delightful fragrance.

Mrs. Cooper set a large wooden bowl of stew in front of John and, turning to Jeff, said, "Get you up to the table and don't forget to thank the Lord before ya eat."

As the boy let go of the rope, the dog immediately ran to John's side growling. Mrs. Cooper swatted at him with a hearth broom and the dog quieted down. The dog lay beside John sniffing at his moccasin, but the hairs on the back of his neck stood up for a long time before returning to normal. Even then, the animal was still quite wary with this stranger in the cabin.

John bowed his head as Jeff said a quick blessing. The boy grabbed his wooden spoon and dug into the thick stew. John also took a spoonful and let it swirl in his mouth. With only wild meat to eat the past nine months, this beef was manna from heaven. The beef was very tender compared to the venison or tough, stringy bear meat he had been consuming. He could tell the stew had spent many hours on the hearth as the carrots and potatoes had been drenched with the flavor of the gravy. John had to restrain himself from gobbling down his bowl of stew. The bread had indeed been hard, but as Mrs. Cooper said, it was delightful once swabbed deep into the thick gravy. As they ate Mrs. Cooper and John had casually chatted about the local area.

"Where ya hail from, Mr. Doyle?" asked Mrs. Cooper as John cleaned up the last bite of stew from his bowl. Before he had time to answer, she asked, "Another bowl?"

"Oh, no thank you, Maam. That was the best food I've had in months, but that was a big bowl and I'm stuffed."

"Well, don't be too stuffed yet," she replied. "I have an apple pie in the cupboard. And how about a cup of coffee with it?"

John was stunned that a cabin in the wilderness could offer such splendid fare. "Mrs. Cooper, that would be more than a man could ever want."

Wiping his chin on his sleeve, John said, "As to your question, I came from Ireland and worked in the shipyards of Baltimore for several years." He decided he didn't want to share his tale of woe regarding the events in Virginia. "I decided I wanted to do some exploring in the west," he added.

"Hello, Mrs. Cooper!" A man's voice called from outside the cabin.

"Why that will be Mr. Hawthorn from the next farm," Mrs. Cooper explained as she went to the door, lifted the heavy wooden latch and opened the door.

Mr. Hawthorn was a tall man with very muscular shoulders. He stopped short when he noticed the stranger sitting at the Cooper's table. Another man pushed by him and stopped as well when he noticed John.

"Mr. Doyle is visiting us from up on the mountain to the south," explained Mrs. Cooper. "He's been living there for almost a year now."

"I'm Sandy Hawthorn and this here is my hired man, Jim Fellows." He propped his rifle against the wall beside the door and stuck out a big beefy hand. He shook John's hand, but his voice had an air of suspicion. "We were checking in on Mrs. Cooper while her husband's away."

"Get yer coats off," Mrs. Cooper told the men. "We're just getting ready to have apple pie and coffee. I'll throw a couple more beans in the water and there will be plenty to go 'round." She went off to her fireplace to tend to the coffee.

She stopped half way there and asked; "You didn't see Maggie and Jim on yer way here, did ya? He should have been home by now." She turned back to the hearth mumbling aloud, "Wonder what's keeping him?"

"How did you happen by this place, Mr. Doyle?" Sandy Hawthorn eyed up John with skepticism. John sensed the tension in this man.

"I've been living south of here a few months and was out hunting when I noticed the smoke from this cabin. Just thought I'd stop by and say 'Hello' to whoever lived here." John smiled hoping to relax this man's distrust.

The two men chatted for a while as Mrs. Cooper boiled the coffee and then began warming her apple pie on the hearth of the large fireplace. It bothered John that the entire time the two men visited, the hired man stood behind John's chair with his rifle in his right hand, his left hand on the hilt of his hunting knife. As the two men talked, John noticed that Mr. Hawthorn kept asking John questions about himself and why he was in this part of the country. There was a strong air of mistrust throughout the cabin, but Mr. Hawthorn seemed pleased when John told him of joining the militia and defending Baltimore from the British.

A short time later Mr. Hawthorn nodded to his man. Jim Fellows rested his rifle against the wall beside his employer's and strolled to a chair at the table and sat down. Both men seemed more relaxed as Mrs. Cooper served her pie along with steaming mugs of strong coffee. The subjects of conversation lightened as well. They discussed the game in the mountains, fishing and trapping.

John told them about the incident with the Indian boy, but no one could guess what tribe he would have been from or who could possibly have shot him with an arrow.

"With all the trouble the Indians have been causing around here," Mr. Hawthorn stated firmly, "I think I would have just let him lie there and let nature take its course!"

Trying to lighten up the atmosphere a bit, John related the tale of the frozen bear he shot in the tree. "And thanks to his misfortune I have a nice, warm coat!"

Everyone laughed and John's story did seem to release the tension in the cabin. John wasn't too pleased with Mr. Hawthorn's remarks about letting the child die in the snow. It was a strange assertion to make.

Mr. Hawthorn related the story of his wife's experience with a bear a few years earlier, "She was alone with our son when she heard someone banging around in our barn. The cows were bawling loudly and the chickens were squawking up a storm. I was out hunting and had our rifle with me, so she grabbed an axe and headed for the barn expecting to find someone out there stealing chickens. She threw open the barn door and there was a large bear with his back turned toward her. There was a big hole in the back of the barn where he had ripped through the wall. With all that commotion the bear never heard her open the door.

"He had a chicken in his mouth and another in his claws. Well, Mrs. Hawthorn was in a rage and struck that black bear with all her might right in the middle of his back. Sunk that axe deep, she did! Dropped him on the spot.

"I came home empty handed from my hunting trip a couple hours later to find my barn in a disheveled mess and Mrs. Hawthorn calmly frying up what chickens the bear had killed and not chewed up too badly. That bear must have been 450 pounds. Killed by a little slip of a woman."

Everyone laughed at the story. Then Mr. Hawthorn stood up and said, "Jim, give Mrs. Cooper a hand cleaning up here. Mr. Doyle and I will go out and bring in firewood for the night fire."

They donned their coats and went out the heavy wooden door heading for the woodpile next to the barn. When they got to the woodpile, instead of picking up any logs, Mr. Hawthorn turned to John and said, "Mr. Doyle, I guess you noticed we were a bit suspicious of you at first. We had good cause."

John looked at him in surprise and asked, "Why did I give you any cause for concern?"

"Mr. Cooper isn't coming home and will never come home again. Last year, in the spring, Mrs. Cooper and Jeff were over at Brownstown for supplies. Mr. Cooper and their thirteen-year-old daughter, Maggie, were here at the farm when an Indian raiding party came through the valley from the south. Up at my place we saw the smoke coming from the Cooper's and sent out an alarm. About two dozen of us got here too late."

John stood in stunned silence as Mr. Hawthorn continued.

"We found Jim Cooper tied spread-eagle to a wagon wheel. Those damn redskins had cut him open from rib cage to crotch and his insides were spilled all around on the ground in front of him. He was still alive when we got here...well, there was no hope for him so we put him out of his misery. Maggie was lying in front of him naked. Before he died, Jim said that they each took their turn with her making him watch. She was hysterical when we found her. We took her into the barn before we helped poor Jim escape his misery."

"Is the girl all right now?" John asked.

"It was too much for Maggie," Mr. Hawthorn continued. "We turned away from her for a moment so she could put on a dress. She grabbed one of the men's pistols and shot herself in the head."

"Oh, Lord," John replied as he shook his head. "But, Mrs. Cooper said they were due back any day now."

"Mrs. Cooper can't accept the truth. She's still in a state of shock. When Jeff and Mrs. Cooper got back here we had both Jim and Maggie already buried. She refused to believe what happened and has been telling everyone that Jim is due back any day now."

Sadly he added, "She goes to their graves once a day and talks to them, but keeps telling everyone she knows that they will be back real soon.

"Everyone pitched in and rebuilt the cabin the redskins burned. All the neighbors have been watching out for her ever since that day. We share our food with her and help tend the livestock. One of my men and I come over a couple times a week and chop wood for her fireplace in the winter.

"We've had some unscrupulous men pass through the valley and try to move in on Mrs. Cooper when they find out she's here all alone. A couple of the pushy ones are buried out in the woods! That's why Jim and I were so apprehensive when we found you here. We feel we have to protect her until she can come to her senses.

"We never found the Indians that raided this farm. The heathens that killed Jim and Maggie Cooper got away before we could catch them or we would have strung 'em up," Mr. Hawthorn bluntly stated.

"But what about their son, Jeff?" John asked.

"He knows and understands what's happening. The local parson explained to him why his mother is acting this way and for such a young boy, he seems to understand the way things are," Mr. Hawthorne told John as he picked up an axe and began splitting wood for the fireplace.

It didn't take the two men long to fill the log rack beside Mrs. Cooper's hearth. She and Jim had everything tidied up by the time they were done.

"Mr. Cooper will really appreciate what you men have done for me," she smiled as she removed her apron. "He and Maggie will be returning home any day now. I don't know why they's taking so long in town."

"Well, you rest easy, Mrs. Cooper," Mr. Hawthorn responded. "We'll help out wherever we can until your husband returns."

"Mr. Doyle," she addressed John. "I want you to take a piece of beef and a loaf of my bread with you when you return to yer place."

John was about to protest, but Mr. Hawthorn, standing behind her, nodded silently letting John know that he approved.

"Thank you so much, Mrs. Cooper," John smiled. "It will certainly be a change from my diet of wild meat."

It was mid-afternoon when Mr. Hawthorn and John told her that they had to be on their way. As the men departed the cabin John profusely thanked her for her hospitality and the food she had given him.

When the men had walked away from the cabin John said, "I didn't realize that there are such hostile Indians in this area."

Mr. Hawthorn explained that the tribes in the area were being relocated further west in the Indian Territory. Some Indians had refused to go and were rebelling. Even though the Army was in hot pursuit, there had been continuing raids at many locations. The Cooper farm was one of their many victims.

He gestured toward his hired hand as he asked John, "Did you take notice that Jim here never takes off his hat?"

John nodded. He had noticed that Jim Fellows didn't remove his fur cap inside the Cooper cabin, but hadn't given it much thought.

"Take your hat off, Jim, and give Mr. Doyle a look," Mr. Hawthorn told him.

Jim removed his cap and turned around so John could see the back of his head. There in the middle of his skull was a deep gash healed over with angry, scarred, red skin. The five-inch gash ran from the top of his head to mid-way down the back. It was almost two inches deep and an inch wide at the widest. John stared in shock.

"Tomahawk!" Exclaimed Mr. Hawthorn. "Notice that Jim never says anything? He was attacked by a renegade band of redskins. One of them hit him in the back of his head and left him for dead. He hasn't spoken since that time and has lost any memories he had before the attack. He doesn't remember his family or farm at all!

"They raided his farm last year and killed his wife and two children. They left Jim for dead, but when we found him he was still alive with a tomahawk stuck deep in his skull. We thought he'd die, but after he lingered on for a week the doc decided he should remove the tomahawk. Everyone thought Jim would die when the doc pulled it out, but he kept breathing and carries that wound to this day."

John had been thunderstruck and didn't know what to say. Jim put his cap back on and turned to John with a big grin. Face to face no one would ever suspect this smiling man had suffered such a brutal attack and wore a vicious wound beneath his rabbit skin cap. The ugly opening seemed to be a thing of amusement for Jim Fellows. Perhaps it was because he couldn't see the wound for himself or remember the pain when it happened.

"Those redskins made one big mistake at the Fellows farm. They found a couple kegs of whiskey in Jim's storehouse and took them along when they left. A group of local men trailed them into the mountains west of here and caught up with five of them so drunk they couldn't run away. Indians fear being hung more than anything, so the men tied them up and let them sober up over night. The next morning they hung them all. They were still hanging from the trees hours later when the Army got there. The commander wasn't too pleased about them being hung without a trial, but didn't say much when they found some of Jim's possessions in their campsite and heard about the murders of Mrs. Fellows and the children. You see, they grab the children by the feet and swing them around until they bash their heads against a tree. It's a horrid sight!

"Well, the Army went off looking for the rest of the raiding party and caught them near the Illinois border. Last we heard the Indians were still sitting in prison waiting for a trial." Mr. Hawthorn spat upon the ground, "Justice! They should have hung them on the spot!"

"Have many people been killed by the Indians?" John asked.

"Yes, there have been several raids by different renegade tribes. Two weeks ago there was an incident over in Scott County at the stagecoach stop. Mrs. Hale was there alone with her three young children when she heard the Indians coming up the Louisville Pike whooping and yelling. She grabbed the children and hid in the wine cellar beneath the taproom. Mr. Hale had fixed a trapdoor so if they had to hide down there a cord would pull a rug over the entrance. That way no one would suspect there was a secret opening in the floor.

"Mrs. Hale got down there and had just pulled the rug in place when the Indians broke in the front door. They were above her drinking the rum and beer they found when her baby began to cry. She knew that if the Indians heard the baby they would find the trapdoor. She held the baby close to her breast to muffle the crying. Once the Indians left, she checked the baby and discovered that it was not breathing. In order to save the other children, hiding in the cellar with her, Mrs. Hale lost her baby. She had accidentally smothered the child. It was a very sad incident, indeed."

As an after thought he added, "The Army caught those Indians and they were sent off to the Indian Territory."

"That's so terrible," mumbled John. He was shocked by the ferocity of these actions by the Indians. The Cherokees around Shenandoah had been very peaceful and blended in well with the settlers. There was rarely a problem between the two.

Mr. Hawthorn told him, "Mecina, the leader of a band from the Kickapoo Tribe, has been preying upon settlers in Illinois looting isolated farmhouses, stealing horses, and shooting cattle and hogs. There seems to be no end to it."

"And this all started with the Indians being moved further west?" John asked.

"The Indians were promised some land for reservations here in the east, but I guess negotiations broke down and the Army was ordered to move all Indian tribes west. I don't know if it's right or wrong, but there's no reason for Indians to be killing innocent women and children. No one around here has sympathy for the redskins now."

The two men talked a bit longer, but John had to get started if he wanted to return to his cave by dark. While Mr. Hawthorn and Jim Fellows only lived a mile away, John had a five-mile hike through the dense forest to return home.

John arrived back at the gorge about an hour before dark. In the deep forest it was very dim, but he could see that something was terribly wrong at the cave. His corral was knocked down, the door to the cave was torn away and one of his horses lay dead at the bottom of the gorge. He wasn't sure what to do. Deep in the gorge it was almost too dark to see, but there wasn't a sound coming from within.

He crept silently along the frozen creek to where his horse lay. Upon arrival to that spot he discovered that it was his packhorse. In the faint light he could see that her side was torn open, her ribs poking through a large gash. It was then that he heard a noise from the cave some twenty feet above him. He froze to the spot just as a large, dark figure exited the opening and started slowly down the trail.

As the figure neared the lighter end of the gorge John could see that it was a very large black bear. Every few feet the animal would stop, stand up on his hind legs, sniff the air, and growl. He realized that the bear had probably picked up his scent.

John stayed kneeled behind his packhorse and waited. Almost at the bottom of the trail, the bear suddenly jumped down into the bottom of the gorge and started up the frozen stream to where John lay in wait. His nose in the air, the bear was gradually nearing John. Very slowly and quietly John cocked his flintlock and readied the flash pan. The bear kept advancing warily. It seemed to be only aware of the dead horse. When the huge bear was twenty feet from John, he raised his rifle and took aim.

The bear spotted John just as he fired. Lunging forward, the bear took the solid lead bullet right between the eyes. His forward momentum sent the huge animal sprawling over John and forcing him into the frozen stream. The ice broke with the weight of the two and John was plunged into the icy water pinned beneath the dead bear.

Only John's head was not submerged. He gasped for air as the weight of the bear crushed him deeper into the mud at the bottom of the stream. The bulk of the bear's weight lay on the dead horse, but the bear's upper body was heavy enough to pin John in the icy water. If the rocks hadn't been slippery beneath his body, he could have been trapped and frozen to death in the ice-cold waters. It took John a couple minutes to squirm from beneath the heavy carcass.

John was stiff with the cold as he crawled and dragged himself up to the cave entrance. Thankfully finding embers still glowing from the morning fire, he soon had a roaring fire going. Shivering profusely he removed his soaked buckskins and wrapped up in his bearskin. Once warmth returned to his limbs he took a burning log from the fire to investigate the darkened corners of the cave to discover what other damage the bear had caused.

He found his mount dead in her stall with her throat opened from a nasty bite from the bear. Wood from the stalls lay shattered everywhere. John guessed that the bear must have attacked her first by trapping her in her stall against the solid rock wall of the cave. The horse never had a chance.

Amazingly his living area was almost intact. The stacked stones between the two areas was knocked over telling of the fight that had occurred between the bear and the packhorse. The bear must have finally caught her outside the cave and killed her within the corral. A powerful strike with his claw apparently forced her through the corral and over the ledge to the streambed below.

John's store of dried meat hadn't been disturbed causing him to wonder what ill wind of fate would have it that all that stored meat was untouched while the bear killed his horses?

With the loss of his horses, John's plans to continue west at the end of winter faded. He spent a week putting the cave back together and came to a decision. The life of a mountainman was no longer for him. There was no pleasure in living alone in these mountains. He had lost the heart for such a life of solitude. And Indians murdering innocent women and children?

Thoughts of finding gold no longer drew him west. The way people struggled to survive out here in the wilderness told him that there was no easy gold to be found. When the first break in the winter weather came, he would head back to Baltimore and the sanity of civilization.

That night he fell asleep in exhaustion. To John the frontier seemed a hostile, unfriendly place. He wanted to put all this behind him. In the solitude of his cave, John rolled up in his bearskin beside the fire. He dosed off thinking of his home back in the lush hills of Ireland.

During the night he dreamt again of Katherine, but this time he saw her as he remembered her the first time their eyes met beside the gentle Shenandoah River. Her long golden hair draped over her shoulder glistening in the afternoon sun. Her blue eyes were the color of the sky and they sparkled as she laughed. She stood there alone, giggling at him as he struggled to free himself from the waters that entrapped him. He strained to reach Katherine as she stood on the distant shore, but the more he struggled the further away she seemed to be. The more he pushed against the waist deep water, the more it resisted his effort. Slowly, in a rising mist, she vanished into the distance just as the waters pulled him deep beneath the surface. He awoke gasping for air.

He had lain there trembling and thinking of his future. After a while, a calm came over him and a short time later he fell into a deep sleep. Once again he was in the embrace of his mother, surrounded by his brothers and sisters. The aroma of the peat fire and his father's pipe drifted sweetly through the night air. He was at peace with himself.

John visited Mrs. Cooper and the Hawthorn family twice during the month of March 1819. Mrs. Cooper still watched out her window for the arrival of her husband and daughter. It was sad to see her in this state. She insisted each time that John take some beef with him when he departed, but he felt guilty, as he knew that she only had the beef because her neighbors shared what little they had with her and her son. John brought her many furs he had shot and trapped on the mountain. He hoped she could use them in trade for other necessary items.

Mr. Hawthorn gave John paper and pen during his first visit and John wrote home to his parents. He hadn't written since his engagement to Katherine and there was much to tell. Writing about her untimely death wasn't easy for John, but he felt he owed his parents an explanation since he hadn't written for almost a year. Mr. Hawthorn promised to mail his letter the next time he was in Brownstown.

He told Mrs. Cooper and Sandy Hawthorn of his plans to return to Baltimore late in March. John told them that he felt he would do better as a carpenter in the shipyards than as a trapper and hunter. While he liked the mountains, he preferred living closer to civilization. He explained to them that the past winter of loneliness in the mountains hadn't sat well with him.

The first week of April John packed his fox skin backpack for his journey. He picked up his flintlock and, leaving the cave that had been his home these many months, started walking down the eastern slope toward the rising sun.

Chapter 10

John had a long walk back to Baltimore. Because he had no money, there were many delays during the trek. He spent many days hunting and trapping, tanning hides, and trading furs for necessities along the way. The further east he ventured, however, the less game there was to be found. The well-worn trails he was following offered no pelts, thus he went back to crossing the more heavily forested areas of the mountains. Even then, he was surprised by the number of people he met who were hunters from local towns and communities.

The latter part of June 1819, he finally reached Baltimore. He thought his best bet would be to visit his father's cousin, Captain Robinson, for advice. John had been gone for over a year and had sent no word to the Robinson family. He wasn't sure how well they would accept him.

The Captain was at sea when John arrived. Mrs. Robinson didn't have room for him to stay in their small house, but was still pleased to see him. She suggested that he sleep in the hayloft in their stable behind the house. The evenings were warm and the loft offered a dry and cozy place to sleep. John felt certain that the stable would be much more comfortable than his cave had been. However, he decided it would be wise not to mention having lived in such a manner to Mrs. Robinson. He also felt it was better not to tell her of the terrible depression he had suffered.

The biggest bonus of his new lodgings was that Mrs. Robinson and her adolescent daughters were excellent cooks. In a short time he had regained his strength and the thin layer of skin, that had barely kept his protruding rib bones covered, was filling out. He was building up some much needed girth.

Mrs. Robinson tried to encourage John to attend Mass with her and the girls, but he politely resisted. He was hesitant about returning to weekly Mass. He felt he had a grudge against God and didn't know how to handle it. His upbringing required obedience and loyalty to the Catholic Church, but the incident in the Shenandoah Valley certainly challenged his faith. He didn't want to discuss the events of the previous year with anyone, especially a priest. Mrs. Robinson finally abandoned her efforts trying to persuade John to attend church. She decided to leave that dilemma up to her husband to deal with upon his return from the sea.

John found small carpentry jobs in the neighborhood, earning a few dollars here and there. Eventually, he started building small pieces of furniture that he felt were suitable for the middleclass homes of the area. Unfortunately, he lacked the proper tools to create finer pieces of higher quality. Nevertheless, his reputation as a first class craftsman soon spread and the demand for his furniture grew. And so, John embarked upon a new business enterprise.

Captain Robinson arrived home at the end of the following month and was quite pleased to see that his cousin's son was in Baltimore. John's mother had sent two letters to him and the Captain had held them in hope that John might someday show up at the Robinson home. Mrs. Doyle had also written the captain expressing her fears for her son's safety. However, she had not mention the incident in Virginia. She had only written that something of great sadness had happened to her son, causing him to depart Shenandoah in haste the year before.

John was pleased when he read his mother's first letter. She had received the letter he had written at Mr. Hawthorne's cabin in

Indiana telling her of the loss of his true love. His mother's words caused him to understand that she truly shared his heartache. She wrote that she wished she had known Katherine for she knew that her son would only fall in love with a girl who was undoubtedly very special. She urged her son to write the Reverend and Mrs. Smythe as they most assuredly shared the same grief as John.

There was still no word of Kevin's whereabouts. The British Admiralty had written the Doyle family and said that they had no record of his conscription or of his serving in the British Navy. Family and friends searched for any sign of him and Mr. Doyle continued to make regular inquiries along the docks of Belfast.

Michael would be sixteen soon and was now yearning to leave home for America. John's mother wrote that she hated to see her three oldest gone from home. Michael was greatly troubled because he could find no employment in Ireland. She added that she was so saddened that John was so far from home and hadn't written in almost a year.

In her second letter, written a month later, she wrote that Michael had left home for America. He was still a few months from turning 16, but had taken a position aboard a Dutch cargo ship and was sailing for New York City as a deckhand. She was very concerned about his welfare.

She wrote that the other children were all doing well and the youngest, Mary, who was now nine years old, was quite concerned about her eldest brother. The news from home made John feel a little homesick, but the letters also cheered him. He now knew he had made the right decision when he left the wilderness and returned to Baltimore.

When the Captain returned from sea, John had good news to tell him. Just a few blocks from the Robinson home, he located a small building for rent. He could practice his carpentry trade on the first floor and use the upper loft for his living quarters. John made plans to move into the building the following week. The Robinson's had a few extra pieces of furniture in their attic and they were more than pleased to help him set up housekeeping.

The biggest prize of all was a real bed. He hadn't slept in a bed for over a year. The small bed had been a youth bed for one of the Robinson girls. All John had to do was add longer sideboards, re-rope the bed and stuff a mattress with fresh straw. He was very pleased and the Robinson girls took great pleasure in helping John move into his new lodging. In a few days, it was home! The girls had sewn curtains for his windows; something John wasn't too concerned about, but it did make his living quarters seem quite special.

Woodworking tools would be expensive, so John borrowed a saw, plane and chisel from Captain Robinson. He was soon well underway creating a table and chairs for a neighbor. Business was good and within a few months, he could afford to start purchasing his own carpentry tools. Before long he had bought additional precision woodworking tools and could then begin to create more refined pieces of furniture.

One evening, in the fall, Captain Robinson called on John. They sat on a bench outside the carpentry shop and chatted. After socializing for a time, the captain finally came around to the reason for his visit.

"John, can you talk about what happened the year you were gone?" the captain asked. "Everyone is concerned about you and the fact that you refuse to attend Mass."

John sat quietly for a few minutes thinking. He took the knife out of his belt and began whittling on a stick that had lay nearby. Whittling had always been John's way of unwinding at times of great tension. After a few moments he replied, "I wrote my mother about the incident, but I didn't tell her that I no longer attend Mass."

"I have not written to your mother about you not attending Mass, but Mrs. Robinson and I are both concerned as to the reason why. Your mother never mentioned what happened to you in her letters. Only that she is worried about you. She wrote recently that your letters don't sound as positive as they once did," Captain Robinson explained. "She is very concerned about you, John."

After a pause, the captain went on. "Mrs. Robinson and I have also noticed that you aren't the same person you once were. The last time you lived in Baltimore you attended Mass every Sunday. You sang all the time and were very friendly. Now my friends tell me you have become a bit of a recluse. I'm not your father, but perhaps you would feel comfortable talking to me. I only want to help."

John was a bit hesitant, but he really did feel depressed much of the time. Life just seemed to have nothing to offer. Working from dawn to dusk kept him busy, but he just couldn't find the satisfaction in his carpentry that he had in previous years. After a long pause, John slowly began to relate the story of the time he spent in the Shenandoah Valley. It was difficult to tell. He told the captain about meeting Katherine and their plans to marry. Darkness had fallen by the time he reached the end of his tale and sadly told Captain Robinson about her death.

The captain put his arm around John's shoulders, "Son, I can now see why you have been so quiet and depressed. Mourning is a difficult thing when you suffer it alone. Mrs. Robinson and I only want to help you, but you really need to discuss your doubts of faith with a priest."

Casting the stick aside, John sheathed his knife and leaning forward, held his head in his hands pondering what the captain had said. "I stood at the altar with Katherine's lifeless body at my feet and vowed to the Lord that I would never forgive him for taking her from me," John mumbled as a few tears flowed down his cheek. "Katherine was my life. She was my only reason for living. When she died, my heart died."

"I truly understand your loss of Katherine," Captain Robinson said. He paused for a moment and then continued, "When I first arrived in America I settled in Provincetown on Cape Cod. I fell in love with and married a beautiful, young girl named Bess Thomas. We had a year of marital bliss and were expecting our first child the following summer. We were deeply in love and looked forward to the birth of our child. I was totally devastated when Bess and our son died from complications during childbirth. Oh, how I mourned my loss."

With a deep breath, the captain continued, "I was terribly distressed over Bess' death. I signed onto a whaling ship and went to sea for five years before returning home to Cape Cod. I had lost my wife and child and faith in the church as well. My years at sea were not a time I would ever be proud of. When I returned to the Cape, a priest helped me understand that we are not to question the Lord's plan. With the Blessed Father's guidance I once again found the right path.

"After moving to Baltimore I met Sarah Good at church. I courted Sarah for a year and then we married. I lived in fear as the birth of our first child neared. I prayed hard for Sarah and our unborn child. With God's blessing we now have two beautiful daughters and we are a devout Catholic family. The Lord listened to my prayers and we have had a wonderful marriage the past fourteen years. I sometimes think about Bess and the way things could have been, but we should not question God's plan."

Standing up Captain Robinson turned to John and placed a hand upon his shoulder, "John, won't you please visit Father Baylor?"

Nothing more was said. The men shook hands and the captain returned to his home. John lay awake for hours that night thinking about Katherine and his loss. Maybe the captain was right. Perhaps Father Baylor would be able to snuff the burning in John's tormented soul.

That night, for the first time in a long time, Katherine came to John dressed in her gauzy white gown with a flowing sash. She pulled her veil aside and smiled at him as she knelt down beside him. Leaning down to kiss him, her golden tresses tickled and teased as they fell across his face and chest. He could feel the sweet warmth of her breath as her lips neared his. But just before their lips made contact, she pulled back. John reached up to pull Katherine back into his arms, but she vanished. He jolted awake.

He sobbed for a long time, but once the remorse in his heart eased, his tears no longer flowed. From this day on, he thought, he would lovingly remember Katherine and no longer cry out for her. He knew that his undying love for her would endure forever.

Gently John drifted to sleep thinking about his lost love and in his dream she appeared in a dark blue skirt with a white bodice. Her blond hair was pulled back, tied tightly with a blue ribbon at the nape of her neck. Her long tresses hung down over the gray shawl draped over her shoulder. As she looked deeply into John's eyes her own blue eyes sparkled. He dreamt of her smile as he held her in his arms and kissed her. Now he remembered the taste of her lips. The kiss was that of a strawberry that had been dipped delicately in honey. He felt the soft, sweetness of her tender lips as they touched his.

John helped Katherine onto a swing suspended from the limb of an enormous willow tree and gently pushed her. As she swung back and forth, her laughter brought new joy and pleasant memories to his heart. John slept well that night.

Father Baylor was sympathetic to John's plight. He patiently listened as John related the events of the past year. The priest didn't say much while John talked, but offered words of wisdom near the end of their visit. They went into the church, knelt before the altar and prayed silently together. John departed feeling relieved of all the pressures that had ridden on his shoulders for a long, long time. He once again had hope for a better future. He now understood that he should treasure the moments he shared with Katherine and not question her death.

The desire for gold no longer held such a significant importance to John. As the priest had said, if it were really there, more men would have found it by now. He added that if John found joy in his carpentry he should take pleasure in the trade, as did Jesus.

John returned to his habit of attending Mass every Sunday. He was hesitant at first because of his almost marrying a girl that was not of his faith, but Father Baylor had told John that since there had been no Catholic Church in Shenandoah, he did nothing wrong by not attending Mass while living there. John began to feel close to the church once again. However, it was several months before he responded to an invitation to join the choir. He finally relented and added his voice in singing praises for the Lord.

One morning John read an article in the Baltimore newspaper about the many canals that were being built in the United States. The nearby Susquehanna (Port Deposit) Canal had been built years earlier, in 1802, commencing in Baltimore. Officials planned to extend the canal to Wrightsville in Pennsylvania. However, Pennsylvania officials fought the idea of any shipping being sent into central Pennsylvania via Maryland. Those officials wanted to build their own system, a canal system that ran from the Schuylkill River to the Susquehanna River. They intended that Pennsylvania commerce would remain within their own borders. Due to the conflict, Maryland's Susquehanna Canal system had gone bankrupt two years earlier in 1817.

Moving huge amounts of freight by inland waterways fascinated John. He was especially intrigued by the idea of using water within a canal or lock that allowed thousands of pounds to be raised or lowered from one level to another. There was a lock system currently in existence not too many miles away in Pennsylvania. The Conewago Falls were bypassed by just such a system of locks. The article reported that they had been built many years earlier and were quite successful. John decided that some day he must travel to Pennsylvania and visit this remarkable feat of engineering.

John accepted many invitations to share Sunday dinner with the Robinson family and even carved dolls for the two young girls. He also thrilled the girls when he created a doll crib for each of them at Christmas. That Christmas he created a small dresser top box for Mrs. Robinson's jewelry and a tobacco box for the captain. The Robinson family became John's family away from home.

In January John wrote Pastor and Mrs. Smythe expressing his regrets for leaving Shenandoah without a word to them. He briefly told them that he lived as a trapper in the west, but had now returned to Baltimore and had opened a cabinet shop. John was truly at a loss for words, thus his letter was short and to the point. He explained in his letter that he understood their anguish over the loss of their only child and expressed his undying love for his lost fiancé. Katherine, he added, would always be in his heart.

Pastor Smythe wrote back thanking John for his sincere letter and expressing concern for his well being. He wrote that John had departed Shenandoah so quickly that the townspeople were at a loss as to what to do with his properties: the Doyle Carpentry Company, the lumber mill and the half constructed house on Second Street.

Pastor Smythe added that friends had completed the house and were currently renting it out. The bank, which held the mortgages, had sold his lumber mill and carpentry business. However, their value far exceeded the balance due on the mortgages. Those assets had been deposited into John's Shenandoah bank account. Pastor Smythe urged him to contact the bank president with instructions.

John no longer wanted involvement in the Shenandoah Valley. He wrote back to Pastor Smythe, with an enclosed letter for the bank, instructing them to sell the house and deposit all assets in his account. He then requested that a new Presbyterian Church be built in the memory of Katherine Smythe. The new building would replace the log built church that Pastor Smythe was currently using. If there were not enough assets, John would make up the difference.

Pastor Smythe's response was an ecstatic one of deep appreciation. He enclosed a statement from the bank indicating that John's wishes would be completed and that quarterly reports of the new construction sent to him. The pastor stated that construction would begin in the spring. He added that the new church would be an everlasting tribute to Katherine's memory. John was pleased with this arrangement.

At a church social, the following spring, he was introduced to Marie Palmer, daughter of a real estate investor. Marie, at 17 years of age, was much younger than John. She was an attractive girl with long black hair and deep hazel eyes. She was considered a real catch by those in the know.

The couple shared a few dances at the social. Between dances they spent a few minutes chatting a bit. While she seemed a bit silly, John enjoyed her company. However, when he asked if he could call on her the following week, she politely declined. Marie had other suitors her own age that held more interest for her.

Many members of the congregation were surprised by Marie's attitude. John had a thriving business and was considered an up-and-coming member of society. He was a tall, blond, handsome young man who drew admiring peeks from many ladies in the congregation, young and old. His cabinets and furniture were in great demand. Many who ordered his products had to wait months for an item to be completed. The busy bodies of the church were also aware that John was now a person of means and maintained a handsome bank balance. But Marie was more interested in the younger, more adventuresome boys her own age. John didn't give a second thought to her refusal.

As the Doyle Cabinetry business grew, John hired two helpers. He had enjoyed working in solitude, but now his good business sense dictated that he must forgo that selfish pleasure. Because of the demand for his furniture, it was time for him to expand his thriving enterprise. A larger building was needed, so he purchased a lot on the outskirts of Towsontown, about five miles north of Baltimore. There beside a stream, he began construction of a large two-story building where he could use waterpower to operate a waterwheel. That, would in-turn, operate his saws and lathes.

The fall of 1820 John moved into a room at Ezekiel Towson's Tavern to oversee the construction of his factory. By the following spring the Doyle Cabinetry mill was in full swing with a total of four employees. A short distance from the mill he constructed a two room log cabin, which was just the right size for a confirmed bachelor.

John was busy at his desk at the Towsontown mill in early May when there was a knock at his door. He looked up and recognized a familiar face; it was his brother Michael. What a pleasant surprise this was!

"Michael, come in. Come in." John rose up and hugged his younger brother tightly. "I haven't seen you in ten years and you haven't change a bit." He jokingly added, "Well, maybe you look a bit older now!"

Both men laughed as Michael returned the embrace. John gestured for his brother to sit as he returned to his desk. "Where have you been? Mother wrote months ago that you were still in California searching for gold. My God, Michael, the family hasn't heard from you in almost a year!"

Michael flushed as he replied, "I've made a mess of it, big brother. I never made it to California."

"What happened?" John asked.

"I started west, but ran into Indian troubles near the Mississippi River," Michael explained to him. "We were a small party of twelve heading west. The group included three women and one young boy. Indians attacked our party early one evening and killed several men instantly. The savages captured the other men and tortured them. By morning all the men were dead. The Indians took the women and child with them when they departed. I escaped the attack with only the shirt on my back."

"How terrible," John said. "How did you manage to escape?"

"I was down by the river getting water for the camp when the Indians attacked. I didn't have my rifle with me, so I hid in the water under some brush until the mayhem was over. I was in the river all night. I'm sure the Indians never knew I was there."

"You were indeed fortunate not to be discovered," John commented.

"In the morning the Indians left taking the pack horses and their captives. What they couldn't take with them they destroyed. The men they had tortured were a gruesome sight. Those barbarians did terrible things to them.

"I couldn't find much at the campsite, so I started back east for the last trading post we had passed days earlier. When I got there I was cold and starving. The owner wasn't much help other than offering me some food. I struggled back through Kentucky and then remembered that you lived in Shenandoah. I headed there, but you had already moved on.

"I remembered father's cousin, Captain Robinson, in Baltimore and hoped he could secure a position for me. He told me that you were living here."

"I'm glad you found me, Michael. I can use some help with my business. I am planning to expand. I'm about to purchase some land north of here and open a lumber mill," John said.

"What can I do? I'm sure I'm not a business man such as yourself," Michael said jokingly.

"The land is ten miles to the north of here and you can oversee the workers. I'll take care of the paperwork, but I need someone I can trust to run that operation," John explained to his brother. "I know it's a lot of responsibility, but I am sure you can handle it. Our parents raised us to think for ourselves."

John obtained a room for his brother at Ezekiel Towson's Tavern and the two began planning how they would run the Doyle Lumber Mill so that it would fulfill the needs of the Doyle Cabinetry business. It seemed like the perfect arrangement.

Two weeks later a letter from the bank president arrived from the Shenandoah Bank explaining that the new church had been completed and there had been an excess balance still in John's account. Enclosed in the letter was a note that transferred that sum to him. John was quite surprised by the amount, as he never realized that his assets in Virginia were so large. Along with the money he had in the Baltimore account he could now easily pay for the forestland and begin the new Doyle Lumber Mill business.

The following week he and Michael traveled to the new plot of land and, after inspecting the stands of hardwood, began the transactions for the purchase. When he and Michael returned to Towsontown, John prepared a Power of Attorney so Michael could complete the transactions with the Baltimore bank. Michael would take the Shenandoah note to Baltimore, deposit the money and withdraw the appropriate amount for payment to the seller of the forestland.

Michael departed for Baltimore the following morning and was expected back by nightfall. Night came and went — and no Michael.

By noon that next day, John was becoming very concerned about his brother's well being. He saddled his horse and headed for Baltimore, a two-hour ride away.

"I'm sorry," the Baltimore Bank manager explained. "Your brother came in here yesterday morning with your Power of Attorney and closed your account. We thought it strange that he requested the balance in cash, but he did have your signature on the appropriate document. He also transferred a note from a bank in Virginia into cash."

John sat in stunned silence. How could Michael do this to him? How could his own brother rob him of all his money? It didn't seem possible. He thought to himself, "This can't be Michael." But the manager described Michael to John and he certainly fit the description.

John had no choice but to go to the police and report the incident. There he received another shock.

"Michael Doyle?" the crusty old desk sergeant asked. "Why we have warrants for his arrest. Seems he brutally beat up a storeowner at a trading post on the frontier and stole a horse, rifle and some supplies. Left the man in bad shape."

"I can't believe it of my brother," he told the policeman. John shook his head in disbelief. He thought to himself, how could a Doyle do such a thing?

"Oh, but that's not all the lad's been up to," added the sergeant. "Seems he robbed a bank in Shenandoah, Virginia, as well. Says on the warrant they knew it was Michael Doyle because he came into town looking for his brother and told several people his name. A short time later, he robbed the bank and hightailed it out of town. The sheriff there notified us because they knew you lived here. Thought he might be heading this way."

With a smirk, the sergeant asked, "You the brother he was looking for?"

John left the police station in shock. He couldn't comprehend how his brother could have become so bad. How could one brother do this to another? Where was Michael's Catholic upbringing? He vowed that he would never tell his parents of this shameful business. It would be more than his poor mother could bear.

John needed someone to talk to about this terrible situation. His mind was spinning with so many confusing thoughts. He headed to the church and hoped that Father Baylor would be available.

Chapter 11

The Doyle Cabinetry Company continued thriving, but its owner was now more suspicious of others than ever. It was months before John's lighthearted demeanor returned. Captain Robinson's questions about Michael's whereabouts remained unanswered. John had vowed to himself that no family member would ever know what evil deed Michael had carried out. The local police were stymied by John's statement that he had "given" his brother the funds. But Michael was still wanted by the law on the other assault and robbery charges.

John's land deal had fallen through and his aspirations of starting another business had disappeared with his bank account. Without sufficient funds, he couldn't think of launching another business. But his cabinetry business was good and he now found great pleasure in creating furniture.

As each piece was completed, he would often think of Frank Moss, who had taught him carpentry at Kemp's Shipyard years earlier. He fondly remembered how Mr. Moss would gently run his fingers across the finely sanded wood grains and take pleasure in his finished work. John shared that kind of love for woodworking and relished in the creation of each item his shop produced. His goal was to instill his workers with that same pride of craftsmanship. Recently he had hired a shop foreman, Bill Mulholland, and was pleased that the man shared the same interests in working with fine woods. When it came to the finer details, John found that Bill's expertise was remarkable.

Top quality woods were in great demand. As the new country grew, the prospering population wanted furniture constructed with the finest woods and of the highest quality. John was constantly seeking better, finer grades of walnut, cherry and oak.

Recalling his years at the Kemp Shipyard, he knew that they insisted on purchasing only exceptionally grained woods, used to finish the interior cabinetry of the cabins. These better hardwoods came from the northern mountains of Pennsylvania. He decided to take a trip to that area and investigate the lumber mills of the region. Thus, on a warm day in May of 1822 John ventured north into Pennsylvania where he was certain he would find the hardwoods he desired.

Remembering an interesting article he had read in the newspaper a year or so earlier, he decided to follow the Susquehanna River north and make use of the canal system that bypassed the Conewago Falls near Wrightsville in Pennsylvania. Arriving at the canal dock two days later, he and his mount continued up river by mule drawn barge.

John fell in love with canal travel that day. He sat at the bow of the barge as it lazily traveled up river. The leisurely pace was indeed slow, but the scenery was magnificent as they passed by small farms, towns and forested areas. John had been so busy with his carpentry business the past few years that he hadn't thought of taking any time for himself. He relaxed aboard the barge and thought about his life. While he would always miss Katherine, he felt pleased with things the way they were now. He missed his parents and siblings, but he always felt welcomed each time he visited the Robinson family. They were his family in this country. He thought about Kevin and Michael and wondered what had become of them. He was ashamed of Michael and worried about Kevin's disappearance. Surely Kevin would have contacted the family by now if he were still alive. Smiling to himself he thought of his baby sister, Mary, who was now almost a teenager. "Why, she'll soon be twelve years old," he thought aloud and chuckled to himself. He must send her a special gift for her next birthday. Perhaps a gingham dress would please her or perhaps a delicate silken scarf woven in the Orient. Yes, the scarf it would be, for his blossoming young sister.

As the barge neared the Conewago Falls, John's attention was brought back to the canal. Barge travel was a novel idea for the new nation. John knew that it was a popular method of transport in Europe, but the barge industry was just beginning to catch favor in this country. An avid reader, he was well aware that Benjamin Franklin had pursued the idea of linking up the country with canals as a system for moving cargo as well as passengers. In 1690 Mr. Franklin submitted a proposal to link the Schuylkill and Susquehanna Rivers in Pennsylvania with an inland waterway. From reading history books, John had also learned that the early Egyptians had built canal systems along the Nile River for the transport of goods within short distances from the river. However, it was during the 15th Century that Leonardo DaVinci designed the first practical canal lock gate for raising and lowering boats to various levels. Thus began the popularity of barge travel for commerce and passenger transport in Europe.

Upon arriving at the Conewago Falls, north of Wrightsville, John's barge entered the Conewago Canal Locks. He had purposely planned his trip to travel by way of this canal. The system had been built a quarter of a century earlier to bypass the falls and rapids on the Susquehanna River. The experience thrilled John and he studied every action of the locks and the canal itself, making detailed notes of his adventure.

Crossing the Susquehanna River on Harris' Ferry, John arrived in Middletown where he spent the night at a hotel. There he discovered that the Union Canal Company had recently been formed with the intent of starting construction of a canal from Middletown to Reading. In some sections, construction had already started.

John read in a local paper that Samuel Mifflin, the president of the Union Canal Company, was commencing construction on the waterway. The company was also building an unusual canal tunnel through a ridge dividing the waters of the Quittapahilla Creek and Clark's Run. Simeon Guilford would be the engineer in charge of the project. The article stated that the digging would be completed using gunpowder to blast through limestone, which contained veins of hard flinty slate. The completed tunnel, 80 feet below the summit of the ridge, would be an amazing 729 feet long. Being the longest tunnel of its kind, it would be considered another "wonder of the world." John was fascinated and captivated.

The trip to northern Pennsylvania was fruitful and yielded the hardwoods that the Doyle Cabinetry Company required. Rather than having the quality hardwoods floated down the Susquehanna River in the usual fashion, John made arrangements to have rafts built of lesser woods useable for framing and other projects. The hardwood boards would then be transported on top of these rafts and kept out of the water. His reasoning was that as the hardwoods floated down the river, the lengthy soaking caused some warping and splitting. Keeping the boards dry would improve the quality of the wood and produce a finer finished product with less waste.

Back at his Towsontown mill a few weeks later, John studied his notes and drawings he had made on his trip through the Conewago Canal. He had noted one problem with the way the heavy wooden planks were being cut for the gates. It resulted in frequent breakage if a barge happened to ram into a closed gate. The lock keepers were required to keep a supply of extra boards on hand in the event of damage. The replacement of broken gates was expensive as well as time consuming. John felt that instead of using one heavy board, two or more thinner boards bolted together would offer more resistance to a severe impact by a heavily laden barge. He was sure of his facts, but wanted to do some tests before addressing this problem to the Union Canal Company.

Much to the amusement of his workers and some local folk, John began building a small lock beside the dam at his mill. He drew up blueprints for a lock that would hold a single rowboat or canoe, but could be used to bypass the six-foot high waterfall at the dam where his waterwheel had been constructed. He began digging the ditch for the canal in the evenings. Many local people came to watch. While not fully understanding the significance of the project, some even picked up a shovel or pick and participated in John's undertaking. The project quickly became the neighborhood novelty and more people showed up each week to watch the events. With all that help, the canal ditch was dug within a few weeks and John began to line the bed and walls with local limestone. For the lack of anything else, John used barn door hinges on the four gates. The lock gates were constructed using his theory of several thin boards bolted together rather than one heavy plank. He wanted to make them as strong as possible.

By the middle of August the canal was ready to be flooded. He and several friends carefully removed the dams at each end of the canal. The water slowly entered the sluice gate and filled John's mini-canal. It was a warm Sunday afternoon and people came from miles around by horseback and in their buggies to watch the first test. Blankets were spread on the ground and picnic baskets appeared. Whole families showed up for the big event. This was going to be a festive experience for the citizens of Towsontown.

Bill Mulholland, John's burly foreman, wanted to be the first to test the new lock. John closed the two lower gates and opened the sluice gate. This allowed the lock to be slowly filled with water from the upper stream. Once the water in the lock was the same level as the upper area of the dam, John opened the two upstream gates. With a large crowd cheering him on, Bill came rowing downstream. He was dressed in his Sunday best and wore an old top hat. He sported an enormous grin, a huge black cigar tightly clenched between his teeth. Bill's wife had draped white ribbons on the bow of the freshly painted Kelly green rowboat and tied a bright pink parasol to the stern. The spectacle caused the crowd to stand and roar with laughter. Bill entered the lock and stopped rowing.

John cranked the upper gates closed behind the gaily-adorned rowboat. Opening a small sluice gate at the lower end of the lock, John allowed the water to slowly drain from the lock. Bill and the rowboat began slowly sinking down to the six-foot level of the stream at the lower end of the dam. The crowd let out a cheer as Bill tipped his hat as he slowly disappeared from view. John cranked open the lower gates and Bill, with parasol in hand, stood proudly in his boat as it drifted out onto the stream. The test, to the glee of all on hand, was a grand success. From nowhere a bottle of wine appeared and all involved in John's project celebrated the successful test whether they understood the significance of the experiment or not.

By now, John's canal was the talk of the town and many people stopped by to gawk or arrive in their boats to give it a try. On Sunday afternoons the lock was kept busy ferrying rowboats and canoes back and forth between the two levels of the stream.

Building the lock was fun for John and seemed like child's play. The important fact he wanted to test was the construction of the wooden gates. A small-scale canal barge was constructed and loaded with stone. The model barge was constantly bashed into the canal gates, occasionally with great force, to test the strength of his new design. John was pleased with the results and felt that his changes would greatly strengthen the full sized gates planned for the Union Canal now under construction.

After weeks of studying his scaled down lock, John sent a letter off to the Union Canal Company indicating that he might have a suggestion to improve the strength of their lock gates. He didn't go into detail, but offered to travel to their Lancaster offices and address his theory. The response was immediate. He was invited to an appointment with Mr. Mifflin. John packed his bags, gathered up some wood samples and headed for Lancaster the following morning. He was quite elated that the company would consider his suggestions.

John arrived in Lancaster to find it a bustling, busy city. Pioneers traveling west came here to begin their long trek into the wilderness.

He discovered that the Lancaster 'Conestoga Wagon' was considered the best money could buy for the arduous journey. The demand for this desirable covered wagon was bringing prosperity to the rapidly growing city, which ten years earlier had been the capital city of Pennsylvania. Many wagon trains began their odyssey in Lancaster and followed the newly built National Road between Baltimore and Wheeling in West Virginia. Every imaginable supply that a traveler could need for the long trek could be found in the stores and shops of the city.

Finding Mr. Mifflin in his office was a stroke of luck as he was indeed a busy man. At their very first meeting John pointed out to Mr. Mifflin that if the wood materials used in the lock gates were assembled differently, the gates would have more strength and not crack as often under the heavy pressure of the water or impact by the barges. Standing on two planks bolted together, each end atop an office chair, John bounced up and down demonstrating how two boards, secured together, had an increased strength. He explained to Mr. Mifflin that by using layers of wood the shock of an impact from a wayward barge could more easily be absorbed by the gate.

Mr. Mifflin was impressed by John's presentation and summoned Mr. Canvass White, the preeminent canal engineer of the day, and Mr. Simeon Guilford, the engineer in charge. A lengthy discussion ensued regarding John's suggestion. The three men spent hours poring over John's notes regarding his tests. They were pleased with what they heard. Based on the recommendations of this panel, Mr. Mifflin arranged for Mr. White and Mr. Guilford to travel to Towsontown the following week. The two engineers wanted to see John's scaled down lock, which used the improvement he recommended.

For a week the two engineers and a team of helpers rammed, strained and forced John's lock gates testing their strength. Many local citizens came to watch the fun and row their boats back and forth through the lock as it was tested. Then one morning, the engineers packed up their equipment and departed telling John only that he would hear from the Union Canal Company once their results were analyzed.

It was a long, anxious wait for John. He kept himself busy with his business, as the back orders were slowly building. The Doyle Cabinetry Company now constructed the finest furniture in the area and people wanted to buy John's products. But waiting to hear from the Union Canal seemed an eternity. It was difficult keeping his mind on the furniture business as the hours and days slowly ticked by. The results of the engineers' tests of his canal gates seemed to take forever. In the meantime, the cabinetry workload increased daily. John had to increase his workforce to ten men and had added an extension to the factory for his growing business.

Early in June several wagons from Havre de Grace arrived delivering the first shipment of hardwood from the lumber mill near Danville, Pennsylvania. The mill had shipped the materials down river exactly the way John had contracted. All the workers at the Doyle Cabinetry were impressed with the quality of the hardwoods. None of the boards were split or warped from an immersing in water. Keeping the hardwoods dry during the float down the Susquehanna River meant the final drying time was now greatly reduced. The poplar and pine logs used for the raft were still somewhat water logged, but that had been expected.

After many pensive weeks, a letter finally arrived early in August from the Union Canal Company. They were enthusiastic about the suggested modifications. John was urged to come to the Lancaster office at the earliest possible date for a conference with Mr. Mifflin and the project engineers.

Putting Bill Mulholland in charge of the Doyle Cabinetry Company, John rode off for Lancaster a few days later. The entire way to the meeting, John was thrilled with the aspect of his suggestions having importance in the construction of the Union Canal Company lock gates.

The meeting with Mr. Mifflin was a short one. Mr. White and Mr. Guilford were sitting in Mr. Mifflin's office when John arrived. The men welcomed John and invited him to sit down at the end of a long meeting table. "John," Mr. Mifflin said. "We want you to come work for the Union Canal."

John was stunned. "I'm not an engineer. I only wanted to make suggestions about a problem I discovered and thought I could help solve."

"Mr. Doyle, you don't know how much of an impact your Towsontown canal has been on our overall design for our lock gates," Mr. Guilford stated. "Not only will your recommendations improve the configuration of the wood in the gates, but the use of barn door hinges greatly impressed us."

"You see," explained Mr. Mifflin as he lit his pipe, "we have been paying a contractor in Europe to construct our gate hinges in the same fashion as used in their canal locks. Making and shipping a special hinge is a slow and expensive operation. Your lock showed us that we can use a common barn hinge and they can be produced locally by any blacksmith."

"I never gave a thought to the hinge assembly," John replied.

"Your small lock successfully used only two hinges per gate," Mr. Guilford added. "We have tested common barn hinges and found that the pressure asserted by a full size lock will necessitate the use of four or more hinges per gate. While your design requires more hinges, the company will still save a lot of money by having them made locally."

"And, that's why we want you working for us, Mr. Doyle," Mr. Mifflin stated as he stood and walked to the window looking down on the constant stream of covered wagons passing beneath. As he puffed on his pipe, he could envision the day when these travelers would cross Pennsylvania on barges owned by his company. He realized that each passing day was giving more business to the Erie Canal in New York or the Chesapeake and Ohio Canal in Maryland. Pennsylvania also needed her share of that commerce.

Turning to John, he added, "I think that we are all in agreement that you have an eye for detail. You may not be a trained engineer, but we think that your observations and suggestions would be a great asset to the Union Canal Company."

"I do have a business in Towsontown," John reminded him.

"Take a day or two and think about it, Mr. Doyle," Mr. Mifflin suggested as he reached out to shake John's hand. "We can offer you a nice compensation package and I think you will find the work extremely interesting."

John returned to his hotel room after the meeting. What to do? It was a dream come true, but he also hated to give up his cabinetry business. He thought of himself as more of a hands-on person, rather than management. Still undecided, John went to a nearby tavern for dinner.

He sat beside a window at the tavern enjoying his meal. On King Street, outside his window, he watched the famous Conestoga Wagons pass by the restaurant in an almost continuous string. Whole families marched beside the wagons, which were packed with all their worldly goods. John marveled how these families could begin such an adventure without knowing what the future would hold. The women walked proudly beside their husbands while smiling children, gleefully jumping and skipping, followed behind. Surely these smiling young faces had no inkling of the enormous journey that lay in store for them. The faces of the parents glowed with hope for a brighter future. How brave they must be. John had recently returned from the frontier and knew of the dangers that lurked there, and yet he knew that these families were following their dream.

"Following their dream," he spoke softly to himself. While sitting in the tavern, pondering the future of these pioneers, John came to his decision. Wasn't he seeking his dream when he came to America? Perhaps the gold he had sought as a young man was actually to be found in a different form, in the form of his involvement in building an inland waterway that traversed Pennsylvania. He decided then and there that Benjamin Franklin's dream would become his. He was elated that he now had a new goal, a new dream. To John, his future now looked brighter.

The following morning he enthusiastically returned to Mr. Mifflin's office. After a few negotiations, John accepted the Union

Canal Company offer. He would return immediately to Towsontown and settle his business affairs. Returning the following week, John would begin working with Mr. Guilford.

On the return trip to Towsontown he decided his course of action. John would ask Bill Mulholland to accept a promotion from foreman to administrator of the Doyle Cabinetry Company. He trusted the man, but decided to have the Towsontown Bank business office manage the company finances and payroll. By splitting responsibilities within the company, John hoped that he would not experience the problems such as his brother had caused.

The following day John held a meeting with Bill Mulholland, the bank president and the bank business manager. Those three men would serve as the board of directors for the cabinetry business. The appropriate contracts were drawn for all to sign and, to be on the safe side, John appointed a local law firm to review the contracts and witness the procedures. The law firm would also be placed on a retainer when the necessity arose to oversee the legal operations of the company.

In addition, John required quarterly reports from the bank business manager to keep him apprised of company business affairs. By the end of the day, John felt satisfied with the control of his company assets. He knew he would often be far a field while working for the Union Canal, but the Doyle Cabinetry Company business must be kept going in his absence.

The net profits from the business were to be deposited in an account John set up separately with the Towsontown Bank. From those profits, John assigned 50% to be sent to his parents in Ballylee each month. He may not be able to send gold back to his family, but he would certainly share his newfound wealth. The remainder would be held in his private account for future business endeavors.

Bill Mulholland would live in John's cabin free of rent as long as he remained an employee in good standing. John generously presented Bill with enough money to immediately enlarge the two-room cabin to accommodate Bill's wife and two children. He felt that this perk would certainly instill Bill's loyalty for years to come. John truly liked Bill and put a lot of faith in the man's sense of priorities.

The second week of September 1822, John reported to Mr. Guilford and began working on the Pennsylvania Canal project. The issue at hand was the tunnel near Lebanon. The contractor, John Ives, had begun digging the 729-foot long tunnel and the progress was slow. While it was thought that they would be tunneling through limestone, the workers had immediately run into an extremely hard vein of slate. John would travel with Mr. Guilford to the job site and see what recommendations could be made.

It would have been more practical to take the long way around the 80-foot high ridge, but a competing canal company, The Schuylkill Navigation Company, was digging a tunnel for their canal along the Schuylkill River near Auburn. People traveled in droves from Philadelphia to see the awesome sight. A man-made underground river for boat traffic; what a wonder it would be! The Schuylkill tunnel was to be 450 feet long and the directors of the Union Canal wanted an even longer tunnel; whether it made sense or not! Thus the Lebanon project would go on regardless of expense.

Mr. Guilford and Mr. Ives were in conference for hours discussing the best method of completing the tunnel. John, on the other hand, went to the job site to review what was being done. He felt completely out of his domain as the men working there knew mining and understood the handling of explosives. John didn't understand any of this, so he mostly watched and asked questions trying to stay out of their way.

Later in the day Mr. Guilford and John met to discuss what findings they discovered. John admitted his inadequacies, but Mr. Guilford said, "You just keep your eyes open, young man. With your keen interest you just might find a better solution. Sometimes we engineers overlook the simplest things in our haste to complete the job."

Back in Lancaster, Mr. Guilford explained to Mr. Mifflin the problems that Mr. Ives and his miners were having digging through the mixture of slate and limestone. The two concluded that the tunnel should be completed within two years. John stayed silent during the meeting.[3]

It was decided that the bulk of John's time would be spent in the Middletown offices, thus he found an apartment in town on Susquehanna Street. His duties did keep him on the move and he didn't spend much time in the apartment.

The next several years found John constantly traveling back and forth along the proposed twenty-four mile length of the Eastern Division extension between Middletown and Duncan's Island at the mouth of the Juniata River. The Eastern Division had begun at Columbia many years earlier and John had traveled upon that portion, bypassing the Conewago Falls, on his first venture into Pennsylvania. Now that division would be extended to Duncan's Island by a canal dug parallel to the Susquehanna River.

As the canal construction to Duncan's Island went into full swing, John was mostly concerned with the construction of those fourteen locks. The locks were naturally much larger than his demonstration lock in Towsontown. These locks would be built 90 feet long and 17 feet wide. Each lock would raise or lower a barge an average of seven and a half feet using diverted waters from the Susquehanna River.

Picks and shovels were used to remove tons and tons of dirt. Mule teams pulling scores of wagons hauled the dirt to other portions of the canal where the dirt would be used for levees. During the dry seasons the levees would maintain the water levels inside the canal route. The levees also helped maintain water levels within the canal during periods of moderate flooding. Massive amounts of stone were cut for the limestone that lined the base and sides of the locks. John was amazed at the manpower involved in the early preparations.

As each gate was constructed, John was on hand supervising the progress. He oversaw the construction and installation of the huge gates on each lock. When the time arose for the filling and testing of a completed lock, John closely examined the project. The completion of each lock gave him satisfaction and he felt proud to be involved in this endeavor. John often wrote his parents describing and extolling the wondrous changes the Pennsylvania Canal system would bring to the growing population.

Construction slowly progressed north. The summer of 1826 the surveyors ventured even farther north from the Eastern Division. They began planning the Susquehanna Division, which would begin at the Clark's Ferry Dam near Duncan's Island. This extension would extend 39 miles north to Northumberland.

The Susquehanna Division would require thirteen locks, the highest lift being an enormous twelve feet at Duncan's Island. John was concerned about such enormous gates holding back that much water pressure. Then the surveyors decided that another twelve-foot lift would also be required at the Northumberland end of the section. John immediately got busy with the engineers to design those massive gates.

The Susquehanna Division of the Pennsylvania Canal System opened an office in the town of Liverpool late in October of 1826. John and Mr. Guilford moved their operations there. Liverpool was deemed the best location, as it was about the halfway point between Duncan's Island and Northumberland.

In the meantime, back in the Lancaster office, Mr. Mifflin and his engineers were busy planning the Juniata Division, which would begin at Clark's Ferry Dam and extend up the Juniata River continuing westward toward Pittsburgh and beyond. Benjamin Franklin's vision was slowly becoming reality for Pennsylvania.

Chapter 12

John looked forward to moving to the small town of Liverpool. It was a busy farming center and even offered several nice inns that catered to river traffic. A beautiful, lofty mountain lay on the eastern side of the Susquehanna River painted with every color a tree could offer. He was pleased that Mr. Guilford and the company had chosen Liverpool as the sight for the next canal office as the area reminded him so much of his home, far away in the hills of Ireland.

John had passed through Liverpool several months before on business. The surveyors had been there laying out plans for the canal route and had determined that a thirteen-foot rise in the river might be too high and expensive for a single lock due to the lay of the land. The surveyors had requested Mr. Guilford's presence and suggested he consider building two locks at Liverpool, one six feet high and the other seven. Mr. Guilford and John agreed to their suggestion that if the locks were located a mile and a half apart, one at each end of town, it would avoid barge congestion at a single lock. In addition, Liverpool offered a convenient overnight location for travelers at one of the inns. The town also had a low rise in the land at the edge of the river. That would offer an ideal location for a barge maintenance facility.

The first week in town John stayed at Meyer's Inn on Front Street, but immediately began looking for an apartment or small cottage away from the hustle and bustle of the riverside business district. While his room in the tavern was much quieter than the one he had rented with Jacque above the Ox and Plow Pub in Baltimore, John preferred quiet evenings where he could relax and read. Quarters away from the nightlife of a pub were more to his liking.

Midweek he found a small, partially furnished cottage on Locust Street for rent. It was only two blocks from the canal office, a building that the company had purchased at the edge of the river. Although sparsely furnished, the cottage met his basic requirements. John was able to pick up a few extra pieces of used furniture and had soon made himself a cozy place to live. He felt true contentment once he organized his books on the two bookshelves in the parlor.

The town leaders held a special assembly so they could meet with John. They wanted him to feel welcome and invited him to attend the monthly town meetings. They were aware that the new inland waterway would have a great impact on their community. By having a canal official involved in their meetings they hoped to be kept up to date on the progress of the construction.

At the meeting, John was disappointed when he learned that the nearest Catholic Church was in Harrisburg, 26 miles to the south. However, the mayor explained that Father Barrett, the circuit priest, came to Liverpool about once a month to administer the Mass.

At his first regular town meeting, a few days later, Mr. John Huggins, a wealthy landowner, invited John to attend the next Mass at his house. He explained that Father Barrett held Mass at someone's home when he traveled up the river. Since Mr. Huggins had the largest house in Liverpool, it just seemed natural that the church service would be held there. John looked forward to meeting Father Barrett and attending his next Mass.

John and Mr. Huggins soon became good friends, as community projects were important to both men. John would be the chief canal official in the immediate area, thus Mr. Huggins wanted him involved in many of the local social functions. He knew that having John's favor would do well if the town needed assistance from the

Susquehanna Canal Division with its plans for the future. In fact, the town leaders had already discussed a new community park. The canal channel would be built right through the current riverside park. Mr. Huggins briefly mentioned the subject to John, but being a shrewd businessman, knew that this wasn't the time or place to go into details.

The winter and spring flew by quickly as John made preparations for construction on the Susquehanna Division to commence. There was land to procure all along the route the surveyors had plotted for the canal. Arrangements had to be made at every site a lock would be built for workers' lodging as well as storage facilities for numerous supplies and livestock. The summer of 1827 found John finally taking a short vacation, but it was a working vacation. He traveled to Towsontown to check on his business there and then toured the tunnel being built at Lebanon visiting various construction sights along the Union Canal. While most construction was going well, it was disappointing that the tunnel near Lebanon was still not completed.

The engineers told him they were also not pleased with the slow progress on the tunnel. There had been a multitude of problems including cave-ins resulting in injuries. Slate was a hard material that often shattered under pressure when least expected. Often an explosion would free more material than had been planned. The digging went on slowly. Already two years behind schedule, there was a hope that it would be completed and opened for barge traffic by the end of the year.

By mid August John was back in Liverpool preparing for the arrival of the construction crew that would begin the digging from Mount Patrick to Dry Saw Mill. John was responsible for the construction of the four locks in this area, but would be required to inspect all twelve lock gates from Duncan's Island to Northumberland. He would be a busy man from now until the canal was completed.

Around midday, the first week of October, John left the company office for a short time to visit the town mayor. As he walked past

Huggins General Store on Market Street a young woman of small stature caught his eye. She had the greenest eyes he had ever seen. Her long dark brown hair hung down over her shoulders, blowing gently in the warm fall breeze. John was stopped short in his tracks by her beauty. Since Katherine, no other woman had even come close to capturing his attention. He instantly knew that he had to meet this stunning young woman.

"Good day," he boldly spoke as he slowly approached her.

She glanced at him, but coyly looked away continuing to stack her parcels into a blue farm wagon.

"It's an absolutely lovely day," John continued undeterred by her act of indifference. "The air smells so crisp and clean."

John received no response from this vision of loveliness. So, he casually continued being as genteel as he could, "Why the trees are so full of color it takes ones breath away."

"Sir," she quizzically looked his way and responded with an icy tone, "I don't know you. Why are you approaching me?"

"I am captivated by your beauty," John said softly. "I thought you might be a nymph or fairy from yonder wood."

"You are far too bold," she responded as a slight smile began to form at the corners of her petite lips.

John could see that he now had drawn her attention and interest. He continued with his sweetest Irish accent, "My name is John Doyle. I have lived in this lovely town for over a year and I am sure that I have never laid eyes on such a exquisite young lass as yourself."

Her hardened shell began to melt a bit and John instantly sensed her interest growing. But an older man, appearing from nowhere, protectively placed himself between John and the young woman. His intrusion quickly drew their attention away from each other.

"Who are you young man," he demanded, "speaking to my daughter in such a manner?"

Just then Henry Minor, the store manager, came out onto the wooden sidewalk and spoke loudly, "Ah, Mr. Thompson. I see you've met John Doyle, the superintendent of the canal project.

John, this is Samuel Thompson and his daughter Patricia. They have a farm up on Toad Hollow Road."

Samuel Thompson backed off from his hostile stance. He instantly realized that, rather than being some ruffian, this was a gentleman of some standing. He put his hand out and said, "Mr. Doyle, it's a pleasure to meet you."

John, returning Samuel's firm handshake, replied, "Mr. Thompson, the pleasure is all mine." Nodding to Patricia he went on, "And I'm very pleased to meet you Miss Thompson."

This strange man's poise and demeanor captured Patricia's attention. At first she was annoyed by his approach, but now she found him fascinating. His soft-spoken, lilting words drew her further into his charming charisma.

John could see that her eyes now sparkled as she peered into his. His inattention barely caught the end of what Mr. Minor was saying, "…is overseeing the construction of the canal here in Liverpool, Samuel. He's also working with Mr. Huggins and the town leaders on a plan for a new community park. It sounds like it will be a really nice place for the children to play and for Sunday picnics."

John realized that Mr. Minor obviously was on his side in his acquaintance with this young lady. John mumbled something in response to the store manager's words, but wasn't quite certain what he had said. He was slowly being drawn into Patricia's penetrating green eyes. At first John wasn't even aware that Mr. Thompson and Henry had returned into the store, but suddenly became conscious to the fact that he and Patricia stood alone on the street gazing into one another's eyes.

Snapping out of his trance, he stammered, "I'd like to call on you." And after a long pause, "If you don't mind, of course."

"Why, Mr. Doyle," she smiled demurely. "You really are quite forward." A slight flush appeared on her cheeks.

But then she quickly added, "I'd feel honored to have you call on me. However, we live quite far out of town."

"I'll find you," John grinned with his conquest. "I'd never let such beauty escape me now."

Patricia giggled as her father descended the steps from the store. "Patricia, we'd better be on our way. Mother is expecting us for dinner and it's a long, long way home."

John noted that Mr. Thompson emphasized the "long, long way home." John stepped forward and, placing his hands on her slim waist, gently lifted Patricia up onto the wagon seat. He marveled how light and tiny she really was.

Patricia blushed as John stepped away from the wagon just as Samuel snapped the reins and the team of horses bolted forward into a fast walk. John wasn't too sure just where he stood with Patricia's father, but he was deeply captivated by this beauty.

"Mr. Doyle," Henry Minor stepped out from the doorway, "Don't let Samuel's manner deter you. I can tell he likes you," he laughed as he added, "and so does Patricia from what I've seen."

John watched the wagon disappear around the corner onto Race Street and without turning to look at Henry, asked, "Can you give me directions to their farm?"

Henry laughed and said, "Come on in, John. It's easy to find."

The following Sunday John slipped his guitar strap over his shoulder and set out early to walk the five miles to the Thompson farm. He was glad that this wasn't one of the Sunday's that Father Barrett would be in town holding Mass or it would be too late in the day for a walk to the farm. He could have ridden his horse, but he preferred to take the long walk. Long walks reminded him of all the miles he and his brothers walked together back in Ballylee years earlier. John loved the slow pace along a country road as he adsorbed all that nature had to offer.

Late in the morning he approached their farm. A white picket fence surrounded the small white farmhouse. Chickens scratched and pecked inside the fence. John barely noticed the green shutters with matching front door.

His attention was focused on Patricia, who was sitting on a bench on the front porch. John was certain that she was waiting for him as she wore a very pretty tan dress. Her long brown hair delicately hung over the front of her left shoulder, tied with a black velvet ribbon. Even from the road, fifty feet from the house, he could see those deep green eyes. His heart beat profoundly as she eagerly rose from the bench and delicately stepped down the porch steps onto the front yard.

John quickly entered the gate scattering squawking chickens in all directions. The couple met in the middle of the yard. Neither spoke, but just stood breathlessly a few feet apart peering into each other's eyes. John's blue eyes held Patricia in rapture like a hawk about to grab a small sparrow.

The door of the house opened and Mr. Thompson stepped out, "I see you found the place. It's a beautiful day for a walk." Obviously Patricia's father had watched John walking up the road for some distance. He was followed out the door by a woman John assumed to be Patricia's mother.

"Good day to you both," John responded with a big smile. "It is truly a lovely day with the trees so full of fall colors. The countryside here is so magnificent that I looked forward to enjoying such a vision of beauty every step of the way."

John looked back into Patricia's eyes hoping that she would understand the double meaning in his statement. Her eyes silently told him that she understood the compliment.

"This," Mrs. Thompson spoke up, "must be Mr. John Doyle. I have heard so much about you."

John, realizing that he and Patricia only met for a few moments in town, recognized the sarcasm in her voice. He instantly decided that he must win this woman over quickly.

"Ah, Mrs. Thompson," John gave her his most sincere look. "What a pleasure it is to meet you. I absolutely love your house. I can see that you take great pride in your home and your lovely family." After a moments thought he added, "And I can see where your daughter acquired her beauty."

And that's all it took; she was his. John had another ally on the spot.

As they all sat on the front porch, they begged John to entertain them with a few Irish ballads. Thus, John further endeared himself as they enjoyed his soft voice and music. Mrs. Thompson insisted that he partake of dinner with them and, of course, John could not refuse such a delightful offer. Disappearing into the house, Mrs. Thompson called them inside a short time later.

A wonderful meal of fried chicken, corn on the cob and baked potatoes had magically appeared on the Thompson's table. Everyone enjoyed the scrumptious meal and Mrs. Thompson's blueberry pie simply melted in John's mouth.

They sat at the table and talked for a short time after the meal. Samuel told John about farming and John told them about the canal and how it would financially improve business in the Liverpool area.

A short time later, Mrs. Thompson told the young couple to go for a stroll while she cleaned up the remnants of the meal. She refused Patricia's offer of help and Patricia didn't protest, as she was mesmerized by John and looked forward to spending a few minutes alone with this interesting man. The Thompsons could see that their daughter was indeed captivated by this handsome young man.

After a few exchanges of formalities Patricia led John to a bench swing suspended beneath a large oak tree beside a small pond. Mr. Thompson sat on the porch a short distance away from the couple dozing, seeming to ignore them. John and Patricia spent the afternoon quietly watching the ducks and geese play in the cool waters of the pond.

John sang a few love songs to her, but mostly the couple just enjoyed each other's company. John boldly touched her hand several times with little or no objection from Patricia. He thrilled at the softness of her skin. Patricia felt little goose bumps rise on her arm and the small hairs on the back of her neck tingle in excitement with each touch. Little was said until late in the afternoon when John told Patricia that he must head back to town.

Mrs. Thompson came out on the porch as John approached the house. "I'd like to thank you for such a delicious meal, Mrs.

Thompson. That was the best food I have had in years. It truly reminded me so much of my dear mother's cooking."

"Oh, the pleasure was all mine," she responded almost with a giggle.

"Mr. Thompson, I'd like permission to call on your daughter," John spoke with hope of a promising response.

Samuel replied, "I'd be honored if you would, Mr. Doyle."

"John, please," John smiled as he responded. "Please call me John."

As he went out the gate, John waved to Patricia. She gave him a big smile and her cheeks flushed once again. John now knew her heart belonged to him. He floated on a cloud the entire way back to Liverpool.

The middle of October of 1827 the first construction crews arrived in town. The project foreman, Mike Quinn, quickly got his men settled in a nearby tavern and immediately began making preparations to build a cabin on canal property to lodge the workers. John was busy farther north when the crew arrived, but Mike was a very accomplished supervisor who got things done. He was firm, but his men liked his impartial method of supervision.

Mr. Guilford arrived in Liverpool the same day John returned from his trip to Port Trevorton, 14 miles north of town. There had been a question about the location of the lock there, but John reserved judgment until the engineers reviewed the surveyors' plans. The next day Mr. Guilford departed to that location to oversee the layout himself while John headed seven miles south to New Buffalo to be certain that the digging began on time at that lock. Both men were kept very busy during the winter of 1827.

Fall and early winter brought a whirlwind romance for John and Patricia. John showed up at the Thompson farm almost every Sunday to visit his newfound love. He began riding his horse so he could spend more time there. He was not only enjoying Patricia's company, but also her mother's home cooking.

On Sundays when Father Barrett arrived in Liverpool to hold Mass, the Thompsons came to town. After they attended Mass together, John would fix them something to eat at his cottage. Compared to Mrs. Thompson's cooking, it was meager fare, but they all enjoyed the meal. After dinner John would take the family on a tour of the canal, proudly showing off the work that was completed since they were last in town.

While canal work did not attract the best mannered of men, they were indeed welcomed by the population of Liverpool, as the canal would bring even greater prosperity to their small town. The workers would be missing their families during this holiday, so the townspeople did what they could to make the men feel at home. On Christmas Eve, the town held a party for the canal workers. Mike was pleased that his men, for the most part, behaved in a gentleman-like fashion. It was a pleasant evening for all that attended.

On Christmas Day, John arrived at the Thompson farm with handcrafted gifts for everyone. He had worked feverishly the past month creating his masterpieces. John presented Mr. Thompson with a pipe and tobacco stand that he had designed with a pinecone carved onto the sides. For Mrs. Thompson John made a blanket chest with a delicate filigree carved into the lid. And John had created a small chest for on top of Patricia's dressing table, to which he had intricately carved vines of violets, Patricia's favorite flower. Everyone was quite pleased with the gifts that John had created.

But for Patricia, John had the biggest gift of all; John asked Mr. Thompson's permission to marry his daughter. He received an overwhelming approval from both parents, as well as Patricia.

In spite of the fact that John was ten years older than Patricia, the Thompsons were pleased that their daughter would marry. At twenty-two, they were beginning to worry that she might become an old maid. Patricia had shown no interest in any suitor her own age. She simply had no interest in any man until John showed up.

It was a busy Christmas Day as the young couple made wedding plans. The wedding date was set for March 16th, when Father Barrett's schedule would permit him to perform the ceremony. Since there was no Catholic Church near Liverpool, the rites would be held at the Thompson farm. There was much to be done in the meantime. Patricia's mother and aunts would gather and create a wedding dress for her. The entire family thrilled at the thought of the upcoming event. Little Patricia would finally marry.

Digging began at Liverpool the day after Christmas. Once their work was completed, the surveyors returned to Lancaster. However, several of Mr. Guilford's engineers remained on hand to explain the location of the survey markers to John and Mike Quinn. Mike would be responsible for the digging and John would oversee the construction of the locks. As the digging progressed, rock for lining the canal was hauled from Girty's Notch near Mt. Patrick. At Girty's Notch, the canal was being cut through solid rock, rock that would be used to line the sides and bottom of the locks at both Liverpool and New Buffalo.

In the evenings John was busy rearranging his bachelor's house on Locust Street to accommodate his new bride. He would move Patricia there immediately after the wedding. He sold the single bed he had built and created a new rope bed with a violet design carved into the headboard. As the months passed slowly by, he also created several more pieces of furniture with Patricia's favorite design. But, he didn't tell her or the Thompsons about his endeavor, as he wanted to surprise Patricia.

On January 9, 1828 disaster struck the construction site. While digging the southern most Liverpool lock, a collapse of the rain-softened ground trapped Nicholas Madden beneath tons of mud. The men dug frantically, but by the time they reached Nick, he was dead. It was a shock to the entire crew.

John discovered that Liverpool Cemetery was non-denominational and thought that Nick deserved to be interred in blessed Catholic soil. He immediately went to Mr. Huggins's office requesting information on a plot of land that could be purchased for this purpose. Mr. Huggins owned a large lot beside the town cemetery and would be willing to donate the land to the Catholic Church. He and John walked the few blocks to the lot. Once John saw the location, he liked the idea. The Catholic Cemetery would look down over the town and the Susquehanna River Valley.

'Digger' O'Dell, the local undertaker, buried Nicholas Madden the following morning in the new cemetery. A week later, Father Barrett arrived in Liverpool to bless and dedicate the cemetery and also hold a funeral Mass for Nick.

A week after Father Barrett departed there was another accident. Bill Williams was killed in a similar accident on January 17th. Sadly, Liverpool Catholic Cemetery had its second customer. To John, it seemed unfortunate that 'Digger' might be a busy man during this construction.

By this time there were about 70 men working on the canal at Liverpool. Mike called them all together and urged them to use the utmost caution. Two deaths, eight days apart, was not a good safety record. Mike worried about each and every one of his employees and tried to make the construction site as safe as possible. However, it had been a rainy fall and digging in the soft, wet dirt was very hazardous.

John was sitting in the canal office early in the morning on January 31st when there was a bright flash followed by an explosion that rattled the windows of every house in Liverpool. He rushed outside to see a large cloud of black smoke rise into the steel gray sky south of town.

"What happened?" John asked the first workers he came upon at the digging.

Mike was standing nearby, his face coated black and his clothing lightly charred. "Several men were setting a charge to remove a large boulder when something went wrong," he sputtered. "I don't know how many men were in the ditch when she blew."

Mike turned to another man nearby, "Charlie, get me a check of who is still alive in that crew. Make it quick!"

John and Mike were not too pleased when 'Digger' arrived in his black hearse a short time later. It seemed to many of the workers that he could sense an impending death. None of the men liked giving the undertaker any more business than was necessary. The workers, while extremely stressed, wryly joked that business was certainly good for 'Digger.'

John's report to Mr. Mifflin in Lancaster sadly stated that Thomas Gannon, George Donoghou, and two men only known by their nicknames, Hawk and Pat, died that day. Many men working on the project only went by nicknames for one reason or another. And it was unfortunate, as the families of these two workers would never know what became of their loved ones. They were buried in the Catholic Cemetery because they were known to attend Mass, but no funeral Mass was held for them.

John's report stated that the men had drilled several holes into the huge boulder and were pouring gunpowder from a ten-pound keg into the holes. Something had gone terribly wrong and the keg exploded. Two workers, who had been standing above the ditch, had suffered some injury, but were able to return to work the following morning. Mike, who had been standing a short distance away, suffered minor burns on his face.

The middle of February brought illness to many workers. It was suspected that cholera was the cause as the disease was creating havoc throughout central Pennsylvania. Many in the area had contracted the disease and 'Digger' was busy filling the Liverpool Cemetery. John hoped that the Catholic Cemetery would not be used for any victims of the disease. Then Edward Nolan and John Hays fell ill. 'Digger' took Edward Nolan to the Catholic Cemetery on the 29th and returned for John Hays just a week later. In Mike's opinion the Catholic Cemetery was receiving far too many of his workers.

Three more men died of cholera in March. Again they were only known by their nicknames, but had attended Mass. Thus, 'Digger' buried them in the Catholic Cemetery. Father Barrett was concerned about their souls and the loved ones they left behind, but his hands were tied by Canon Law. They did not receive funeral Masses.

Near the end of March Father Barrett announced that the number of funerals he conducted within his circuit were becoming less and less. Throughout the Susquehanna River Valley the feeling was that the cholera epidemic was ending. Many parents were relieved, as the epidemic had taken the lives of far too many babies and young children.

March 16th turned out to be a very cold, snowy day, but no one would be deterred by the weather. Many relatives arrived at the Thompson farm by horse drawn sled from many miles away. Father Barrett and John had ridden together on their horses from Liverpool. The Thompson's friends and relatives were pleased to see the priest arrive, as there was much concern that the weather might cause him to be delayed.

Most of the furniture had been removed from the downstairs of the small farmhouse and stored in the barn for the occasion. Father Barrett placed his small travel altar on a narrow table in the parlor and all waited for the bride to descend the stairs. John and Father Barrett stood by the altar waiting patiently for Patricia.

All eyes turned toward the stairs as the bride came down the steps on her father's arm. One of her uncles had brought his violin and played softly as she neared the makeshift altar. Patricia's mother and aunts had spared no detail in her white wedding dress. The women had embroidered dainty violets on the ends of the sleeves and collar of her gown. Patricia wore a gauzy veil that failed to hide her sparkling eyes. John's breath was taken away by the loveliness of his exquisite bride. His heart pounded so hard he was certain that everyone in the room could hear.

Samuel guided Patricia to the altar and placed her small hand into John's large strong hand. The young lovers didn't realize the Mass was over until they heard Father Barrett announce, "I'd like to introduce Mr. and Mrs. John Doyle." Everyone in attendance applauded with glee for the newlyweds.

Hot rum punch and fresh baked cookies were on hand for the attendees, however Father Barrett had to depart immediately for town. The storm wasn't lessening and he had other obligations that evening. Gradually, the friends and relatives loaded themselves into their sleds and the sounds of sleigh bells were heard jingling as they headed out into the storm for their individual farms.

Samuel knew that some of the mischievous young men were planning a shivaree for John and Patricia. When the newlyweds had gone to Patricia's room to change their clothing, Samuel went to the barn and brought John's horse underneath Patricia's window. He quickly reentered the house and quietly ascended the stairway. He tapped on her door and advised the young couple of the planned prank, explaining that John's horse waited beneath the back porch roof for them.

John and Patricia quietly climbed out her window and onto the porch roof. John dropped down onto his saddle and caught Patricia in his arms as she slid off the roof. He quickly turned his horse and rode out the back gate of the house before the revelers knew what was happening. The newlyweds headed out into the snowy afternoon for Liverpool.

Rather than risking pranksters that may lay in wait at his house, John had made arrangements to spend their first night together at the boarding house run by Mrs. Gensler in the center of Liverpool. In a heavy snow, they approached town on Chestnut Street from the south. John quickly hid his horse in Mrs. Gensler's barn and the newlywed's deception was complete.

As John carried his bride across the threshold of their room, they were pleased to discover that Mrs. Gensler had prepared a meal for them, along with a bottle of wine, which she had placed on a small table by their front window. John swept his tiny bride into his strong arms and the world belonged to them.

The next day their little cottage was filled with love as they moved into their first home. Patricia was excited about all the preparations John had made. She loved each and every little detail of the house that John had readied for her. She marveled at the furniture that he had crafted. Patricia was deeply in love with John and their home.

John returned to work the following Monday and Patricia began her life as a wife. There were curtains to be hung on the windows and carpets for the floors. Details that a bachelor didn't concern himself with. Patricia stood at the door at the end of each day waiting to throw her arms around John the minute he came home from work. As time passed, their love and passion for each other deepened.

A bitterly cold, rainy morning in early April found John at the northern end of Liverpool examining the final stages of the lock. The men had finished lining the walls of the lock with heavy stone. He looked on as a dozen men placed the stone floor in the bottom of the lock. Suddenly there was a loud rumbling. It seemed to come from a temporary dam a hundred feet away. The dam kept the icy waters of the Susquehanna River out of the canal ditch while it was under construction. Everyone stopped to look, but the rumbling stopped and all was silent. The men continued working on the floor.

Then suddenly, with an explosion, the dam collapsed. Thick muddy water and chunks of ice poured into the ditch and headed straight for the workers in the lock. Most of them managed to jump out of the way, but three were caught in the onslaught. Workers at the top of the wall grabbed two of the men by their coats and pulled them to safety, but a third man's feet were pinned to the floor of the lock by the deepening mud. He struggled frantically to free himself. The water had reached his chest and was still rapidly rising. In horrified shock, he realized that he was only seconds from death. With a desperate plea for help on his face he looked up at the men standing above him on the wall of the canal.

Without hesitation, John took a deep breath and jumped into the icy water. He dove down to the muddy bottom and with his bare hands, furiously dug into the foot deep mud pulling at the man's legs. Finally one foot freed. John was almost out of air as the man's second leg pulled loose. John reached the surface gasping for air. The workers on the bank quickly pulled the two men out of the lock. A few more seconds and the trapped man would have drowned in the six-foot deep waters of the lock.

John awoke several days later. It was nighttime. A single lantern revealed that he was in the company cabin wrapped in a multitude of blankets. He felt strange, as he had no feeling in his body. It was as if he was floating above the cot.

As he slowly became more aware of his surroundings he saw Patricia asleep in a chair at the foot of his bed. Her sweet face looked exhausted and ashen. Her beautiful hair hung down uncombed like snarled, matted ropes. John was confused, but dozed off again into blissful oblivion.

When he awoke again, a man was changing his blankets. He knew the man, but couldn't think of his name. He spoke to John, but his words didn't make sense. The man called out behind him and suddenly Patricia was there by his side. She wept openly as she hugged John tightly. John was thoroughly confused. What was wrong? Why was Patricia crying? He drifted slowly into unconsciousness once again.

John was lying back against a tree enjoying the warm summer sun as he watched the sheep that grazed about him. He watched the leaves on the large tree limbs as they swayed in the afternoon breeze. He was suddenly troubled by something tugging at his sleeve. Was it one of the sheep nibbling on his wool jacket? He tried to shake the nuisance away.

"John, John!" The voice demanded. He struggled to awaken. Then he became aware that the voice he heard in the distance was Patricia. "John, please. Oh, John come back to me," she begged. The words were spoken in fear and frustration.

Slowly John became aware of his surroundings. Several people were in the room. Then he recognized that he was in the bedroom he and Patricia shared. A friendly face came near him and said, "John, you have to wake up. You must fight this fever."

He knew that face. Why it was Dr. Armstrong. What was he doing here? Patricia stood on the other side of the bed grasping John's hand, afraid to let go.

"Talk to him, Patricia," Dr. Armstrong was saying. "You've got to bring him out of this. Try to get John to understand he must wake up."

John looked at Patricia. Tears streamed down her soft, white cheeks. She looked terrible. What had happened to her? Who had made his beautiful wife cry?

"Patricia," he spoke. But his words jumbled and he had to strain to make the sounds. "What's wrong with you, Patricia? Are you alright?" John tried to sit up, but had no strength to do so. Dr. Armstrong put his arm around his shoulders and helped him sit up in bed.

Patricia laughed with joy and everyone seemed so pleased. There was another man in the room and John knew his face, but couldn't remember his name. The man looked so worried, so concerned. What was wrong with this man?

"What's wrong with everyone?" John asked in a clear voice.

Patricia threw her arms around him and wailed loudly as she released her pent up tension. Dr. Armstrong and the other man shook hands with great glee. John was totally confused. "What's going on?" he murmured.

"John, dear," Patricia asked him through her tears, "do you remember the accident? Oh, my love, you have been so sick. I was so afraid that I had lost you."

"The accident?" John thought for a few moments. Then he began to realize what she spoke of. He remembered that the dam broke and a man was trapped in the water. Why, that was the man who was standing next to Dr. Armstrong. John remembered the look of horror on his face as the water rushed into the canal. He now remembered that he dove into the water, but that was the last thing he remembered.

"John," the man spoke to him as he gently touched his shoulder. "You saved my life. You risked your life and dove into the water and saved me. Do you remember that? Do you remember the accident?"

"Yes," John whispered. "I remember the accident now, but why am I here?"

"You have been in a coma for several weeks, John," Dr. Armstrong was saying. "We didn't think we could save you. You certainly gave Patricia a scare!"

John looked at Patricia, who now sat on the edge of their bed. She held his hand tightly to her lips, kissing him gently. She looked exhausted and emotionally spent. John took her into his arms and held her tightly as she wept uncontrollably.

"Am I alright now, Doctor?" John asked.

"Well, John," Dr. Armstrong replied somberly, "You have lost a lot of strength these past weeks. It will take months to recover your health. I'm afraid that you'll be out of work for sometime to come. I wish I could offer a better outlook, but the important thing is that you're finally rid of the fever. Patricia is the best medicine for you now. She has been at your side these many weeks and wouldn't leave you for a moment."

Dr. Armstrong and Patrick Hurley left the couple alone. John just sat holding Patricia for a long, long time. Not a word was said. The love they shared at that moment was enough; words couldn't express the depth of their love any more than just holding tightly on to one another.

The recuperation was indeed slow. John couldn't believe how weak he was as he had always been a powerful man. He was worried. He and Patricia needed an income. The canal company had no interest in him once he could no longer work.

Another worry for Dr. Armstrong and Patricia was that John had lost large portions of his memory. He did not recognize some of his friends and had forgotten the names of other friends. Many memories from his past were lost forever.

To keep busy and create some income, John began making a few pieces of furniture to sell. His hands seemed to work magic with a knife and chisel, but he couldn't remember where he learned the trade. Mysteriously, it seemed, the craft simply arose from a misty past.

A few weeks after he awoke from his coma, John was sitting on a bench in front of their cottage when Mr. Huggins came up the street. "John, I'm so glad to see you are able to get outside. You had the entire town worried. You were unconscious for a long time. How are you feeling?"

The two men sat and visited for a long time. But, before departing, Mr. Huggins made John a proposition. He owned an inn at the north end of town and needed a couple to operate the business. Mr. Huggins offered the position to John and Patricia. Without hesitation, they eagerly accepted his offer.

They moved their belongings from their rental cottage on Locust Street to the pub on a warm spring day in mid May. The newlyweds were very pleased with their stroke of fortune and Patricia blossomed as she watched John grow stronger every day. While John still struggled to recall memories from his past, he seemed to be well on the road to recovery and growing stronger every day.

On Friday and Saturday nights John sang and played his guitar at the inn. From the songs, and his accent, he realized that he must be from Ireland, as Patricia had told him, but remembered little else of his homeland. He drew quite a crowd from all along the river. In a short time, a group of friends brought their instruments and joined John in providing the entertainment. The inn soon became a popular place with its lively music, and Saturday night dances were a regular event. Life was good again.

One evening, in the middle of September, sad news arrived at John's inn. Mike Quinn was dead. He was one of the few friends from John's past that he remembered. He was told that his friend was trying to break up a fight between two workers. Knives were drawn and Mike tried to intercede before the fight became deadly. He was stabbed by one of the workers as the man lunged at his opponent. The man hadn't meant to stab Mike, but unfortunately, he was the one who received the fatal wound. He was dead before Dr. Armstrong could arrive. John was despondent for days over the loss of his good friend.

Conclusion

Winter arrived early in 1828. A cold, bone-chilling wind passed harshly through the Susquehanna Valley. The river froze over earlier than usual. Many farmers lost livestock to the bitter freeze.

John came down with a bad cold early in November. Within a few days, Dr. Armstrong worried that John had contracted pneumonia. By the end of the first week of November John was so sick that he slipped into a coma once again. Nothing Patricia or Dr. Armstrong could do seemed to help.

On November 17th John passed away while Patricia sat by his bedside holding his hand. John Doyle was buried in the Catholic Cemetery the next day.

Summer, ten years later, a pale green cargo wagon with a white canvas cover creaked as it slowly headed toward the hills west of Liverpool. Constable Deckard urged the two dapple-gray horses along the rutted road taking his wife and Mary Doyle to the Thompson farm five miles to the west on Toad Hollow Road. It was a hot August day so the horses moved slowly down the dusty lane. Mary marveled at the many farms along the road. She had expected Liverpool to be a small village lost in the forests of central Pennsylvania, but she was discovering that this was a thriving agricultural valley hidden between two high ridges of the Blue Mountains.

The morning air was warm, but crisp and bright without a single cloud in the sky. Individual trees on the distant mountains were clear and distinct in the lush green canopy. Cows, cattle and horses grazed casually as far as the eye could see. White dots on some of the higher hills revealed a few sheep grazing contentedly. Cornfields were full and begging to be harvested. Some farmers were already cutting the fields of golden wheat and green alfalfa to be stored in their barns for livestock fodder during the upcoming winter. Here and there small farmhouses and large red barns dotted the landscape. Yes, Mary told herself, this was a thriving farm community.

Mary had awakened early as the first light of the day rose over the mountain on the far side of the Susquehanna River. By the time the sun had peeked into the window of her room at Mrs. Gensler's Boarding House, Mary was dressed and ready to partake of the delightful smells of breakfast emanating from the kitchen below. The aroma of fresh baked bread permeated her room as she opened the door into the hallway and the heavenly fragrance of frying bacon wasn't far behind. The aroma of the baked bread reminded Mary of her family far, far away, back home in Ireland. She could almost envision her mother baking bread on the hearth in their little cottage.

She arrived at the long breakfast table to discover several hotel guests already there enjoying a scrumptious breakfast. Mrs. Gensler was hustling around making sure everyone had hot coffee and plenty of food. Mary quickly discovered that Pennsylvania housekeepers were very generous with their portions and took great joy when a big appetite appreciated their foods.

The talk of the morning was about the wondrous crops the local farmers were reaping. It had been a perfect spring and summer for farming. Many of the canal boats were heading south burdened down with an unusually large portion of this years bountiful harvest to feed those in the towns and cities along the river.

Mary settled in at the table and chose hot tea to enjoy with her breakfast. Mrs. Gensler placed a hot plate before her piled with bacon, hot cakes, fried potatoes, and fried eggs. "Oh, my." Protested Mary. "I'll never be able to eat so much food!"

All at the table chuckled at the slender young woman's remark. "We have to build you up, Miss Doyle," replied Mrs. Gensler as she set down another plate with two thick slices of homemade bread. "Such a thin thing as you needs a big meal. Are you off to the Thompson farm this morning?" Without waiting for an answer she placed a jar of strawberry preserves on the table in front of Mary and then scurried off to serve another guest a similar plate filled with delightful morsels.

"Oh, yes," Mary enthusiastically replied over the clatter of plates. "Mr. and Mrs. Deckard said they'd be along early to take me there. I am so looking forward to the trip."

"Well, it will be quite a surprise for your brother's wife and son." Mrs. Gensler responded. "I don't think they have received word yet that you are on the way."

That astonished Mary for it seemed by now everyone in Liverpool knew of her visit and the circumstance that brought her there. Everyone in town was being so kind and considerate to Mary. They worried over her and watched out for her well being. Small towns are that way, Mary thought to herself. Everyone is always interested in what someone else in town is doing. It certainly wasn't that way in New York City where people went on their way without much thought of those around them. Mary liked the small town way of life much better, but for the time being she would have to continue to earn her livelihood as a maid in the big city.

Mrs. Gensler disappeared into her kitchen and the talk around the table returned to farming and the cornucopia of foods available on Mrs. Gensler's breakfast table.

Shortly thereafter the Deckard's arrived to gather up Mary for the five-mile trip west. As Mary started out the door, Mrs. Gensler gave her a bouquet of flowers to place upon her brother's grave as they passed the Catholic Cemetery.

Mary's thoughts of the early morning activities were brought back to the present when the farm wagon bounced harshly in a deep hole along the dusty road. "Would you bounce us out on our heads?" Mrs. Deckard jokingly asked of her husband. All three laughed at the comical way they all were jostled in the air from the bump.

Coming down the road from the other direction, a man on horseback tipped the brim of his hat as he passed the wagon. The Deckard's greeted him warmly as he passed. Mary noted the very dark complexion of his skin and the straight black hair. He wore beads around his neck and a large feather stuck out from the beaded hatband on his black felt hat. He wore a large pistol in a black holster on his hip. Mary watched him with deep interest as he passed by.

"That's Captain John," Mr. Deckard spoke up, noting Mary's interest. "He's the head of the local Indian police. Most of the Indians live near Loysville at Cisna's Run."

"Oh, my," Mary remarked. "I've never seen an Indian before. Are they hostile?"

Both the Deckard's chuckled. "No, Mary," Mrs. Deckard answered. "Our local Indians are very peaceful. They are great hunters and trappers. The furs they trade are of the best quality and so very soft. I wouldn't want to spend a winter here without a nice warm fur wrapped around my shoulders."

"There are hostile Indians further to the west," Mr. Deckard added. "Every once in a while we hear of Indian troubles, but not near here. A few local farms in our valley are owned by Indians and they are respectable members of the community."

After an hour in the summer heat Mr. Deckard stopped the wagon beside a small stream to rest and water his team of horses. Mrs. Deckard spread a blanket out on the ground in the shade of a large elm tree and opened a picnic basket. She set out bread and a jar of her strawberry preserves then opened a bottle of wine. Mary sat on the blanket sipping her wine and simply enjoyed the moment. She felt too full from the enormous breakfast that had been served at Mrs. Gensler's place to eat a bite.

The air was sweet with the mixed smells of wild flowers and newly cut alfalfa. Bees buzzed all around them busily collecting honey.

Melodious songbirds enhanced the surroundings taking Mary back to her home far across the Atlantic sea; back to her home in Ballylee. For a moment she was there in her mother's arms. A tear gently trickled down her cheek as she fondly remembered the good times at home with her family.

"You mustn't feel so bad about your brother." Mrs. Deckard said not realizing what thoughts were actually passing through Mary's mind.

Brought back to the present, Mary responded, "I wish I could have know him. I was still a babe in swaddling when he left home. I have read his letters over and over, but just could never picture him in my mind. I think that when I do imagine my brother I see my father, as he would have looked when he was younger. But John's face is still a mystery for me."

Mr. Deckard strolled over and sat on the blanket with the ladies. He accepted a cup of wine from his wife. She spread strawberry preserves on a slice of bread and handed it to him. As he nibbled on the bread, he spoke to Mary. "I did look in the town records for any information on your brother, but there wasn't much recorded." He stopped to shoo away a bee that was taking delight in the slice of bread in his hand and then went on, "There is a listing of his marriage to Patricia Thompson of Perry County on March 16, 1828."

He paused as the Deckards waved to a buggy passing by on the road and salutations were exchanged as it continued down the dusty road. Constable Deckard continued, "Your brother's death is recorded as happening on November 17, the same year, but there is no mention of the cause of death. It is also recorded that Patricia and John had a son, Andrew John Doyle, born on June 20, 1829. That would make Andrew nine years of age now.

"My wife told me that Mr. Perkins at the cemetery told you of the circumstance of your brother's passing as he knows it. We had a fire in town several years ago and many records were destroyed or damaged. Unfortunately, that's all I can help you with. I'm sorry that I don't have more information for you."

Mary smiled as she dabbed at her tears, "But you and Mrs. Deckard have revealed so much! I can't begin to tell you how pleased that I am to know that my brother married and had a child. I can't wait to meet them."

"Then let's be on our way, David," Mrs. Deckard gleefully spoke as she jumped up and began to gather the picnic leftovers. "Mary Doyle is on her way to a most wondrous reunion!"

It was another mile before the Thompson farm came into sight. Mr. Deckard saw a man working in a field of straw away from the house, which lay in the distance beside a small pond. There wasn't another soul in sight at the small farm and Mary hoped that their journey hadn't been in vain. Someone just has to be home, she thought to herself.

Mr. Deckard stopped the team by the fence. He stood up in the wagon and, cupping his hands, called out to the man in the distance. "Samuel! Come and meet someone special I know you'll want to be acquainted with!"

Mr. Thompson stuck his pitchfork into the pile of straw he was raking and strolled over to the split rail fence as he removed his wide brimmed straw hat. He mopped his brow with a large handkerchief as he asked, "Good morning, Mrs. Deckard. David, what brings you all the way out here?"

The constable turned to Mary and gestured saying, "Samuel, I want to introduce you to Miss Mary Doyle, young Andrew's aunt. She's come all the way from New York City to visit him."

Mr. Thompson's mouth dropped open with the news. In his mind he quickly thought of his daughter's short marriage, the accidental death of his new son-in-law, and the arrival of his grandson the following summer. He and his wife never realized that John had any relatives in this country. They were only aware that he had come from Ireland and they didn't have any details about his family. The short time they knew him, John hadn't mentioned any kinfolk.

"Oh, glory be to God," he stammered. "Come, come quickly to the house. What a glorious day this will be for Patricia and Andrew."

His horse was tethered to the fence nearby in the shade of a large chestnut tree. Samuel quickly climbed on his horse and joyously led the farm wagon up the hill to the farmhouse. When they came within earshot of the white farmhouse he called out, "Patricia, Andrew! Come quickly! Come quickly!"

A petite young woman, with concern on her face, emerged from the small white farmhouse drying her hands on her apron. She looked at the wagon approaching and wondered what all the commotion was about. Her father quickly dismounted and tied his horse to the hitching rail just outside the picket fence. He rushed inside the gate and took her arm. Gently escorting her down the porch steps he walked her to the wagon that was just now arriving in front of the farmhouse. He was full of excitement and smiling from ear to ear, which caused the young woman to be slightly hesitant.

As the Deckard's wagon stopped, Mary studied the woman as she was guided across the front yard of the farmhouse. Mary saw she was quite comely and about five or six years older than herself. The woman had very dark brown hair with eyes as green as the sea. Deeply tanned skin told of the many hours spent in the field working the family farm. She held herself proudly erect with poise.

An older woman followed her out the door and hastily descended the few porch steps to the front yard. Just as the swirl of dust from the wagon settled to the ground, a young boy came running from behind the farmhouse, a yipping puppy close at his heels. Mary saw he had blond hair and blue eyes, a Doyle family trait. He quickly hid behind his grandmother. Putting his arms around her waist he stood there peeking shyly from behind his protector at this stranger.

Mary was stunned with the Doyle family resemblance. There was no doubt in her mind that this was her brother's child. Mary and this child had the same deep blue eyes and blond hair. He looked so much like her brothers and sisters that Mary's breath was almost taken away.

"What's all the commotion, Samuel?" Mrs. Thompson asked her husband as she broke the stunned silence, quickly adding, "Hello,

Constable and Mrs. Deckard. Welcome to our home." She looked at Mary with curiosity, startled at the similarity between this woman and her grandson. "And who do we have here?"

Mr. Thompson went to the wagon and helped Mary down from the high seat. With an enormous grin he said, "Mother, Patricia...I want you to meet Miss Mary Doyle, John's sister, come all the way from New York City!"

Both women were stunned into silence. After a moment or two Patricia dashed to Mary and threw her arms around her. They hugged tightly and cried with joy. Mrs. Thompson tearfully went to the two women and hugged them both as the three regaled in this moment of bliss. Mrs. Deckard, still sitting on the wagon, wiped a tear of happiness from her eye as well. Long moments passed before anyone could speak.

Young Andrew stood inquisitively a few feet away not fully understanding what all this commotion was about. His mother broke free from the embrace and turned to him, "Andrew, this is your father's sister. Oh, darling, you never knew your father so I'm sure you don't understand all this. I have missed your father so much."

Mary dried her eyes and held her hand out to the young man. She softly said, "It's a pleasure to meet you, Andrew." She envisioned this young lad being exactly what her brother had looked like in his younger years. Her deepest fantasies of seeing her brother were answered as she laid eyes on the handsome face of his son.

Andrew stood quietly for a moment bewildered by this reunion. This was all so strange for him. He thought back over the many years of his young life when his mother had told him stories about his father. Quite often she sat by his side, holding him in her arms, and told him how much she had loved his father. He had heard about the day his father had the fatal accident and about his mother sitting by his father's side the last few days of his life, holding his hand, watching him slowly slip away. While Andrew never met his father, he loved him and missed him from the stories he had heard from many people who did know him.

Long moments passed as Andrew tried to understand what was going on. Finally his grandfather spoke. "Andrew", his grandfather said softly, "say 'Hello' to your Aunt Mary."

Andrew ran to her and threw himself into Mary's arms hugging her tightly. He clutched her as if he was holding the father he yearned for. There wasn't a dry eye on the Thompson farm during the wondrous reunion. Even the tough ol' constable swabbed away a tear or two.

Once composure returned to the assembled group, Mrs. Thompson told everyone to come into the sitting room for tea. Mary and Patricia held each other's arm tightly as they sat on the old, horsehair settee while Mrs. Thompson served the tea. They were like old school friends reunited after many, many years. There was so much to say and hear, but the moment was held so precious that no one dared to speak.

Andrew sat closely beside his Aunt Mary. She put her arm around him and hugged him closely. Andrew broke the silence first by asking, "Did you come all the way from New York City just to see me?"

Everyone laughed and the ladies all had to wipe away tears of elation once again.

Mary kissed him on the forehead and spoke softly, "Well, Andrew, I really came to visit my brother's gravesite. You see we never knew that your father had married or that you were born. You can't imagine what joy there will be back in Ireland when I write and tell the family the wonderful news. Your Grandfather and Grandmother Doyle will be so pleased. They thought that they lost a son, but they now have a fine grandson to hold dear in their hearts. Oh, will they celebrate back home!"

Mary squeezed him tighter and kissed his cheek. "Why you have cousins, aunts and uncles both here in this country and in Ireland that will rejoice with the news. Oh, my there is so much to tell you" she hugged him again placing a kiss on his forehead just below his golden bangs. Mary's heart exulted in this moment. It was as if she held her long lost brother in her arms. The brother she had yearned for these many years.

"Mary," Mrs. Thompson interrupted, "you must move from the boarding house in Liverpool and stay with us here on the farm for the remainder of your visit. We all have so much to learn and I am sure you will want to hear all about John and what happened to him since he last wrote back home. It is such a long way in to town. You can sleep in Andrew's bed and he will sleep with us."

"Oh, how wonderful," Mary replied. "I do hope that it's not too much trouble, but there truly is so much to share. I want to spend every moment I can with Andrew." She squeezed Patricia and added, "And I want to learn all I can about my brother."

Mrs. Deckard suggested, "I'll go back to town with Mr. Deckard and explain these events to Mrs. Gensler. I'll pack your bags and have them sent here this afternoon. We'll have them brought by horseback. The wagon is far too slow." She poked her husband in the ribs jokingly.

"Everyone is being so kind," Mary exclaimed. "I don't know how I could ever express my appreciation to everyone."

Mary hugged both the Deckards as they departed and all agreed that since Mr. Thompson was so busy with the harvest season in full swing, the Deckards would return in four days to take Mary back to Liverpool for the packet barge heading south.

The harvesting needed to be done, so Mr. Thompson returned to his field. Mrs. Thompson went back to her canning in the kitchen after reassuring Patricia that her time would be well spent with Andrew and Mary as they shared their memories, thoughts and dreams.

With Andrew in tow, the young women strolled down to the pond and sat on a bench swing suspended from a limb on a huge oak tree. They sat for several minutes watching ducks splash about in the pond as Andrew skipped a few rocks across the water.

"Aunt Mary," Andrew suddenly said with childish glee. "I have something to show you." Without further word, he ran back toward the farmhouse, blond hair trailing behind like the tail of a racehorse.

He quickly disappeared inside returning a few minutes later with something clutched in his hand.

"These were my father's and mother says that now they belong to me." He held out a small leather bag and dropped it into his Aunt Mary's lap. Mary slowly untied the leather strap and looked inside. Three British coins were in the bag. Mary was confused.

"John told me that his mother gave those to him the day he departed Ireland," Patricia explained. "They meant more to him than life itself over the years as those coins were the only thing John had from home. He told me that all through his travels he kept them close to his heart. When Andrew was born I decided that he should have them to remind him of his father."

She quietly added, "You see, at the time of John's death, neither of us knew that I was with child. As John weakened he told me to safeguard his coins so I would always remember him and his home in Ireland. John never knew he had a son. When Andrew was born I decided that he should have his father's legacy."

"I'll keep them forever!" Andrew announced proudly.

Mary smiled at the boy. "In my next letter I will tell your Grandmother Doyle that very thing. She will be so proud of you!"

Andrew tightly tied the leather bag closed and ran to the farmhouse to return his treasure to its safe hiding place.

"Patricia," Mary solemnly asked, "tell me about John's death."

"Well, I was at our cottage on Locust Street when there was a commotion out on the street. I rushed outside where I heard that there had been an accident at the lock that the men were constructing. By the time I reached the canal site, John and several others were lying on the ground beside the lock. It was full of water…and it shouldn't have been so. John was covered with mud and soaked through and through. Someone rushed up with blankets and quickly covered the men, but it was a very cold, snowy morning in early April.

"The other workmen took the drenched men into the company log cabin and got a big fire going in the fireplace. Most of the men recuperated that very day, but John seemed to go down hill. When he didn't get better, Doctor Armstrong suspected that he had contracted Cholera. There was an epidemic going around in some parts of the valley. No one was allowed in to see John except the man he saved and myself.

"This man, Patrick, had been trapped in the mud at the bottom of the canal and couldn't free himself. John was in charge of the construction and couldn't let something happen to one of his men. I was told that he risked his life jumping back into the canal lock to save this man as the water and mud rushed in. Patrick was so thankful for his life that he wouldn't leave John's side. He was ordered back to work, but he stayed with us doing whatever he could to make John better. He kept a huge fire going and took care of our every need. John was constantly slipping in and out of a coma the first week, but kept forgiving this man whenever he was awake. Patrick just cried so.

"John finally regained some strength and the following week I was allowed to take him to our cottage and care for him. He was still so very weak and the accident had stripped him of many memories. I was frightened at first that he may not remember me." Patricia dabbed at her eyes as she remembered the events of ten years earlier. "Patrick stuck by us and any time he wasn't at work at the lock, he came to our cottage and did all sorts of tasks John could no longer do."

"John could no longer work for the canal and that meant no income for us. John had met a wealthy landowner, Mr. John Huggins, when he first moved into town. Mr. Huggins stepped in and helped us. He saw to it that food was sent from his store for our kitchen during April and May.

"When Mr. Huggins was told by Doctor Armstrong that John would never be able to work for the canal again, he arranged for John to rent an inn he owned on Front Street. We moved from our cottage to the inn late in May. Oh, we had such wonderful support from all the townspeople. There were many inns in town, but John drew the travelers into our pub almost every night with his singing. It was strange, he could remember the words to many, many songs, but he couldn't remember anything beyond a few years. I tried to ask him about his family in Ireland, but those memories were gone forever.

"Well, a group of the men from the canal got together and formed a small band and they played almost every Saturday night. We had wonderful dances on those nights. The entire downstairs of the inn was used for the dancing." She gave a slight smile remembering the good times.

"When John was the supervisor of the lock construction, he became busy with the social activities of the town. Mr. Huggins was very interested in helping the citizens of the town develop the town into a fashionable community. He felt that Liverpool would certainly grow with the arrival of the canal system. John had worked with Mr. Huggins on some of the projects around the town over the previous year and even persuaded Mr. Huggins to donate a parcel of land to the Catholic Church for a cemetery on the hill overlooking the town, right beside the town cemetery." Patricia bit her lower lip as she added, "Little did John know that he would soon be interred in that very plot of land.

"Fall of that year brought very cold weather with terrible snow and wind. John began to weaken. His fevers returned during the night and he would often awaken in cold sweats. Doctor Armstrong did what he could, but by early November John could no longer rise from our bed. The doctor couldn't understand what his malady was, but suspected it could be pneumonia or Cholera. He ordered our inn closed and no one was allowed to visit us while John was sick once again. Father Barrett was in town the week before John's death and performed the last rites for him.

"With the inn closed, we were once again without any income. Things seemed so bleak, but Mr. Huggins stuck by us and was so understanding through all this."

Patricia wiped a tear as she added, "I was holding John's hand when he died early in the evening on November 17. They buried him the next morning."

Mary put her arm around Patricia and held her close. Both women wept quietly. Nothing on earth could have bonded these two women more closely together than the emotion of the tragic loss they shared.

The women wiped away their tears as Patricia went on, "That day Patrick packed his bag and disappeared. He didn't come to John's funeral. Patrick had left town by then and no one has heard from him since.

"I know he was full of guilt. Perhaps, at the moment of John's death, I should not have blamed Patrick for the loss of my husband, but it was a terrible time for me. I lashed out at Patrick and screamed while I pounded my fists on his chest. I felt so sorry for the man afterward, but I had just lost my husband and had reached the depths of despair." Patricia put her head in her hands and sobbed. Mary gently rubbed Patricia's shoulders in supportive understanding.

Patricia paused to regain her composure, and then continued. "I returned to my parent's farm after the funeral. There was no reason for me to stay in town. It was two months later that I actually realized that I was with child. I was so confused back then. I had lost my husband, but still I carried a part of him within me. My parents were so very tender and understanding through it all. They helped me through my depression and soon had me looking forward to the birth of my baby. They never gave me any need for concern. I was assured that they would always be there for me.

"Since his birth his grandparents have loved Andrew as much as I love him. To me he is a large part of John. He looks so much like his father," Patricia smiled as she watched Andrew playing with his puppy down by the pond.

"And," she smiled as she added; "Andrew has the voice of an angel when he sings. His father sang all the time. He loved to sing and sang to me often during our short time together. No man could ever replace him.

"I have always wanted to send a letter to John's family in Ireland, but our time together was so short that he never told me his parents names or where they lived." She paused in retrospect, "Or, if he had, I'd forgotten. My head was spinning with my love for John. We had such a whirlwind courtship. I only knew John was from the north of Ireland.

"Our wedding license doesn't show our parents names. A few years after John's death someone suggested using our marriage registration to obtain his parents' names, but an unfortunate fire destroyed many records at the registrar's office several months after we were married. I also inquired at the Canal Office, but they had no listing for a next of kin. He hadn't even had time to record my name as his next of kin."

After a pause, Mary told Patricia, "My family was so concerned about John's death and not knowing the cause of it. You see my three older brothers have been lost to the family. Kevin, my parent's second son, was kidnapped on the streets of Belfast two years after John left home for America. He hasn't been heard from since that day."

"How awful for your family," Patricia responded.

"Then there was Michael, my parents third son. He departed for America a year after Kevin disappeared and we haven't heard from him since. We know he reached Baltimore, as father's cousin wrote that he had visited him several years after he left home, but nothing has been heard from him since. It has been very hard on mother."

"I can understand your parent's concern, Mary," Patricia replied. "To have three sons lost so far from home would be tragic. I wish I had known your parents names so I could have contacted them when John passed away." After a pause, she added, "Its so sad."

They sat there silently for several minutes watching Andrew playing with his puppy. The boy was full of energy and such a joy to watch at play. Yes, Mary thought, this was indeed John Doyle's son.

"Patricia," Mary asked, "How did you and John meet?"

"My father and I were in Liverpool early in fall for supplies when this brash young man approached me and asked if he could talk to me. Well, I was aghast! My parents had warned me about these Canal men. Why they drink and swear and even spit on the street!" Patricia laughed as she remembered her parent's words.

"But John's voice was soft and pleasant. He wasn't forward at all. I found him handsome and rather interesting. My father returned to the wagon while I was talking with John. Father wasn't pleased, of course, but within a few minutes John's demeanor gave father the assurance that this wasn't one of the canal troublemakers.

"I was surprised when John showed up at our farm the next Sunday. He had walked all the way out here to see me. Mother invited him in for dinner, which was another surprise." Patricia laughed, "I knew then that Mother and Father liked him.

"After lunch John and I sat here on this very swing. It was a warm, fall afternoon. As we sat here, under the watchful eye of my parents on the front porch, he played his guitar and sang songs he learned here and back in Ireland. I was deeply in love with John from that moment on.

"Toward evening John approached my father and asked if he would be permitted to call on me. That impressed Father even though John was much older than me." Patricia chuckled, "Father was beginning to think I would always be an old maid for none of the local men interested me at all. Why my mother even invited John here for our Harvest Meal on Thanksgiving when all our relatives would be visiting." Both women tittered at the thought.

"Well, to make a long story short, John asked my father for my hand in marriage Christmas day. With father's approval John proposed to me in our parlor. We were wed here at our farmhouse on March 16th. We moved to John's cottage, in town, that very day.

"We were so very much in love…and then his untimely death." Tears streamed down her cheeks and Mary sobbed softly with her. Andrew strolled over to them, sat between them and hugged them both. He was his father's son!

After a few minutes, Patricia asked Mary, "Did you know that John almost married once before?"

"Why, yes." Mary replied. "He did write home about a young lady in Virginia."

"Oh, he told me all about Katherine shortly after we met. He thought it better I find out about her from him before someone else told me. John said he was very young and fell in love with her the first time he saw her. It happened about ten years before he met me. They were engaged and were planning their wedding when she died. He said a stray bullet killed her shortly before they were to be married."

"John wrote home about a year after Katherine's death," Mary added. "He had disappeared for a long time and the entire family was so concerned about him."

"He said he was so depressed that he became a hermit. Can you believe that about John?" Patricia laughed as she asked Mary. "He was so friendly with everybody and everybody liked him. It doesn't seem possible that a man like John could live alone like that in the wilderness."

"Did John tell you how he ended up in Liverpool?" Mary asked.

"He had his own carpentry business near Baltimore and was doing quite well for many years. He had heard about opportunities with a new canal system being built in Pennsylvania. John found canals fascinating. There was really no reason for him to stay in Baltimore.

"John made some inquiries and took a job working here in Pennsylvania on the construction of the canal system. John could read and write. They said that was critical for a canal construction supervisor. He understood all kinds of construction.

"He started working near Harrisburg and was there on the planning committee when the canal began. He had moved to Liverpool a year before we met and was overseeing the locks being built on this section. That's when I met him."

"Didn't John tell you about the company he owned in Maryland?" asked Mary.

"Oh, I didn't know he owned a company. He just said that he built and sold some furniture while he lived in Baltimore," Patricia replied.

"Well, my dear, I have a very pleasant surprise for you. The Doyle Cabinetry Company has a factory in Towsontown, Maryland. When the family received word of John's death, my parents inherited the company, as they were his next of kin. Now that we have discovered that John married, the company rightfully belongs to you!"

"I...I don't know what to say," Patricia stammered. "If your parents own the company, how could it possibly belong to me?"

"Yesterday, when I found out that John had married and has a son, I wrote home to tell my parents the good news. I know my parents well and I know that they will insist that the company ownership be transferred to you," Mary excitedly told Patricia.

She continued, "Mr. William Mulholland is the president of the company. He has done wonders for the business. Doyle Cabinetry has over 200 employees. They ship furniture all over the country."

Mary went on, "John sent money back to our parents for years. They bought a lovely cottage and father retired. John was very generous with our parents."

Patricia just sat there with her mouth open not knowing what to say. She and Andrew were just managing to get by as the small farm did not offer that much of an income. Her mind spun with a thousand thoughts.

Mary interrupted her thoughts when she happily added, "Patricia Doyle, your husband left you a wealthy lady!"

The women hugged and cried over this revelation. Patricia just couldn't seem to comprehend it all at once. The two women talked on endlessly for hours. There was so much to say to each other, so much to share.

That evening, after supper, Patricia took Mary to her bedroom and showed her the furniture John had created for her as a wedding gift. Mary daintily traced her fingers over the intricately carved violets on the headboard. Their perfection and the hours it took to create the designs truly demonstrated his love for Patricia. Mary never had imagined her brother being such an artist.

Patricia went to her dresser and emptied the contents of the small wooden chest on top. The box was carved the same violet design as the bedroom furniture. She turned to Mary with tears in her eyes and said, "This was the first thing John made for me. Our first Christmas after we met John gave it to me on Christmas Day. Mary, I want you to have it so you will always have something your brother created."

"Oh, no!" Mary protested. "John made it especially for you. I wouldn't dream...."

"Please," Patricia interrupted, placing the small box in Mary's hands. "You lost your brother a long time before I lost him. I want you to take it with my love. It contains your brother's love and I know he would be pleased that I gave it to you."

Mary held the small box to her heart and with tears in her eyes, responded, "Patricia, I will cherish this forever. Words can never express my gratitude to you for sharing something so very special to your heart."

The days passed far too quickly and the Deckard's returned to gather up Mary for her long voyage home by way of the Pennsylvania Canal to Columbia.

Patricia and Mary parted as the best of friends. Andrew had a new aunt and she a special nephew. Little could any of them suspect that there would not be too many more trips for Mary by canal packet as the railroad began building tracks up the Susquehanna River a few years later bringing the two families closer together. In the near future Mary's six-day trip would take her only two days. She promised to return the following summer and perhaps someday Andrew and his mother could visit her in New York City.

Early one morning in August 1838 Mary started home from Liverpool. She stood on the fore deck of the packet as it passed through the southern lock of Liverpool and felt proud knowing that her brother, John, had built the lock, and each successive lock the packet boat would pass through the whole way to Columbia. She took comfort in the accomplishments of her brother, John. Her parents would be proud.

[1] *Father Barrett, in his research, could find no record of the town of Ballylee in County Down. Today, there is a "Thoor Ballylee" near Galway. However, during a visit to Northern Ireland it was suggested to Fr. Barrett that there once was a town of Ballylee in County Down located south of Belfast near the southern end of Lough Neagh.*
[2] *There is no record of women or children being interred in the Catholic Cemetery at Liverpool.*
[3] *Little did the engineers know what problems lay ahead for it was actually the spring of 1828 before the tunnel was opened for barge traffic*